A Christmas to Remember

Also by Beverly Jenkins

BLESSINGS NOVELS

HISTORICALS

ROMANTIC SUSPENSE

A Christmas to Remember

A BLESSINGS NOVEL

Beverly Jenkins

AVON

An Imprint of HarperCollins*Publishers*

A CHRISTMAS TO REMEMBER. Copyright © 2023 by Beverly Jenkins. All rights reserved. Printed in the United States of America. No part of this book may be used or reproduced in any manner whatsoever without written permission except in the case of brief quotations embodied in critical articles and reviews. For information, address HarperCollins Publishers, 195 Broadway, New York, NY 10007.

HarperCollins books may be purchased for educational, business, or sales promotional use. For information, please email the Special Markets Department at SPsales@harpercollins.com.

FIRST EDITION

Library of Congress Cataloging-in-Publication Data has been applied for.

ISBN 978-0-06-301821-1
ISBN 978-0-06-311925-3 (hardcover library)

23 24 25 26 27 LBC 5 4 3 2 1

To Gwendolyn E. Osborne (1949–2022).
She will always be remembered. Always.

A Christmas to Remember

Great dinner, little brother."

Chef and restaurant owner Thornton Webb responded to his sister, June, with a smile. "It'll be our last meal together for a while so thought I'd make it special."

"And you did. The gumbo was superb, but I still can't believe you're selling your restaurant."

"Time to try something new."

"By relocating to Nowhereville, Kansas?"

His amusement showed. "Yes. Nowhereville, Kansas. The real name of the town is Henry Adams, Kansas, by the way."

She shook her head as if his decision was a difficult one to understand. "How about I help you clean up, we make some coffee, and you can fill me in on the details."

A short time later, Thorn's stainless state-of-the-art kitchen was sparkling again, and with coffee cups in hand the siblings took seats outdoors on his balcony. The sun was setting over the San Francisco Bay.

"Million-dollar view," June said, raising her cup in toast.

"One of the things I'm going to miss when I move." His large sprawling house positioned high above the bay was on the market, too.

"Have you found a buyer for this place yet?"

"The Realtor has had a few nibbles." Thorn would've put the house up for sale even if he weren't moving. He'd owned it for almost twenty years, and now at age forty-eight, he'd matured enough to no longer measure his worth by the prestige owning it once represented.

"So why Kansas?" June asked.

"I feel as though I've been in a rut, and this could be the life reboot I need. Launching a new restaurant from the ground up will be a challenge. The owners are naming it the Three Spinsters after three women who helped found the town. I've never been to a place where Black folks have lived and flourished for over a century. I could almost taste the history in the air."

"Never known you to be a history buff."

"Me either, until I went for the interview a few months ago." He found it hard to explain why Henry Adams, Kansas, touched him so deeply because he couldn't explain it to himself. "I felt as though I belonged there, if that makes any sense."

"I suppose," she replied softly. "How historic is it? Never mind. Google is my friend. I'll look it up when I get home. Is all the paperwork done for the restaurant sale?"

"Almost. Lawyers are still doing their thing. My financial people keep asking me to reconsider accepting Sean's bid and take the counteroffer from a private equity firm, instead. But my gut says a group like that will only be interested in the bottom line, not the quality of what comes out of the kitchen.

I won't have to worry about that with Sean as the owner. He's been the manager since we opened and has earned the right to keep it going."

"What's the witch have to say?"

Thorn smiled. "When are you going to stop calling her that? I did love her at one point." The witch was his ex-wife, supermodel Helena Winston.

June countered, "I didn't love her at all, ever. So I can call her what I damn well please."

Helena, born Harriet Williams, was as narcistic as she was beautiful. In her mind, the sun rose daily for her alone. She and Thorn had married eight years ago. It only took him three to realize it wouldn't work. June had never liked her, and the feeling had been mutual. Even though photo shoots and fashion runways necessitated Helena traveling all over the world, she'd been angry at playing second fiddle to his restaurant and demanded he make a choice—her or his work. He chose lawyers, then moved out. She'd been so confident he'd come crawling back to kiss the soles of her Louboutins she'd stalled for over a year before finally signing the papers. His freedom had been as sweet as his grandmother's pecan pie. "She has no say in the sale. I bought her out after we divorced."

"Good."

Junie was a year and a half older and always took great pride in pointing that out. Their parents were retired, still madly in love, and living out their golden years in Savannah. Thorn, who'd always wanted a brother too, once asked his mom why she hadn't had more kids. She explained, "On the measly money your daddy and I were making, we were too busy trying to keep food on the table and a roof over our heads." She added, "At one point, things got so bad we tried to sell you and Junie to the circus, but they kept bringing you back." He smiled at the memory.

"What are you smiling about?"

"Mama and her selling us to the circus story."

"I think she's finally going to let go of that old tall tale."

At his puzzled look, June explained. "When we visited them this summer, she told it again, and Saria, thinking she was serious, burst into tears, ran from the room, and hid."

"Why?" Six-year-old Saria was June's youngest child.

"She said she didn't want Gramma to sell her to the circus. Mama felt really bad. Daddy started fussing about having told her to stop telling that story. Mama clapped back that she should've sold him to the circus. Then Saria yelled, 'STOP SELLING PEOPLE TO THE CIRCUS, GRAMMA!' It was a mess."

Thorn laughed. June and her husband, David, a former NFL defensive lineman and Thorn's teammate when they both played for the Oakland Raiders had five kids: two sets of twin boys, ages eleven and eight, and Saria the only girl. "Poor Saria."

"Poor Mama. She was so shocked at being checked by a six-year-old—you should've seen her jaw drop. The twins, Daddy, David, and I were on the floor."

Thorn wiped at the tears of mirth in his eyes. He loved his nephews, but Saria, Junie's mini-me, held a special place in his heart. The family lived in nearby Oakland. One of the downsides of moving away was that he'd not see the kids as often as he'd become accustomed to. He was already missing them. He'd miss Junie and David, too. "I'll have to remember to ask Mama if she's sold anybody to the circus lately when I talk to her tomorrow."

"She's going to reach through the phone and smack you." Junie's voice and demeanor grew serious. "Who am I going to pester if you move, Thorn? How will I hook you up with someone who'll love you as much as I love David if you're living so far away?"

"I don't need somebody like that. I can't afford five kids."

She leaned over and punched him in the arm. "Stop it." She settled in again and said wistfully, "The moment I saw that big ol' man I said I wanted to give him babies."

"I know. I was the one you said it to." She'd met David at Thorn's restaurant. The retired NFL lineman took one look at the statuesque, former NCAA champion shot put queen and it was love at first sight. They'd married six weeks later.

"I hate that witch for stealing your joy and wasting your love, Thornton."

He gave her a look.

"Okay. Shutting up."

"Thank you."

They sipped their coffee in silence. He knew June cared about him. She always had. Yes, Helena broke his heart, but he was over that and her. Cooking became his life at the age of nine when his mother showed him how to make spaghetti and meatballs. Any woman interested in him would have to be okay with knowing his love for food would always come first. He'd yet to meet such a unicorn and had no expectations he ever would.

When their visit was done, he walked his sister out to the driveway. She gave him a strong hug. "Going to miss you."

"Ditto, but I'm only moving to Kansas, not Kazakhstan. There are phones these days, you know."

"Yeah, smart-ass, I know, but you'll be so far away."

"I'll stay in touch. Promise."

"You better."

She opened the door of her silver SUV and got in. "You are coming to Savannah for Christmas, correct?"

"Correct." It was now early November.

Seemingly pleased by that, she started the engine. "How soon are you leaving for Nowhereville?"

"Probably right after Thanksgiving. The restaurant owners want my input on the blueprints and some other things so I'd like to get there and get settled in as soon as I can."

She nodded. "We'll be spending Turkey Day with David's folks this year. Travel safe and call me when you get to Kansas."

"I will. Love you, Junie."

"Love you back."

He stepped aside and she backed her vehicle down the driveway. With a parting wave she drove away, and Thorn walked back inside.

"Y ou may now kiss your bride."

Bernadine Brown, the owner of Henry Adams, Kansas, dabbed at her wet eyes with a tissue as Gary Clark gazed down at his bride, Eleanor "Nori" Price. The love they radiated melted hearts all over the packed church. The sweet kiss that followed set off exuberant applause and cheers. Twenty years ago, the former high school sweethearts were ripped apart by circumstances beyond their control. Last summer, they found each other again and realized they were still in love. Now, the Saturday after Thanksgiving, they were married.

Come Christmas Day, Bernadine and the well-dressed man at her side, Malachi July, would be the bride and groom standing before Reverend Paula Grant. They'd come through a lot too and although small seeds of uncertainty seemed intent on bedeviling her, Bernadine refused to let them take root. She loved him. He loved her. As if sensing her thoughts, he gave her a quick smile and a squeeze, and she leaned against his strong shoulder, content.

As the ceremony ended, the happy newlyweds made their way down the center aisle and exited the church to another rousing round of applause and cheers. The reception would follow at the town's diner, the Dog and Cow, so folks gathered their belongings to head over.

Outside, vehicles glistened under a light dusting of fresh snow, adding to the three inches that had fallen overnight. Mal opened the passenger door of his restored, red Ford pickup truck and Bernadine got in. Before joining her, he used the scraper to give the windows and mirrors a quick swipe.

Shivering, he started the engine and hit the heat. "Reason number one for a honeymoon some place warm."

"Amen," she agreed with amusement. Winter on the Kansas plains was no joke, and there were at least three, probably four more months to go.

Mal steered the truck away from the curb and joined the caravan of vehicles for the short drive to the Dog.

"It was a nice wedding," she voiced.

"It was. They deserve to be happy."

Bernadine thought she and Mal deserved the same. They'd had their share of problems. Mal's insecurity regarding her wealth led him down a path that left the town reeling, and her with a broken heart. After owning his mistakes, he'd earned forgiveness. Lingering issues were being dealt with in weekly couples' counseling with Reverend Paula. No relationship was perfect, but she and Mal were working hard to make theirs as close as possible.

Outside of the rough patch with Mal, she had no complaints about the life she'd carved out in historic Henry Adams, Kansas, since purchasing it off eBay a bit over five years ago. The megadivorce settlement she'd received from her now late ex-husband, Leo, helped transform the struggling, poorer-than-a-church-mouse town into a twenty-first-century jewel. It also transformed the lives of five incredible foster kids she'd paired with loving adoptive parents who'd given them homes and places in their hearts.

Henry Adams had offered Bernadine much as well: a strong sense of purpose, cherished friendships with women like her assistant, Lily Fontaine July, and the town's newly elected mayor, Sheila Payne. It also gave her Mal. After her divorce from the adulterous Leo, she'd guarded her heart closely, never imagining she'd end up proposing marriage to the descendant of a nineteenth-century gang of train-robbing outlaws. Yet she had.

The Dog's parking lot was as packed as the church had been. Free spots were hard to find.

"We'll let them keep hunting and pecking," Mal said, referring to all the vehicles slowly circling the lot. "We'll go around back."

"Nothing like having friends in high places."

He flashed her a grin. As part owner, he lived in an apartment above the diner and had a designated parking space for his truck near the loading dock. He pulled into it and turned off the engine.

"Have I told you I love you this morning?" he asked.

"No."

He leaned over and gave her a soft kiss. "Love you, lady."

"Love you back."

They entered the diner through the kitchen's back door and stepped into a whirlwind of noise and activity. The waitstaff clad in their fancy whites were prepping food and zooming in and out of the doors leading to the main dining room. Head chef Randy Emerson was carving a beautiful length of roast beef and calling out instructions while his serious-faced minions handled huge pots of steaming veggies, stacked china and silverware on metal-wheeled carts, and prepared large trays of appetizers and canapes. Over at the dessert station, Mal's co-owner, Rocky Dancer James, glanced up from the sweet potato pies she was slicing. "Mal, can you make sure everything's okay in the dining room?"

"Yes, ma'am." He turned to Bernadine. "See you later."

She nodded and left them to their work.

SEVENTEEN-YEAR-OLD PRESTON MAYS Payne enjoyed Mr. Clark and Ms. Nori's wedding and was now riding with his parents to the reception. For the most part his life was good. After being rescued by Ms. Bernadine five years ago from the often painful world of foster care, he was no longer the asthmatic overweight kid he'd been while living in Milwaukee. He now had two awesome adoptive parents in Sheila and Barrett Payne, was surrounded by the love and guidance of friends and the citizens of Henry Adams, Kansas, and next fall, he'd be attending MIT to study physics. He just wished he knew what to do about his broken heart.

Mr. Clark's oldest daughter, Leah, was Preston's first true girlfriend. They both loved physics, sports, and until meeting her, he never knew talking to a girl could be so easy. He also didn't know girls could be so complicated either until a week ago. They'd be graduating from high school in the spring, but instead of joining him at MIT in the fall, she'd be heading to Stanford. Because they were going to different schools, Leah wanted to end their relationship. She was certain that he'd meet some hot babe at MIT who'd rock his world, and she wanted to save him the trouble of having to end their ties by doing it now.

To him it was the dumbest thing he'd ever heard, but she was convinced this was for the best. He had no idea how to tell the most logical person he knew that she was being totally illogical. He hadn't talked to anyone about the problem—not his mom, not his best friend, sixteen-year-old Amari July, and not town therapist and priest, Reverend Paula—in hopes Leah would come to her senses. So far, she hadn't.

He was determined to change her mind, though. He hadn't broached the issue with her in the past few days, knowing she'd be busy with her dad's wedding. She was calling their breakup distancing, something she thought they should begin practicing now in anticipation of the separation to come. However, Preston had planned to spend as much time with her as possible before college separated them because he cared so much about her, but she wasn't feeling that. They'd gone from sharing kisses and cuddling in his car to acting like strangers, and honestly, he was hurting. A lot of the old-school songs on the Dog's fancy red jukebox were about heartache, and he hadn't really understood what that meant. Until now.

His dad found a free space in the packed parking lot and they got out. On the way to the entrance, his mom asked, "Are you okay, Preston?"

"Yes, just a little tired," he lied.

The concern in her eyes was genuine. He knew he could talk to her about this Leah thing, but he wasn't ready yet because he still believed he could figure it out on his own. His dad, Barrett, was eyeing him now, too.

"If there's something bothering you, son, you know we're here to help."

"I do, but I'm good."

His mom ran a comforting hand down his back, but kept unspoken any concerns she might still have.

Inside, the Dog was on jam. The old-school tune "Celebrate" was blasting from the speakers, competing with the sounds of laughter and the raised voices of a zillion conversations. The wedding party was greeting people on the far side of the room, and there stood Leah wearing a mint-green pantsuit. Her locs were gathered up in a fancy do on top of her head, and to him she looked amazing. As if sensing his interest, she looked up and held his gaze for a long moment before turning away. He sighed inwardly. Spotting Amari and the other kids in a booth in the back, he put on a fake smile, and said to his parents, "I'm going to sit with Amari and the crew."

"Okay. We'll see you later."

The dining room was standing room only so it took him a minute to make his way through the crush to where his friends were. "Man. Everybody in town is here," he said to Amari as he removed his black parka and squeezed into the booth.

"I know. Along with everybody who's ever shopped or worked at the store, looks like."

Mr. Clark was the manager at the town's only grocery. Preston and Amari worked there as stockers after school and on weekends. Preston spotted the store's cashiers, the purple-haired butcher, Candy Stevens, and the head of produce, Mr. Newsome.

"Even Mrs. Beadle is here," Amari pointed out.

The elderly Mrs. Beadle had a habit of opening a bottle of wine and drinking it while she shopped, but not paying for it at the checkout. Preston's dad, head of store security, had turned her over to local law enforcement at least a thousand times. She usually had her crazy chihuahua, Lorenzo, with her wherever she went. "I don't see Lorenzo."

"Probably in her tote bag."

Preston figured Amari was probably right. His eyes drifted to Leah again. She and the wedding party were now seated at the main table. "It was a nice wedding."

"Yes. OG and Ms. Bernadine are next, Christmas Day."

"Would you want to get married for the first time if you were OG's age?" Preston asked. OG was their nickname for sixty-plus-year-old Malachi July, Amari's grandfather, and the unofficial grandfather to the rest of the town's kids.

Amari shrugged. "Ask me when I get to be his age and I'll let you know. At this point, I'd just settle for a girlfriend."

Amari had been sweet on a honey named Kyra Jones but when she moved away, the relationship ended. This past summer he thought he had a thing for Tiffany, Leah's younger sister, but Tiff was all about drama and her jealousy made him break things off almost as soon as they started.

A tap on Amari's shoulder made him and Preston turn around in their seats. It was twelve-year-old Zoey sitting in the booth behind them. She, Preston, Amari, Crystal, and Amari's little brother, Devon, were the original group of foster kids Ms. Bernadine brought to Henry Adams. Since then ten more had been added to the ranks under varying circumstances.

"What's up?" Amari asked.

"Will you tell Devon to stop pouting? He's being a pain in the butt."

Preston took in Amari's thirteen-year-old brother. The bottom lip was poked out, the brown face was set on silent fume, and his arms were crossed tightly over his dark suit.

"What's wrong with him now?"

"Mad that he can't sing during the reception."

Amari sighed. "You can't sing at everything, Devon. People want to hear a DJ or professionals at something like this. No offense, Zoe."

"None taken."

Zoey was a musical prodigy. Devon was the lead singer in her band, Exodusters—named after the people who founded Henry Adams during the Great Exodus of 1879. The band often performed at town functions. Devon considered himself the reincarnation of the Godfather of Soul, James Brown. Preston would be the first to acknowledge how good Devon was onstage, but he didn't want to see him performing at everything, either. He also thought the James Brown pompadour wig Devon insisted on wearing everywhere was dumb looking. And yes, he had it on now.

"I wish you'd lose that wig," Amari said. "It's embarrassing."

Devon gave him a silent snarl and continued to pout.

Amari shook his head. "Sorry, Zoe. He doesn't listen to me."

"Me, either," she replied, shooting daggers at her on and off best friend.

Devon was a pain in the butt twenty-three hours a day. He was spoiled, whiny, and judgmental. Amari wanted to trade him for a draft choice and Preston did, too, but they all continued to put up with him in hopes that one day he'd get his stuff together. As the crowd began lining up for the buffet, Preston set aside the mopey Devon, and said to Amari, "Let's hit the buffet."

"I'm right behind you."

They loaded up their plates and returned to their seats. As

they began eating, Amari asked, "So what's going on with you and Leah?"

Preston froze and replied innocently, "What do you mean?"

"You've been sneaking peeks at her since you got here, and she's been doing the same to you. You both look sad."

Figuring people out was one of his friend's superpowers. "We're good."

From the way Amari studied him, Preston knew Amari wasn't buying it because Amari often knew Preston better than Preston knew himself.

"Okay. My bad."

Although Amari let it go, Preston had no doubts that more questions would eventually follow. Persistence was also an Amari superpower.

REVEREND PAULA LIVED a few minutes from the Dog in a double-wide trailer on the land owned by town matriarch Tamar July. Entering her place, she turned on a light and found the silence soothing after the raucous wedding reception. She'd had a great time as she always did at Henry Adams celebrations. She'd eaten the fabulous food, danced the Electric Slide, Wobbled, savored the laughter, and was honored to have been the officiant that sealed Gary and Nori as man and wife.

She was happy for the newlyweds, but as she hung up her coat and sat to remove her boots, she also admitted to being a bit envious. Her envy was tied to being without a companion of her own. Her holy commitment to her faith offered a joy that would always come first in her life. However, that didn't prevent Paula from wanting someone to share her time with, to laugh with, and who'd offer a comforting shoulder when offering hers to others sapped her strength and spirit, even though she knew the Holy Spirit had her back. It would take a very special man who didn't mind being second to Christ in her life, and so far she'd yet to meet him.

There hadn't been many men in her past, but the one she thought she was in love with said he couldn't see a future with her because he kept picturing God watching their every move. In her ideal world the man she envisioned being with would be someone her age who was settled in life, easygoing, and had a sense of humor. Maybe he'd be a widower with a loving family that would embrace her and help ease the ache she still carried from the mental and physical abuse she'd suffered at the hands of relatives while living her teen years in her late mother's hometown of Blackbird, Oklahoma. After a yearslong on-and-off conversation with God about whether wanting companionship was a selfish failing, she'd come to the conclusion that it was not. And because it wasn't, and because she was certain God would provide, she'd been content to wait, all the while telling herself the person she quietly longed for would show up at the right time. Still filled with that belief, she sent up a silent thanks for the wonderful day and walked to the bedroom to change into her pajamas.

Once she was ready for bed, she took a moment to send a text to her eighteen-year-old cousin, Robyn, currently visiting down in Atlanta. Since moving in with Paula six months ago, Robyn had become friends with Hope Zale, the daughter of Leslie Zale, one of Paula's beloved sorority sisters. When the Zales invited Robyn to spend Thanksgiving with them, she'd jumped at the chance to go. She'd be returning home tomorrow afternoon and Paula wanted to make sure the travel plans were still on schedule.

After a few minutes, Robyn texted back a reply. She'd had such a good time, she wondered if she could stay for another few days? She and the Zales spent Thanksgiving Day working on a Habitat for Humanity build. Robyn relayed how amazing it had been and that further work with the organization was scheduled for the next day. Deciding she needed to talk to her, Paula called.

In the end, Paula agreed to let her stay. It was the first time she'd ever heard Robyn speak so passionately about anything. Like Paula, Robyn's life had been filled with pain and dysfunction living with family members in Blackbird. As the call continued, Paula heard about the work Robyn had done, the family that would be moving in once the house was finished, and that Leslie's sister-in-law was on the Habitat local board. Paula then spoke to Leslie who assured her that Robyn was more than welcome to stay, and how helpful she'd been. After a few more back-and-forths with both Leslie and Robyn, Paula agreed to rearrange the flight and received Robyn's grateful thank-you.

After the call, Paula went online, redid the ticket, and paid the change fee. With that squared away, she got into bed. Although she needed to take one last look at tomorrow's sermon, she found herself thinking about her ties to Robyn instead. Their mothers had had tragic lives. When Paula's mom, Patricia, became pregnant out of wedlock, her furious father, Tyree, responded by driving her to the train station, handing her fifty dollars, and walking away. Robyn's mother, Lisa, disappeared when Robyn was a toddler. Robyn's great-grandfather Tyree, and his daughter Ardella, Lisa's mother, led Robyn to believe she'd been abandoned. Six months ago, Lisa's body had been discovered buried behind Tyree's house. Ardella was arrested for the crime, found guilty of manslaughter, and was currently serving time in an Oklahoma prison. Paula took Robyn in, and since then had been helping her young cousin navigate a life free of the beatings and verbal abuse that were a daily occurrence living under her grandmother Ardella's roof. Paula knew firsthand how awful that life had been because she'd endured the same when her mother's death forced her to move from her hometown of Sacramento to Blackbird at the age of fourteen. The shared experience made Paula want to wrap Robyn in layers of cotton and guard her like dragon treasure to ensure no one ever hurt her again.

The excitement in Robyn's voice earlier when talking about her volunteer work over Thanksgiving warmed her heart. Paula was honest enough to admit how much she missed her young cousin. Having lived alone most of her adult life, she'd grown attached to the teen's presence and woke up each morning grateful to have her near. Robyn had been looking at colleges but so far hadn't decided where she wanted to attend. Paula secretly hoped she'd choose a school not too far away so their connection could deepen and grow.

Paula turned her attention to the sermon on her tablet and once satisfied with the message and the flow, she doused the lamp on her nightstand and settled in for sleep.

CHAPTER
3

Bernadine was up before sunrise on Monday morning. Dressed in her robe and pajamas, she sat in her kitchen with her coffee. The weather app on her phone showed the outdoor temperature to be a sweltering fifteen degrees. Winter often made her reevaluate her decision to tie her life to the plains of Kansas where snow ruled sometimes until midspring. Considering her bottomless bank account, she could have chosen a more soothing place to reside, like maybe the island of Anguilla with its warm sands and crystal blue waters. Instead, she'd picked a place where the cold could freeze your nose hair, and frostbite was a certainty if you didn't cover your hands and ears. However, she loved being in Henry Adams and complaining about the weather didn't change it. Although she turned the world of her small town, Mother Nature ruled the seasons.

Her phone chimed and Bernadine smiled at the heart displayed on the screen. It was Mal's way of saying good morning. His accompanying text said he was driving to Hays to pick up a new freezer Rocky had ordered and would stop by and see her that evening after his weekly card game with Clay and Bing. Sipping her coffee, she realized that once they tied the knot, the heartwarming gesture of hearts and texts about the day's agenda would no longer be necessary, because they'd be waking up under the same roof. She looked forward to it, even knowing that after living separate lives, adjustments would have to be made. Mal had never been married and Bernadine hadn't lived full time with a man since divorcing Leo almost a decade ago. When her adopted daughter, Crystal, moved out last year, Bernadine had admittedly been lonely, but as time passed, she began relishing having the place all to herself. She was concerned about going back to having someone in her space 24/7. Were she and Mal both too old and set in their ways to handle having each other underfoot all the time? They'd agreed it made more sense for Mal to move in with her since his apartment was so small, but what would happen if they needed the privacy and space they were accustomed to having? Would it be considered selfish to voice that?

So far, she hadn't shared her misgivings with him because she didn't know how to bring it up. Although the territory ahead was unknown, she kept telling herself her love for him meant more, even as she prayed that the transition of combining their lives would lead to a positive future and banish her unspoken, lingering doubts.

Bernadine's phone chimed again. Seeing her sister Diane's name on the caller ID made her want to send it to voice mail, but she decided to answer. "Morning, sis," she said. "How are you?"

"Good. How are you?"

"Getting ready for work. What can I do for you?" Bernadine hoped the call wasn't tied to any drama because it was way too early in the morning for that, but this was her sister, after all, and drama had always been Diane's middle name.

"I'm wondering when I'm supposed to get info on my fitting?"

"What fitting?"

"For my matron of honor gown for the wedding. Did I miss an email or a text?"

Bernadine sighed inwardly. "No."

"The date's getting kind of close. Most brides would have arrangements like this locked down by now."

Taking digs at Bernadine was Diana's reason for living and it had been that way since their childhood. "Tina Craig's going to be my matron of honor."

Silence followed that revelation. "Am I the one giving you away?"

"No. I've asked Crystal."

Silence again. "So I have no role?" she asked testily.

"No official role, no, but I do want you there." She hoped she'd be forgiven for lying so early in the morning.

"How can you not ask your sister to be in your wedding? Is this because I didn't want—" She corrected herself. "—couldn't have you in mine because the bridesmaids' dresses didn't come in your size?"

The weight shaming was always the most hurtful sting.

Diane asked, "So is this payback for that?"

"No, Diane. Tina's my best friend."

"I see. Well, I'm thinking about going to Hawaii to see the kids for Christmas and I may have to miss the wedding."

"Understood. How's the job?" Bernadine needed to change the subject before the headache forming got any worse.

"I'm up for a promotion. I'll know in a few days."

"Congrats. I need to get to work. Let me know if you'll make the wedding and if the promotion goes through. I'll talk to you later."

"Bye."

Bernadine ended the call and sighed with frustration. Her sister would never be the loving sibling Bernadine had always needed and wanted. Saddened by that knowledge, she walked her now empty coffee cup to the sink and climbed the stairs to get dressed for work.

In her office at the Power Plant, Bernadine hung up her coat and fired up her single-serve coffee maker. The short walk across the parking lot had been a frigid one and she needed warming up. She'd just inserted the pod into the machine when her administrative right hand, Lily Fontaine July, walked in. "Lord, it's cold out there."

"Tell me about it."

Lily unzipped her white parka. "What's on your plate this morning? Anything you need help with?"

"Can you get me a new sister?"

Lily shed her coat and placed it over her arm. "What's she done now?"

"Mad that she's not my matron of honor."

"Were you hers when she and her ex said I do?"

"No. I wasn't in the wedding party." The coffee was ready. After some sweetener and a stir, she sipped.

"Why not?" Lily asked. "Were you and Leo traveling?"

"No. I was told the bridesmaids' dresses didn't come in my size."

Lily's eyes widened. She took in Bernadine's tersely set

features. "Oh, Bernadine. I'm so sorry. What is wrong with her?"

Bernadine shrugged. "Everything and nothing, I suppose. I reasoned if not having my big fine self in the mix made her feel better about herself, so be it."

"That girl needs a good beatdown. She should've been pushed in front of a train when she stole your prom date back in high school."

Bernadine agreed. That painful episode was one Diane took great pride in boasting about to anyone who'd listen. Last year, after Diane's husband filed for divorce, she'd been forced to move in with Bernadine and Crystal because she had no place else to go. She'd gleefully shared the story during a meeting of the Henry Adams Ladies Auxiliary. Bernadine's friends were appalled. After matriarch Tamar July pulled Diane aside for a frank chat, Diane never brought up the subject again, at least not within Bernadine's hearing. "I always wanted us to be close, especially after my sister CeCe, died, but that's never going to happen, I guess."

"I'm sorry again."

"Thanks. So, you asked about my day. There is one thing you can do for me."

"And that is?"

"Help me come up with a reason to opt out of this bridal shower you all are insisting upon."

Lily laughed. "Really? The woman who wanted to book the Taj Mahal for my wedding? Not happening, sister. You'll be at the shower Sunday afternoon, and you'll like it."

"But—"

She shook her head. "Nope. Not a word from you. Not one peep. Next subject."

"I hate you, you know."

"I do, but you're still having the shower, so don't even try it."

Amused, Bernadine hung her head. She supposed she'd earned the mock scorn. She'd been way over the top attempting to make Lily and Trent's wedding match her own fairy-tale vision of how it should be. Now it was her turn. Luckily everyone involved possessed a lot more sense and restraint than she'd shown. "So what's on your plate today?" she asked Lily.

"First is tracking delivery of the wreaths and greenery Mayor Sheila ordered to decorate the town. Everything should arrive in plenty of time for the big to-do on Saturday, but I want to make sure."

For the first time Henry Adams would be dressed up for Christmas. Mayor Sheila Payne's committee had gone all out ordering garland, red bows, and poinsettias, in addition to a truckload of wreaths to display in the windows of buildings like the church, Clark's Grocery, and the Dog. Sheila said she wanted it to be a Christmas to remember, and with her in charge, Bernadine knew it would be.

"Any word from Chef Webb?" Bernadine asked.

"Yes. I spoke with him a few days ago. Both his house and restaurant have sold and he's ready to start his life here."

"So he'll he here in the spring?"

"No, he says he's coming in a few days. He's driving."

"What? Why?"

Lily shrugged. "I don't know him well enough to ask a bunch of questions, so I didn't. He said he'd call once he was on his way."

"Interesting. Okay. We'll put him in Rocky's old trailer until he finds more permanent housing."

"Sounds like a plan. I'll let Tamar know."

"Thanks."

Lily left for her office and Bernadine sat wondering if Webb had any idea what the plains of Kansas were like in the middle of winter? Figuring he'd find out and hoping Mother Nature would show him some grace, she began her day.

She hadn't heard from Mal since his text, so she assumed his drive to Hays to pick up Rocky's new freezer hadn't run into any issues.

AFTER LUNCH, BERNADINE received a call from Leo's lawyer, Madeline Bush. "What can I do for you, Ms. Bush."

"If it's okay, I want to email you Leo's will."

"Why?"

"He left everything to you. It's a little under four million dollars in stock, property, and cash."

She choked on a swallow of coffee. When she was able to speak again, she said, "What? Why me?" Leo was killed last month by a local farmer he'd cheated in a business deal.

"Were he here I'm sure he'd explain, but since he isn't . . ." Her voice trailed off. Then she went on, "But also were he here, he'd probably be pretty angry."

"Why?"

"He thought he was broke. Now granted, he did manage to keep your financial people from finding all his assets when you divorced him, but when the oil company fired him, he didn't have much of that money left. In fact, when he died, he was living paycheck to paycheck. I think when he made this will and left you everything, it was more of a screw you, Bernadine, you get nothing."

Typical Leo. "So where did this money come from?"

"A financial firm he worked with at the beginning of his career is being sold, and they found notice of it in their records. Leo changed money managers quite a few times over the years and apparently this account got lost, buried, not sure what to call it as his portfolios changed hands. It's an untouched offshore account that's drawn a ton of interest."

"I don't want his money."

"I understand. You could always donate it to a charity or a nonprofit, but it's yours."

She supposed that was an alternative. There were many organizations that would rejoice over receiving such a sum. "What about the ex-wives?"

"He didn't leave them so much as a paper clip, and with his death, the alimony stops. They aren't going to be happy."

"As long as they don't bring that unhappiness here, I'm good." But Bernadine had a feeling one if not both would probably want to challenge things. If so, she'd let the lawyers deal with them. "Send me the will, and I'll have my people look it over."

"Sounds good. Give me a few minutes, but you'll have it shortly."

"Thanks."

After the call ended, Bernadine agreed that Leo had probably thought leaving her nothing would be the ultimate insult, instead. . . . Truthfully, she thought he was broke, too. Based on the last time she'd had her friend Tina Craig peek into his accounts, he'd lost a ton of money in a bad investment overseas and had very little wealth left. Tina was known in the financial world as the Blood Hound for her legendary prowess in unearthing funds corporate capitalists didn't want found, especially during divorce proceedings. Very few money managers had the ability to hide assets from her, and she wasn't going to be pleased to know Leo had.

Tina was also one of the investors in the town's upcoming new restaurant, the Three Spinsters, along with Bernadine and Rocky Dancer James. It was scheduled to break ground in the spring as would the B&B Tina planned to open. On her visits to Henry Adams during the past few years, she'd fallen in love with the people and the peace and quiet. She'd be back in town for Bernadine's bridal shower but was presently in her hometown of Milwaukee riding herd over her elderly mother, Mimi, a former roller derby queen. Last month, Mimi took a bad spill on her skates and after a successful surgery had been sent to a rehab facility to get back on her feet. Tina was there to make sure her force-of-nature mom followed doctor's orders. Bernadine made a mental note to give her a call later about Leo's bequest.

A quiet knock on her opened door pulled her attention away from Leo's downloading will to see Anna Ruiz holding a large box. She was the mother-in-law of town fire chief Luis Acosta, grandmother to his two kids, Alfonso and Maria, and a joy to be around, but her eyes were red as if she'd been crying. Concerned, Bernadine stood. "Anna, what's wrong? Why are you crying?"

She beamed. "They're happy tears. May I show you something?"

Still worried, Bernadine nodded. Anna set the box on the floor, and as she opened it and reached in her tears began flowing freely. "Look at this." She carefully lifted out a huge star that appeared to measure about three feet across. It was painted with a glowing metallic red, green, and white reminiscent of the colors of Anna's native Mexico, and embellished with smaller stars, crosses, bits of glitter, and small gold crystals. Its beauty was absolutely stunning. Bernadine walked closer and the sudden recognition made her smile. "Is that a piñata?"

"Yes," Anna said in a shaky voice. "Eli James made it and sent it to me for our Las Posadas celebration. Isn't it beautiful?"

"Oh, my goodness yes."

"And Bernadine, it's made of clay just like the traditional ones from the days of my grandparents. I just burst into tears when I opened the box and cried even harder when I read Eli's note. There are two this size and three little ones—all gorgeous. I left the others at home. We can't break this. It's too beautiful."

"I agree."

"Here, read the note."

Dear Ms. Anna. Thanks for helping Henry Adams raise me. Please accept these as tokens of my gratitude for teaching me about Las Posadas. Love, Eli James.

Bernadine wiped at her own tears and walked back to her desk to grab tissues for herself and Anna. "How dare that boy make me cry from a thousand miles away." Eli was the son of town teacher Jack James and was now attending college in California.

Anna laughed. "I know."

"Any idea how or where you want to display them? The celebration begins on the sixteenth of December, right?"

"Yes. First, I'm keeping the other one this size. Alfonso and Maria can fight over who gets to keep it after I go to the Lord. But maybe we can put this one in the window of the Dog or suspend it from the ceiling?"

"I like both ideas. Get with Mal and Rocky and the three of you figure out what's best."

Anna nodded. "Not sure about the three small ones. One for the coffee shop window?"

"Yes, and maybe one can go to the church? Don't the stars' seven points represent the seven deadly sins?"

"Yes. And the blindfolded striker represents blind faith."

"Talk with Reverend Paula and see what she thinks."

"Will do."

The gorgeous piñata was carefully rewrapped and returned to its box. They spent a few minutes talking about the logistics of the annual Las Posadas.

Anna said, "Sheila and I will firm up the details."

"Okay. If you need me for anything, you know where to find me."

After Anna's departure, Bernadine made a mental note to get Eli's number from Jack so she could call him and personally tell him how much his gift meant not only to Anna but to the Henry Adams's community. She was proud of him.

Crystal stopped in soon after.

"Hey, sweetie. How are you?"

"Doing good."

"What's up?"

"Do you think I can start an art gallery in the space Detective Langster was using?"

Having not heard any mention of this before, the question caught Bernadine off guard. "An art gallery?" Sandy Langster's small detective agency had been inside the renovated Sutton Hotel. She'd recently relocated to Topeka.

Crystal nodded. "Yes. I know a lot of artists, and it would

be nice if they, myself included, could have a central place to show and sell their work."

Bernadine had a ton of questions but tried to whittle them down to just the essentials for now. "What happened to going away to school?"

"I still want to do that, but if I could sell some of my art, I could make some money and not have to be all up in your pocket for tuition and stuff."

"That's very mature thinking and I appreciate that."

Crys smiled and said proudly, "I want to call it Crystal Art."

"Nice name. Do you have your business plan worked up yet?"

"Business plan?"

"Yes, honey, you need a business plan so you can set your goals, figure out your targeted market, how you're going to make enough money to do things like keep the lights on. That kind of thing."

The smile flattened. "I was just hoping to showcase the art and sell it."

"You can still do that, but if you're going to function as a business you have to do the business stuff, like paying taxes, maybe hiring an employee if you need to, and if you do, then there's payroll to handle."

Crystal sighed.

Bernadine said gently, "I'm not trying to discourage you. In fact, I think your idea is a great one and since Ms. Langster has moved out, I have no problem with you using the space, but if you're going to go into business you have to do all the appropriate stuff that goes with it."

"Oh."

"There are a ton of businesswomen in this town—your

mom included," Bernadine pointed out. "So you'll have a ton of help. However, you need to be up on the details of what going into business entails. You can probably find the basics online to get you started."

Crystal met her eyes.

"And don't be discouraged. You're a force of nature. You got this."

The smile returned. "Okay, Mom. I'll get with Google and see what I need to do. How about I get with you after Christmas and show you what my friends and I come up with?"

"Sounds like a plan. And speaking of showcasing art. Eli sent Anna Ruiz a beautiful piñata for the Las Posadas celebration. Maybe he'll want to sell some of his pieces through Crystal Art."

"Maybe. I talked to him a few nights ago."

"How's he doing?"

"Really good. He loves being back in Cali. Doing a lot of surfing."

Bernadine knew the two had been sweet on each other on and off since Eli and his dad moved to town a few years back. However, she knew better than to ask where they stood on a personal level now.

Crystal added, "And just so you know. Friends and I are going to Lawrence this weekend for a concert."

"Sounds fun. Who're you going to see?"

"Thundercat."

Confused, Bernadine paused for a moment before asking, "Thundercat like the old cartoon show?"

Crystal chuckled. "Sort of. He took his stage name from the cartoon, but his real name is Stephen Lee Bruner. Plays bass and sings R & B. He's deep into anime."

"Ah.

Crystal stood. "I'm hostess today at the Dog, so I need to get going. Thanks for the advice about the art thing."

"Have a great day, sweetie."

"You too, Mom. Bye." With a wave she was gone.

Thundercat. Who knew?

The silence left behind by Crys's exit lasted all of two seconds before the mayor-elect swept in.

"Hi. Are you busy?"

"Always have time for you, Madame Mayor. Have a seat."

Sheila Payne peeled off her bright red parka and sat before taking a notepad and her ever present fountain pen out of her tote. "I have the menu choices for your rehearsal dinner, and for the wedding buffet. Rocky says she needs your decisions back by noon tomorrow."

Bernadine chuckled. "Glad she's giving me so much time."

"She has a lot on her plate with the shower and all the Christmas celebrating on tap. I've spoken with Luis about his fire guys helping with the placement of the tree we're planning to have on Main Street."

"Where's it going to be?"

"I've narrowed it down to either in front of the rec center or the coffee shop."

"How tall is it?"

"About sixteen feet."

"Oh my!"

"Too much? Since this is our first big to-do, we need a big to-do tree."

Bernadine smiled. "You're the mayor and VP for Social Affairs. You get to decide."

Sheila went on to talk about the ornaments she'd ordered

for the big tree, the time frame she'd set for all the decorating taking place on Saturday, and who would be doing what. "Rocky has ordered all the cocoa and marshmallows, but we'll let the kids at the coffee shop do the making of it and the distribution. The staff at the Dog has enough to do." Sheila checked her notes. "Oh, your friend Tina called a bit ago and said some of your girlfriends from the Bottom Women's Society are coming to the shower."

Bernadine sat up straight. "What?"

"Tina didn't want me to tell you. She wanted it to be a surprise but I'm not big on surprises, so hope you don't mind that I let the cat out of the bag."

"Thanks for telling me. Did she say how many are coming?"

"Two. She said twenty wanted to come, so she made them draw straws for two spots because her chopper only seats three."

"I'm still going to kill her."

"Let me know when and where so I can add the funeral to my schedule. Like I said, I don't do surprises."

That Sheila voiced the quip with such a seriously set face made Bernadine say wryly, "I'll give you a heads-up just as soon as I find a place to bury the body where it can't be found."

"Got it."

"Anything else?" Bernadine asked.

"Not right now. The rest of this list is for Lily, so I'm heading to my office and then to hers." Her office was at the end of the hallway. Sheila got to her feet and picked up her coat. "Oh. Almost forgot. Jack mentioned something about the convergence of Jupiter and Saturn in mid-December, and he wants to have a sky watch night so we can view it. He called it the Christmas Star. He and I will be meeting with Reverend Paula to get her involved."

"Is my input needed?"

"I don't believe so."

"Okay. Keep me posted."

"Will do. On to Lily." With a waggle of her fingers, she sailed out.

Bernadine wondered if she was the only person Sheila left breathless in her role as mayor. The difference between the timid little mouse Sheila had been when she first moved to town and the take-charge whirlwind she'd become showed how transforming Henry Adams could be. Glad her town was in good hands, Bernadine turned back to her screen to view Leo's will.

A few of the properties listed appeared to be the homes of his two ex-wives. She shook her head thinking about the drama that would cause once there was no Leo to pay the taxes or the upkeep and wondered how they'd react. She certainly had no plans to pay for either. The stocks now hers were in the ruthless oil company he once worked for. Having learned during Leo's trips to Henry Adams how they operated, she'd be advising her broker to sell immediately and donate the profits. There was also a few hundred thousand dollars stashed in what appeared to be other offshore accounts. She'd have Tina investigate that.

Thinking of Tina made her revisit the surprise Sheila shared. Bernadine certainly didn't mind her friends attending her bridal shower, but she'd firmly told Lily and the rest of the Henry Adams women—no gifts. She doubted they'd listen though, and she knew the Bottom Women's ladies wouldn't, so lord only knew what they'd be bringing. She also wondered when they planned to arrive. Since the surprise was Tina's baby, Bernadine assumed the Blood Hound had a plan to cover all the moving parts, so she decided not to worry. With the town decorating scheduled for Friday and Saturday, and the bridal shower Sunday after church, the weekend would be a busy one.

Later that afternoon, she got a text from Mal letting her know he and the freezer were on their way back to town and that he'd check in after the card game.

Before leaving the office for the day, she put in a call to Tina. After getting an update on Mimi's recovery, she asked, "So what is this about surprising me at my shower?"

There was silence for a moment, followed by fake outrage. "Sheila told you?"

"Yes. She doesn't like surprises any more than I do."

"Neither of you are any fun."

"So who's coming?"

"I made them draw straws. Patty and Gwen."

Bernadine sighed. She loved her Bottom Women sisters, although they tended to be over the top, a trait she also shared, but at least these two were members of the calmer delegation and, more important, good friends.

Tina continued, "We'll chopper in Saturday afternoon and be out of your hair Sunday evening after the shower."

"We're decorating the town on Saturday so be prepared to be put to work."

"Yes, ma'am. You aren't really mad, are you?"

"Of course not. You're welcome to bunk at the house. We'll have a pajama party and catch up."

"Sounds good. Letty's daughter has almost finished your dress."

Bernadine said, "Can't wait to see it." Letty McFarland's daughter, Cynthia, was an award-winning fashion designer. She'd created gowns for Bernadine before and all were lovely.

They then talked over the logistics for the chopper landing, before Tina had to go check on Mimi. "Love you. See you Saturday."

"Love you, too. Travel safe."

Bernadine put her phone aside. She wasn't upset with Tina. However, when your sister steals your prom date, or you go to your husband's office for a birthday lunch and walk in on him having sex with his secretary, you tend to not be a big fan of surprises. This was a good surprise though, and she looked forward to seeing her friends.

"Six."

Mal looked up from the terrible cards in his hand and studied his son, Trent. They were playing bid whist. Clay Dobbs was Mal's partner and Trent was partnered with Henry Adams patriarch Bing Shepard. Trent's declaration of a six meant he either had a world-beater of a hand or he was lying through his teeth. Viewing Trent's poker face, Mal chose the former. It was now Mal's turn to bid. "Pass." He didn't even have a face card.

Clay had already passed. Bing passed too, wearing a catbird seat smile that only added more credence to the butt kicking Mal sensed his team was in for.

"Clubs," Trent called, naming the trump suit. Mal had one club. A five. Definitely not a game changer, but he clung to the hope that Clay had enough to put up a fight.

He didn't.

They were slaughtered. Trent threw down club after club and when he passed the lead to his partner, Bing added to the pain with the ace of hearts, spades, and diamonds. By the time they were down to the last few cards, he and Clay hadn't won a book, and Bing was singing, "We're leaving on the midnight train to Boston."

Boston was the game's mythical destination when one team skunked the other, and Mal and Clay were stinking up the house. "Shut up, old man," Clay groused, tossing in another losing card, which Bing swept up and put in the pile of the winners, called books, on his side of the table.

As the next to the last card fell, Bing added yet another book and reached up and pulled on an imaginary train whistle. "All aboard! Next stop Boston. You and Clay want beans or chowder?"

Mal shot him a mock glare. Bing loved rubbing it in.

"Your turn will come," Mal warned.

"Probably, but it won't be tonight. I love the smell of a good butt kicking in the evening."

The last card fell. One more book for the opposing team and blessedly the game was over. The four men usually played once a week. Hosting alternated between Clay and Bing's farm and Mal's apartment above the Dog. This evening's match was at the farm. It was always a three-game set and because Trent and Bing won two, they'd hold bragging rights until the next time.

"Sorry, Dad," Trent said. "But that was one of the best hands I've ever had in life." He and Bing shared a congratulatory fist bump.

Mal showed his grumble face. "I don't want to talk about it."

Clay gathered the cards and put them back in their box. "You know, we're probably not going to be able to get together like this once you're married, Mal."

Mal was confused. "Why not? You and Bing selling the place and moving?"

"No, but we trade off hosting. Is she going to let us play bid at her place when it's your turn?"

The she was Bernadine. Mal took in the faces of Bing and his son and saw no support for Clay's remark. "Why wouldn't she?"

Clay shrugged. "You know how women are."

This wasn't the first time Clay had voiced an opinion on how Mal's life would be altered once he and Bernadine tied the knot. Mal loved Clay like a brother, always had, but the cuts he kept taking were getting old.

But before Mal could call him out, Bing said, "Clay. Stay out of his business. We all know you don't know a thing about women. Otherwise, that sweet little Genevieve would be married to you and not TC."

Clay huffed back. "I'm glad we broke up. Gen is not the woman I thought she was."

"Learned to think for herself, you mean?"

Clay didn't appear pleased by that, but as always, Bing didn't care. "Mal's a grown man. Bernadine isn't going to keep you two from being friends—because that's what this is really about."

Lips pursed, Clay looked away.

Bing continued, "Do I think they should get married? No."

Mal stiffened.

"I think they should just keep doing what they're doing— loving each other without being tied by a piece of paper. She has a good life. Mal has a good life. Marrying may mess that up. But nobody asked for my opinion, so I'm keeping it to myself. And you, Clayton Dobbs, should do the same."

Mal was stunned by Bing's take.

Trent broke the silence. "This has been one hell of a trip to Boston."

Mal agreed, but before he could respond, Riley Curry, former mayor and town ne'er-do-well, came strolling in, and said importantly, "Guess what?"

"You've found a place to live," Bing cracked. When Bernadine evicted Riley and his hog, Cletus, from a place she owned, they'd had no place to go. Clay offered Riley the farmhouse's spare bedroom and the hog a stall in the barn until their circumstances improved. Riley was grateful but Cletus pitched a fit having to share quarters with the other animals, and for the first three nights he squealed angrily until dawn. The fourth night, Bing, axe in hand, went to the barn and threatened to turn Cletus into hog's head cheese if he didn't pipe down. They hadn't heard a peep out of the disgraced porcine Hollywood star since.

Riley responded to Bing's question with a pleased smirk. "I probably will be moving, and this is why." He passed a photo to Clay. Clay looked at it and his mouth dropped open. He stared wide-eyed at Riley. "Is this real?"

Clay passed the pic to Mal, who instantly went wide-eyed too, before handing it over to Trent and Bing. The photo showed a beaming Riley holding a large, oversize check from the state lotto office. He'd won three million in Saturday night's drawing.

He puffed up and boasted, "Going to buy myself an RV, and then Cletus and I are going on a nationwide tour. Folks all over the country were mad when the studio pulled Cletus's movie. They'll line up from here to Kentucky to get a look at him and I'm going to give the people what they want. We'll get a publicist, call all the newspapers and TV folks, and once the crowds start showing up in droves, Hollywood's going to want me on speed dial. Just watch."

Mal was glad Riley had finally achieved his lifelong dream of being rich but was even happier to hear he'd be leaving town.

Clay asked pointedly, "Is the state making you repay the money you stole from Genevieve?" Riley had been found guilty of embezzling close to fifty thousand dollars from his ex-wife's accounts.

The satisfaction on Riley's face momentarily faded into sheepishness. "Yes. They're taking it off the top. It's just a drop in the bucket compared to what I'll still have, though." He paused a moment as if mulling over his future. "Thinking me and Cletus will relocate after the tour. Maybe Florida. That'll all depend on what happens with Hollywood, of course."

"Of course," Mal echoed. He turned to his son and saw Trent give a tiny shake of his head in disbelief. Trent thought Riley was delusional too, as did everyone else in town because he'd proven it so many times.

Bing said, "I wish you luck. When are you leaving?"

"Hopefully this weekend. The sooner we get on the road, the sooner Hollywood will call. I ordered the RV on the way back from the lotto office a couple hours ago. I can already see Kelly begging me to stay. After all, I'm the best barber in town, but this money is my destiny. She'll have to find someone else."

Kelly Douglas managed the hair salon where Riley worked. Trent replied, "I'm sure she'll be able to find someone."

"Not my worry though because I'm rich! Going out to the barn to let Cletus in on all the details. He's going to be so happy." And on that note, he hurried away.

In the silence left behind, Bing declared, "There is a God!"

Laughter erupted.

BEFORE HEADING HOME, Mal sent Bernadine a text to see if he could stop by for a minute because he hadn't seen her all day. Receiving her yes, he started up his truck and drove to the small subdivision where she and many of the town's families lived.

"Who won tonight?" she asked as he stepped inside.

"I don't want to talk about it."

"Whipped you that bad, eh?"

With his arm around her waist, they strolled into her living room and sat down on the couch. He pulled her close and she placed her head on his shoulder. "Yeah, they beat us to death. Bing was singing his version of 'Midnight Train to Boston.'" He waited while she quietly chuckled before continuing, "Have some interesting news, though."

"And it is?"

"Riley hit the lotto, and he and Cletus are leaving town."

She pulled back. "Shut up!"

"He won three mil. Had a picture of himself with the check. He's ordered an RV and he and the hog are going on tour."

"What kind of tour?"

Riley explained.

"Lord," she voiced in reaction. "Riley, Riley, Riley. Look out, world."

"I know." The doubt-filled words of Clay and Bing about Mal and Bernadine's upcoming marriage also rose in his memory, but he chose not to share them because he knew she wouldn't be pleased. He wished folks would stay out of his business.

"How soon is this tour jumping off?"

"Real soon hopefully."

"Is tomorrow at dawn too early to ask."

He laughed and gave her a squeeze. "Not in my book."

"As long as he and that killer hog are leaving town, I suppose I can wish them well."

"As long as they stay gone."

"Amen."

In spite of the dumb opinions of Clay and Bing, Mal looked forward to sharing life with Ms. Bernadine Brown. "How'd your day go?"

She told him about Mayor Sheila's plan for the upcoming weekend before adding, "And Leo's lawyer called about his will. Apparently, he left everything to me."

That surprised him. "Interesting."

"I thought so, too. Told the lawyer I didn't want it. She suggested I give it to a charity or a nonprofit, so I'll have my people investigate it." She went on to share the news about Anna receiving Eli's beautiful piñatas.

Mal was pleased by that last part. "For a boy no one could stand when he and Jack first moved here, he turned out well."

"He has. We loved him even though he didn't love us back."

"Being snatched up by Tamar a few times will make you reevaluate your worldview and your life."

"Yes, it will. I'm going to give him a call before I go to bed to say thanks and let him know how much he's loved."

"Is he coming home for Christmas?"

"I don't know. I'll ask him." She yawned. "Sorry."

"No apologies needed. Been stifling my own. Let me go so you can make your call and head to bed." He ran his eyes over her beautiful face. "Did I tell you today how much I love you?"

She made a point of thinking about it. "Hmm. I'm not sure. Maybe you should again just in case."

He leaned over and kissed her deeply instead. "I love you, doll," he whispered.

"Ditto," she replied in the same quiet tone and cupped his cheek gently. Their eyes held for a moment. She leaned up to kiss him again and murmured, "It'll be nice when we can float upstairs together on a regular basis. You're welcome to stay."

Mal kissed the tip of her nose. "Driving Tamar to Topeka for her annual checkup with her doctor in the morning. Need to be clearheaded on the highway, not befuddled by all your loveliness."

"Flattery will get you everywhere."

"Good to know." He felt so blessed by Bernadine's love—especially after his boneheaded embezzlement scheme. He'd never forgive himself for the pain and embarrassment his fragile ego put her through.

They left the couch, and he donned his outdoor gear. "Once we're headed back, I'll text you."

"Okay. Drive safe."

"Will do." The love he felt for her had to be the most amazing thing he'd ever experienced. That she wanted to be with him in spite of his tons of baggage left him speechless and very much humbled. As a way to acknowledge that truth he vowed to devote the rest of their lives together to putting her happiness first.

ONCE HOME IN his apartment above the Dog, Mal turned on some quiet jazz and changed clothes. He traded his jeans for a pair of cozy flannel sweatpants and his black turtleneck for a

long-sleeved black shirt with the Tenth Cavalry coat of arms
on the front. Making himself some tea to help him sleep, he
savored the fragrant brew while viewing the snow blanketing Main Street through the big glass door that led out to his
small patio. He also savored the apartment's warmth.

Before Bernadine and her magic checkbook came to town,
the Dog, and his place above it, had been as broke down as the
rest of Henry Adams. During the winter months, he'd relied
on a space heater and layers of clothing to beat back the cold.
From spring to fall, he'd placed buckets in his tiny bedroom
and the even smaller bathroom to catch the rain from the
leaking roof. He'd cooked meals on a hot plate, and a family of
squirrels lived in the walls of the lone bedroom closet.

All that changed after Bernadine's renovations. There were
now two bedrooms. One to sleep in, and the other to house
his books, display his small art collection, and listen to his
music. He also had a working furnace with air-conditioning,
and a small stainless steel kitchen. The roof no longer leaked,
and the squirrels had been evicted. To furnish the renovated
space, he'd sprung for a new bed and a large variety of plants.
Other items like his couch, recliner, and rugs were courtesy of
yard sales, estate sales, and flea markets.

The transformation made it a home instead of the place
he'd used strictly to crash during his years of drinking, and he
loved every inch. Thinking about having to give it up when
he and Bernadine married was disquieting, though, increas-
ingly weighing on him to the point that he knew he needed
to talk to her about it, but how? He didn't know.

CHAPTER
4

It was Preston's week to see to the school's big fish tank, so after putting his coat in his locker, he checked the filters and gauges showing the water temperature and the oxygen levels before shaking in some food. He also took a moment to observe the occupants to make sure no one had been eaten overnight or had babies. Seeing no surprises, he gave the aquarium a satisfied nod and walked down the hallway to the classroom.

The school day opened as it always did with Mr. Abbott's class and Mr. James's class in the room together for the singing of the Negro national anthem, "Lift Every Voice and Sing," while Zoey accompanied on the piano. As the last notes faded away, Mr. James said, "Alfonso and Maria are of Mexican heritage and since we're all about culture here in Henry Adams, I thought it would be nice if we also paid tribute to Mexico when we start our day, so Maria . . ."

Curious as to what this meant, Preston watched ten-year-old Maria Acosta leave her seat and walk to the piano. He glanced at Amari, who replied with a shrug right before Mr. James began to speak again. "Maria has been learning to play the national anthem of Mexico. Can you tell us its name. please?"

"'Himno Nacional Mexicano,'" she said proudly. "It's also sometimes called, 'Mexicanos, Al Grito de Guerra.'"

Her brother Alfonso added, "That means, 'Mexicans, at the shout of war.'"

"Whoa," Preston whispered. The name sounded real serious.

Mr. James said, "After Maria finishes, we'll watch a You-Tube video that features a chorus singing it along with close-captioned lyrics in Spanish and English, so you'll get a feel of the voices and the words. I did some research and many articles on the anthem said only Mexicans are supposed to sing it, so rather than debate whether that's true or not and be disrespectful, we'll just listen." He looked to Maria. "Ready?"

She nodded and began to play. Preston knew she'd been taking piano lessons from Zoey Garland and Zoey's mom, Ms. Roni, so she wasn't very good yet, but her face was set tight with concentration, and the notes she flubbed were made up for with her enthusiasm. She played it fiercely. He looked forward to hearing the choir and seeing the lyrics in English.

When she finished, everyone applauded. She went a little red-faced from the praise and said, "Thank you. I know I messed up a lot, but I'll get better."

"You did just fine," Mr. James told her with a smile, and Preston agreed. He glanced Devon's way. Amari's brother didn't appear happy. Probably mad about someone else being in the spotlight, but what else was new where he was concerned. Zoey, on the other hand, was grinning proudly from ear to ear.

The day began with what Mr. James called Self-Interest Studies. Students could spend the two hours before lunch researching and studying subjects they were curious about. After lunch, everyone was given ten minutes to share what they'd learned with the rest of the class. Usually, Preston and Leah teamed up to check out the latest goings-on at the Large Hadron Collider, the world's largest and most powerful particle accelerator, or findings from NASA's new James Webb Space Telescope. He looked her way, hoping they could still share their love of science in spite of the issue between them, but she was focused on her laptop. He toyed with the idea of walking over and asking if he could sit with her like they used to but decided against it. If she turned him down, he didn't want to be embarrassed and get his feelings hurt in front of the whole class. Sighing, he booted up his screen. Another glance Amari's way showed his friend watching him intently. The concern in his eyes was as plain as it had been at the wedding reception, but he didn't say anything. Thankful for that, Preston opened the bookmarked Hadron website and let his love for physics override everything else.

Because it was wintertime, the students ate their lunch in the gym. Preston joined Amari at their usual spot. Leah had always eaten with them, but she was seated a distance away with her sister, Tiff, and some of the other girls. He removed the Ziplocs holding his sandwich and carrots from his backpack while Amari did the same with his lunch.

"So what's up with you and Leah?" Amari asked nonchalantly.

"I don't want to talk about it."

"You two break up?"

"I don't want to talk about it, Amari."

"You're stressing, man, and when you stress I worry, because you're my best friend."

Preston sighed. "It's nothing. She and I are just going through some things. It'll be okay."

For a moment Amari didn't reply and just studied him. "Okay, but if you need anything, I'm here for you."

"I know. Appreciate it."

Preston was glad Amari let the lie slide. He'd end up sharing the truth with him eventually, just not now.

They ate in silence for a few moments before Amari announced, "I'm thinking about asking my parents to take me to Atlanta so I can check out Morehouse."

Preston paused and excitement replaced his blue mood. "The HBCU Morehouse?"

"Yeah. After living in Kansas, being in that kind of environment for college will be good. I miss living in a big city where stuff's always happening. You know what I mean?"

"I do. I doubt I'll get much stuff happening at MIT but that won't be my focus. Not to belittle your choice."

"No. I didn't take it like that. You're all about the science and a place that oozes that is where you should be. Leah, too."

Preston ignored the obvious hint and bit into his baby carrot. "I'm not talking about it, Amari."

Amari smiled. "Just thought I'd try."

Preston rolled his eyes before asking seriously, "How are we going to deal with me living in Massachusetts and you living in Atlanta? We've had each other's backs for forever, seems like. Not sure how it'll be not having you to talk to and hang with."

"Same here."

That their friendship might go cold once they went to college was a continuing worry for Preston. For all intents and purposes, Amari was his brother, and he didn't want a life that didn't have him in it. Leah, either, for that matter. She was the third part of their triangular friendship and Amari looked upon her as his sister in much the same way he and Preston did Crystal and Zoey. Leah was the one who'd given Amari the book on chess that helped him learn to beat Preston like an old rug every time they sat across the board from each other. She'd become important to them both.

"I say we make a pact to always stay in touch, no matter what," Amari proposed.

"I agree. No matter where we live or what the future holds. Me and you."

"Shake."

They shook hands to seal their pledge.

"Brothers for life," Preston declared.

"For life."

The end of lunch buzzer sounded, and everyone gathered up their trash and belongings to return to their classrooms. As luck would have it, Preston and Leah reached the trash receptacle at the same time. Both paused. Feeling the urge to say something, he began, "Leah, I—"

She didn't let him finish. "I need to get back to class."

She hurried away. Amari stood nearby. Preston didn't bother hiding his sadness. Amari didn't comment, which Preston appreciated, and they joined the flow of students leaving the gym.

"So what did the doctor say?" Mal asked on the drive back to Henry Adams after Tamar's doctor visit.

"To watch my salt."

"That's all?"

"That's all you need to know."

He sighed and wondered if the rest of the world's elderly mothers were as curmudgeonly as his. "I'm your son, Tamar. If you're having health issues, don't you think I should know?"

"You should know what I'm willing to share. Nothing more."

He wasn't sure why he worried about her—she was probably going to outlive everyone he knew—but he did worry. He was sixty-five years old and she was thirty years older if his math was correct. Both their remaining days were numbered.

"Are you looking forward to your wedding?" she asked, deliberately changing the subject.

"I am."

"No second thoughts?"

"Unlike you, I'm willing to reveal what you should know."

She smiled. "Which is?"

"The living arrangements. I don't want to give up my place."

"Have you told Bernadine?"

"No."

"Why not?"

"Don't want her thinking I don't love her. Wanting to keep my place sounds selfish."

"True, but you should talk to her about it."

"I agree. I just don't know how to bring it up."

"You need to figure it out."

"I'm hoping the subject will come up naturally. Last thing I want is to hurt her. Been there. Done that."

"No kidding."

The sarcasm stung but he'd earned it. His dumb embezzlement stunt broke Bernadine's heart as had showing up at Rocky and Jack's wedding with another woman on his arm. It was a wonder Bernadine was even speaking to him, let alone marrying him.

"She has a bigger heart than anyone I know. I'd've fed you arsenic."

"I can always depend on you to tell the truth."

Tamar swung those hawklike eyes his way, but he didn't flinch. After being nailed by them most of his life he was immune—at least for the most part.

"I wish I'd've fed Joel Newton arsenic. Still do."

Mal stilled and glanced away from the traffic to study her face. Her bitterness was plain. Newton was his father. She'd found out on her wedding day that he was already married. "First time you've mentioned him in decades," he replied as nonchalantly as he could.

"No reason to."

They'd rarely discussed his parentage. He'd learned the details from Marie Jefferson's mother, Agnes, and could only imagine how humiliated and furious the prideful Tamar must have been when Newton's wife showed up at the ceremony and outed him as a bigamist. A short time later, Tamar discovered she was pregnant.

Mal took the opportunity to ask a question he'd worried over since being old enough to know the circumstances of his birth. "Did you resent me being his child?"

The silence in the cab grew so lengthy, he thought he'd overstepped. "Sorry if that was too personal."

"It is, but you deserve to know. At first, I did, but the day you were born changed me. You didn't ask to be born."

Relief filled him. "I thought you not wanting me was the reason you were so hard on me growing up."

"No. I was hard on you because you were hardheaded and smart-mouthed. Typical July in other words. It had nothing to do with Newton, even though you favor him so much that when I see you, I see him."

Having never met the man, Mal didn't know that, either. Although Tamar raised him well, he often wondered how his life might have been different had he had a father instead of relying on men like his grandfather, Clay's dad, and Rocky's grandfather for guidance along the way. Maybe his seventeen-year-old self wouldn't have gotten Rita Lynn pregnant. Maybe he would've been less traumatized by Nam and not turned to alcohol to cope with the demons the war left him with. Might he have been a better father to Trent? Would he have married and settled down instead of being a player chasing after women young enough to not know Marcus Garvey from W.E.B. Du Bois? Those unanswerable questions quietly nagged him for years, and truthfully, continued to do so.

He wanted to ask her if Newton was still alive, but she spoke first. "No more questions."

He supposed he'd done well getting her to respond at all, so he bowed to her wishes. "Okay."

A few moments later, he looked her way and saw her nestled comfortably against the door, eyes closed, asleep, or maybe pretending to be. Either way, their conversation was over.

Upon returning to Henry Adams, Mal made sure Tamar got inside her house okay before driving off. The short talk about Newton and his thoughts about fathers made him want to see his own son, so he stopped at Trent's garage.

Trent was the town's former mayor. He had a degree in engineering and held a few manufacturing patents that were lucrative enough to provide a good life for his family and allowed him to retire. One of Mal's biggest regrets was knowing Trent spent his high school weekends crisscrossing the county in search of his drunk dad to keep him from killing someone while behind the wheel. It was humbling knowing he had a much better son than he'd ever deserved.

Entering the garage, he found Trent working under the raised hood of an old sapphire blue and white Packard. "Where in the world did this come from?" he asked eyeing the big curvy automobile with surprise.

Trent straightened up. Smiling, he wiped his hands on a small shop towel. "Hey, Dad. A guy in Topeka found it in his grandfather's barn after his death last month. It was towed here a few days ago."

"Does it run?"

"It does. Drives okay too, but he wants it cleaned up and repainted. It's a 1941, 110 coupe. Six cylinder."

Mal walked closer. "What's it worth? Do you know?"

"Right now, about fifteen or sixteen grand, but will be worth a lot more once I'm done with it."

The car looked like something from an old forties movie.

Trent then asked, "You have time to sit a minute? I'm going to take a break. Amari should be here in a few. School just let out."

"Sure."

They left the bay and walked into the garage's waiting room. Trent pulled two colas out of the old red Coca-Cola cooler and handed one to Mal. They sat and sipped.

Trent asked, "How'd Tamar's doctor appointment go?"

Mal shrugged. "Who knows? She made me wait out in the waiting room. She said the doc told her to watch her salt intake but that was it."

"She stays real closemouthed about her visits. I asked her once if she'd tell me if she had any life-threatening issues. She said, no."

Mal shook his head at her stubbornness. "Kind of frustrating."

"Agreed, but what can you do? Can't tie her up and make her talk. Although sometimes I wish we could."

"We'd never live long enough to hear the answers, though."

Trent laughed. "No, we wouldn't."

Amari sauntered in. "Hey, Dad. Hey, OG."

Trent greeted him and then it was Mal's turn. "Hey, young gun. How are you?"

"I'm good."

Mal watched and listened as Trent and his son talked about the school day while Amari stashed his coat and backpack in a locker and changed into his coveralls. Amari loved cars so he and Trent were a perfect dynamic duo. In fact, before moving to Henry Adams, Amari spent most of his time speeding up and down Detroit's freeways in stolen cars, and being arrested. His young friends nicknamed him Flash in honor of how fast he could steal one. The last time Amari was arrested for car theft had been during his first summer in Henry Adams during a well-meaning, but misguided plan to help Crystal find her birth mom. He'd stolen Mal's truck.

"We had self-study this morning," Amari said continuing to tell them about his school day. "And this afternoon we learned about the confluence with Jupiter and Saturn that's going to be happening soon. Mr. James said it's been like eight hundred years since the two planets hung out together this way."

"That's a long time," Trent replied.

"I know you and OG probably read this online or heard it on the news, but Mr. James said if you go back in time, astronomers and astrologists think the confluence made the Christmas star the wise men were following when they found baby Jesus."

"I did read that," Mal said. "I also read that some people think when those two planets align the world's energy changes and that great men are born or rise to prominence."

"Yeah, we talked about Alexander the Great and Saladin because there was a confluence during their times, too."

Trent said, "Interesting."

"Mr. James wants to have a star watch when they get closer so we can see it. If the weather's good."

"I like that idea. Mom and I can get you a telescope if you want one of your own."

He shook his head. "I wouldn't use it that much, so it would be a waste of money. Mr. James has one and so do Brain and Leah. I can look through theirs." He quieted, then said, "Something's not right with them, though."

"What do you mean?" Trent asked.

Amari relayed examples of what he'd observed.

"Have you asked Brain about it?" Mal asked, concerned about the town's budding scientists.

"He said he doesn't want to talk about it."

Trent replied, "Then as his friend, you'll have to accept that. If and when he's ready to open up, he will."

"But I worry about him and Leah, Dad."

"I hear you, but if the relationship is starting to split apart, there's nothing you can do but be there for him and/or her."

"I care about them both. I don't want to have to choose."

"Understood, but don't try and force an explanation from them as to what's going on. If they want you to know, they will."

Mal knew Trent was offering good advice, but knowing Amari he still wanted to help fix whatever was going on because Preston and Leah were his friends and Amari had a big heart.

Trent's next words mirrored Mal's thoughts. "I know how deeply you care about people, Amari—it's one of your strengths as a person—but sometimes you have to take a seat and just watch."

"It's hard."

"I know."

Mal saw the patience, love, and wisdom he'd grown accustomed to seeing in Trent's face when dealing with his son, and he envied that because he hadn't been there for Trent in that way at that age. It saddened him too because there was no way to go back in time and change it.

"Things will work out, son. They always do."

Amari answered with a half-hearted nod.

"You ready to work?" Trent asked him.

"Yeah."

Mal took that as his cue to leave. He stood. "I'm going to head home. I'm tired after all that driving. You two have fun." He waved goodbye and left them to their work and their love for each other.

Seated in her office, Reverend Paula ended her call and sat back to process the conversation. Robyn wasn't coming home in a couple more days as they had last talked about. She wanted to stay in Atlanta and work for Habitat for Humanity instead. She'd already broached living with Leslie, whom Paula also spoke with, and who said she'd love to have Robyn stay. When Paula brought up the subject of school, Robyn stated she'd get a GED and consider college maybe sometime in the near future. It was a lot for Paula to take in. She loved her young cousin. The two of them had endured much growing up in poverty-drenched Blackbird, Oklahoma. Paula enjoyed sharing a home with her and had been looking forward to watching Robyn blossom and grow. However, Paula was also a firm believer in choosing your own path. Robyn turned eighteen last month, which meant she could legally do what she pleased, so rather than deny her and cause a rift, Paula agreed, even though the plan left her sad. Did she believe Robyn was mature enough to live on her own? She had doubts but took comfort in the fact that she'd be living with a family who'd look after her as if she were their own. Paula also knew how taken she herself had been on her first trip to Atlanta after finally getting away from Blackbird. She'd been like Dorothy in the Emerald City. Everywhere she looked there were wonders: music, people her age filled with dreams and aspirations, plays, concerts, museums, nightlife. She supposed Robyn was experiencing a similar excitement. As much as Paula loved Henry Adams, she'd be the first to admit that due to its isolation and lack of amusements there wasn't much to offer those on the cusp of adulthood. The historic town and its citizens offered a stellar environment to raise and mold children, but to continue their maturation, leaving the nest was a given. Yet another reason to support Robyn's plan.

Feeling blue she began packing up for the end of her office day when a knock on her opened door drew her attention.

She glanced up to see teacher Kyrie Abbott standing there. "Hey, neighbor." Kyrie was a teacher at Marie Jefferson Academy and had lived near her in one of the three double-wides on Tamar's land. This past summer, he'd moved into an apartment in the renovated Sutton Hotel to be closer to the school. At twenty-four years old, he was a handsome, dark-skinned young man. In her day, the ladies would've termed him a babe. From his stylish short twists and small silver hoop earring to his black jeans and Timbs, he was all that. Raised well, whip-smart, and caring, he was going to make a difference in the world someday.

"Hey, Reverend. Can I talk to you for a minute?"

"Sure, come on in and close the door."

Once he took a seat, Paula asked, "What's up?"

"I'm thinking of leaving Henry Adams."

She studied him silently for a moment. "Okay," she said, drawing out the word.

He appeared torn. "I mean, I'm proud to teach at the Academy. The pay is fantastic, but I'm bored to death, Rev."

She chuckled softly and thought back on her musings about Robyn and Henry Adams's shortcomings. "I understand. There's not much to do here for someone your age."

"There's nothing for someone my age to do here."

"Have you talked to Jack about how you're feeling?"

"I haven't talked to anyone yet, so far. I'm worried they'll think I'm ungrateful after all they did to get me here."

"I don't think you have to worry about that." Everyone would be sad to lose him, though.

"Mr. James is a great mentor," he said, continuing. "He's taught me so much. I'd like to take what he's given me and apply it to a school that needs it. There are districts all over the country that could use his methods, and I feel as if I'm sort of wasting it teaching only a handful of kids when I could be reaching twice as many somewhere else."

"I understand, but honestly, finding a district that will allow you to teach outside the box the way Jack does may be difficult due to all the rules and regulations."

"I know, but I'm willing to look for one. His methods could really make a difference in a larger environment, especially an urban one."

"Is there anything I can do to help?"

"I'm not sure, but I wanted to run it by you to make sure I'm not being disrespectful about wanting to leave."

"I don't see it that way, but respect Jack enough to talk to him. The sooner the better. When are you planning on leaving?"

"Ideally, after the holidays. I know it's short notice, but I honestly can't stay here until June. I really can't. Maybe I'll come back when I'm older and I'm ready to settle down with a family because this is the perfect place for that, but not now."

She nodded understandingly.

"I came to talk to you first because I know you're everybody's counselor and I'm hoping you can sort of soften things up for me by letting Ms. Marie know that I'm thinking of leaving?"

She shook her head. "No. If this is your decision, you need to own it. It's part of being an adult."

He sighed. "You're right."

She waited for whatever else he had to add.

"I'll talk to Jack at school tomorrow and see what he has to say."

"I'm sure he'll be disappointed, but he'll also be understanding."

He sighed again. "I've talked to my parents."

"And they said?"

"My mom's happy I want to leave. She's still worried about that drama with the Russians last summer and that they'll come back and shoot up the town again. My dad thinks I should stay and stick it out, but said the decision is totally on me. What do you think?"

"That the decision is yours."

"Team Dad, then."

"No. Team Kyrie. This is your life."

He nodded and cracked a small smile. "Okay, Rev. Thanks for listening."

"Anytime."

After his departure, she hoped all would go well with him, while also hoping Bernadine and the town officials found a way to make Henry Adams more attractive to young people like Kyrie Abbott so it would not only survive but thrive.

WHEN SCHOOL LET out for the day, Preston put in a shift as a bagger at Clark's. Once his shift ended, he walked home and smiled as he spotted his mom's red Jeep in the driveway. As the new mayor she'd been spending a lot of evenings at the Power Plant with Ms. Bernadine and Amari's mom working on town stuff. He and his dad had been trading off doing dinner and housework to help out. Entering the house, he removed his coat, and set his backpack down. She was in the kitchen and the sight of her and the wonderful smell of her pot roast filling the air lifted the gloomy mood he'd been carrying around for the past few days. "Hey, Mom."

She turned from the sink. "Hey there. How are you?"

"I'm good. How are you?"

"Enjoying being home in time to cook dinner for my guys. You and your pops have been doing most of the cooking lately, and I've really appreciated it."

"We haven't minded. Pops hasn't complained, either. I saw him at work. He said he'd be home by six."

"Good to know."

"Can I help with anything?"

"Everything's nearly done, but thanks for asking. How was school?"

"Okay. We're still studying the confluence."

"I talked to Bernadine about the sky watch event. She liked the idea."

"Good. You think we can have hot chocolate?"

She gave him a smile. "I'll talk to Rocky. Her staff has a lot on their plate with all the events coming up. They may not have time."

He knew she was right but held on to his hopes. Being in Henry Adams and having great parents made the Christmas season something to look forward to in ways he'd never experienced in foster care. Although his problems with Leah muted his feelings somewhat, he was determined not to let them ruin things completely. "What do you want for Christmas?"

She paused and seemed to think it over. "Not sure. It's not as if I need anything."

"I have to get you a present."

"Surprise me."

"You're not helping, Mom."

She laughed softly. "You'll think of something, and whatever it is, I'll love it."

Preston heard the front door open and close, and a second later, his pops entered. "Hey, you two."

"Hey back," his mom said. Barrett walked over and kissed Sheila on the cheek.

"Hey, Pops. When I was at work, I heard Mrs. Beadle and Lorenzo were escorted out by Deputy Ransom this morning."

Barrett lifted the lids on the pots on the stove, peeked inside, and gave his wife a smile. "You heard right." Taking a seat at the table he continued, "I don't know what we're going to do with her. On one hand, she's just a harmless, little old lady. On the other hand, after stealth drinking most of a bottle of wine while shopping, she's pretty drunk by the time she gets to the checkout lanes. Can't have her drinking and driving. Not to mention, the Health Department won't be happy if they find out Lorenzo's been on the premises again. We've already been closed down once because of that dog."

His dad was head of security for the store and for the town and was referencing the time Lorenzo got loose in the store and went tearing through the aisles like something out of a *Fast and Furious* movie. The whole place had to be cleaned, sanitized, and inspected by the Health Department before being allowed to reopen for business. Barrett added, "I called the sheriff on her today, and Will said he'd speak to Mrs. Beadles's son again to see if some solution can be found."

"Why doesn't the son move her closer to him?" Sheila asked.

"Doesn't want the responsibility it seems."

Preston knew from being in foster care how it felt to be unwanted. "That's sad."

"I agree."

"Wash your hands and grab a plate, gentlemen," his mom said. "Time to eat."

After dinner, his mother went upstairs to work in the spare room she'd turned into an office and Preston and his pops cleaned up the kitchen. Once they were done, Preston headed to his room to tackle homework, while his dad settled on the couch to watch TV.

One of the day's assignments was to listen to Duke Ellington's *Nutcracker Suite* album. Preston knew a little bit about Ellington from previous lessons on jazz musicians. What he hadn't known was that the Duke and his bud Billy Strayhorn had flipped Tchaikovsky's Nutcracker Suite and composed a jazz version. Mr. James wanted his student to listen to "Sugar Rum Cherry," the Duke's spin on "Dance of the Sugar Plum Fairy," and "Toot Toot Tootie Toot," the jazzed-up "Dance of the Reed Pipes." There'd be a discussion tomorrow. Settling in, Preston listened to the original Tchaikovsky versions on YouTube, made some notes, then brought up Ellington-Strayhorn renditions. The lively beats and swagger made him smile.

He listened to both composers again and while it played, he shot Leah a text asking if they could talk. She didn't respond. Frustrated, it occurred to him that maybe he should let her have her way and go along with the breakup, but he didn't want that. He wanted them to talk this out. Scrolling through his phone to see if maybe he'd missed a text from her, he saw that he'd missed a call from his bio mom.

Dr. Margaret Winthrop and his bio dad, Lawrence Mays, were college students when she became pregnant. Their plans to marry were shattered when Lawrence was killed in a car accident. Margaret's wealthy conservative parents, appalled by the pregnancy, didn't care that she'd loved Lawrence, or that he'd been brilliant with a bright future ahead of him had he lived. They didn't want an out-of-wedlock baby sired by a poor kid from Philly's inner city sullying the illustrious Winthrop name. They demanded she put her son up for adoption. Determined to hold on to her child, she refused, but she'd been twenty years old with few resources of her own, so, after much arguing and tears, she surrendered. Preston went into the foster care system. Margaret moved in with her aunt and cut ties with her parents.

Mother and son were reunited two years ago by her mother, Lenore Winthrop, who hoped a reunion would help close the divide between Margaret and her parents. Margaret hadn't spoken to them since being forced to give up her infant son. It didn't heal the breach, but it did bring Preston and Margaret back into each other's lives.

He sent her a text apologizing for his late reply, and she immediately responded with a request for a video chat. He texted an okay and waited for her to appear.

"Hey, Preston," she said, smiling as she came on-screen. She was in her office at NASA. She was an astrophysicist and as beautiful as a supermodel.

"Hey, Doc. How are you?" It took Preston a while to settle on a name he felt comfortable addressing her by. First it had been Dr. Winthrop, then Dr. Margaret. He'd finally shortened it to Doc, and they were both good with that.

"I'm okay." They spent a few minutes catching up on small matters, like schoolwork, and his prep for entering MIT. Then she dropped a bombshell. "I've been contacted by your dad's sister."

He froze.

"Are your parents home?" she asked.

Shocked and shaking, he nodded.

"Can you ask them to join us for a few minutes? I want them to hear what I'm going to say."

Preston couldn't move at first, but eventually left his room to do as she'd asked. A million and one things swirled in his brain as he walked down the hallway to where his mom was working. The door was open. She looked up from her laptop and, seeing his face, went still. "What's wrong? You look like you've seen a ghost."

"Doc and I are on a chat, and she said she's been contacted by my bio dad's family. She's going to tell me about it and wants you and Pops to come listen."

Her concern plain, she took him in for a moment. "Are you okay with this, Preston?"

"Not sure."

"Understandable. It has to be overwhelming but let's see what she has to say. I'll get Barrett and we'll be right there."

He returned to his room and sat down again in front of the screen on his desk. "They're coming."

Margaret nodded. "While we wait, tell me what you want for Christmas."

Christmas was the furthest thing from his mind, at the moment. "Can I think about it and get back to you?"

"Of course."

His parents arrived. Flanking him, they shared greetings with Margaret. That done, she began. "Lawrence's sister, Cecily Mays Darden, got in touch with me yesterday. She saw me mentioned in last Sunday's *New York Times* article on the women of NASA."

Preston had seen it, too. Reading about her many accomplishments filled him with pride.

Margaret continued, "To make a long story short. The family is overjoyed to learn you and I have been reunited, Preston, and they want to meet you. I spoke with Lawrence's mom, Grace Mays, and she cried hearing that you're alive and well. She said she's prayed for you every night and during church every Sunday since the day you were born."

His heart swelling, he looked up at Sheila, who smiled in response and gave his shoulder an encouraging squeeze.

His pops's face was unreadable when he asked, "Are they good people, Margaret?"

"Yes, Barrett, they are. Lawrence was raised well. I met them when he and I were dating. He was the first in his family to attend college. They were so proud that he'd gotten the scholarship and were devastated when he was killed. I'd be okay with connecting them with Preston, but it's not my decision. You and Sheila are his parents, which is why I wanted you to hear all this."

Preston didn't need to think about it. "Tell them yes," he said quietly. "I want to be contacted."

Just as quietly, his dad looked down at him and asked, "You sure?"

"Yes." Preston looked again to his mom, who offered a smiling nod of approval. He couldn't put his feelings into words, but he felt the rightness of it. He wanted to know his bio dad's family and for them to know him.

Margaret appeared pleased with his decision. "I'll give Cecily your email and you all can take it from here."

They gave her their thanks and she was gone.

Preston sat silent thinking about what this meant. For forever, he'd wanted to know who his biological families were. The question was half answered when Margaret's awful mother, Lenore, hooked them up, and now the last half was about to be answered, too. "Do you think his family will like me?"

Sheila replied, "How could they not?"

Barrett said, "If they're not as proud as Sheila and I are of all you've accomplished, and the strides you've made, then they won't be worthy of your time."

He supposed the colonel was right, but deep inside Preston wanted them to see him as part of the son they'd lost. His intellect and love for science was due not only to Margaret but to the man who'd fathered him. He wondered if he had other family members, like cousins? That would be a question for Lawrence's sister, Cecily, he supposed. A part of him anxiously wanted to be contacted right away, but another part wanted to take a few days to get used to the idea.

His mom said, "If you're having second thoughts, you can change your mind."

"No. I'm just not sure if I want her to contact me right away or wait a few days so I can process everything."

He looked to the two people who'd become the most important people in his life.

His dad said, "Totally up to you. There's something to be said for both choices. Only you get to decide which one you want."

Preston was glad the colonel wasn't being a hard-ass. A few years back, when he first began searching for his biological parents, the retired marine hadn't been very supportive. This time around, he seemed to be handling things much better.

An email popped up. It was from Cecily. *"Dearest Preston. Being contacted by us has probably thrown you for a loop. Although we are jumping with joy at the thought of connecting with you, we're sure this is a lot for you to deal with, so we'll leave when we connect up to you. Take care. Aunt Cecily Mays Darden.*

Preston smiled.

"How caring," his mom said. "I like her already."

He did as well.

CHAPTER
5

Chef Thornton Webb sat on the bed in the tiniest hotel room he'd ever been in and wearily dropped his head into his hands. He'd imagined the fifteen-hundred-mile drive from California to Henry Adams would be scenic and picturesque. Instead, it had turned out to be a nightmare. The first leg on I-80 from California into Nevada had been fine; traffic had been light, the jazz playing through the speakers of his flashy German import had been soothing, and although the sky had been a bit cloudy, the weather had been cooperative. Things began going downhill when he crossed the border into Utah and found himself in a blizzard. For two scary hours, his top speed of thirty-five miles per hour was all he could safely muster as the snow blew so fiercely he could barely see the road ahead. It made for an anxious white-knuckle drive that left his hands sore and stiff from gripping the steering wheel so tightly. Upon seeing signs for Salt Lake City, he'd decided getting off the highway was in his best interest and stumbled onto this tiny motel. There was an even smaller diner attached. He planned to get something to eat but first he needed to recover and let his heart rate return to normal. Sighing, he removed his hikers and fell back onto the thin mattress. Two seconds later, he was asleep.

When he awakened the next morning, it took a few bleary moments to figure out where he was and why he was fully dressed. Remembrance came on a groan, and he sat up slowly. Dragging his hands over his eyes, he stood and walked to the window. Opening the drapes showed a snow-covered landscape stretching as far as he could see. Were he a kid in Chicago he'd be celebrating a snow day, but as an adult, he was not looking forward to continuing his drive.

After a surprisingly good breakfast of eggs, bacon, and the best biscuits he'd had in quite some time, he paid his bill and crossed the freshly plowed parking lot to his snow-covered car. He'd been smart enough to buy a snow scraper when he crossed the Nevada state line into Utah, so he pulled it out of the trunk, turned on the car's engine and defroster, and set to work. He applauded himself for bringing along a pair of gloves, but he'd forgotten a hat. His head and ears weren't happy with the twenty-degree temperature. Raising the hood of the sweatshirt beneath his black parka, he carried on.

According to the route he'd plotted out, I-80 would take him across the southern border of Wyoming and into the city of Cheyenne. From there he'd cross into Nebraska and head south to Kansas. According to his GPS, Cheyenne was about six and a half hours away from Salt Lake City but with last night's snowstorm, he wasn't sure what lay ahead.

As he pulled out of the tiny motel's parking lot, he called Ms. Brown to let her know his location and approximate arrival. He then topped off his gas tank and set out. The sun was shining, making the snow sparkle like a blanket of diamonds, but the wind was blowing, causing moments of limited visibility. The roads were passable, but the pavement was covered by flattened inches of snow, making it necessary to stay in the ruts carved out by the traffic. Trucks whizzed by, but he and his import were forced to crawl. Crossing into Wyoming he had no time to be awed by the state's mountainous beauty; he was too busy slowing down to skirt semis that had slid off the road, gripping the steering wheel to stay in the ruts, and being stuck in several, miles-long traffic backups due to cars spinning out and, at one point, a small herd of bison standing in the road. As a result, the planned six and a half hours turned into eight. By the time he reached Cheyenne it was dark. Were it summertime he might have pushed on and driven straight through to Henry Adams, but he was so tired, and his nerves so shot from worrying about getting into an accident of his own, he opted for a room in a national chain hotel. After a hot shower and room service, he settled into bed and vowed to never drive cross-country during winter again.

The next afternoon, he finally made it to Kansas. After leaving the interstate, he turned onto a small two-lane road. Seeing the sign HENRY ADAMS 25 MILES, he did a fist pump. He'd made it. However, a little more than a mile later the road was so snow covered, he got stuck. His attempts to rock free by alternating forward and reverse only succeeded in burying his fancy wheels deeper. Frustrated, he slammed his hand against the steering wheel, which caused the horn to respond with an angry blare, and got out to see if he could push his way free. No. The snow was up over the wheel wells, and he needed Hulk strength to make it move. He looked around for possible help but saw only open, snow-covered plains. There were no homes, barns, or traffic. Sighing, he got back in the car. Praying there was cell phone coverage, he placed a call to Ms. Brown. When she answered, he wanted to shout for joy. His face hot with embarrassment, he explained his plight. Her concern sounded genuine, and when she promised to send help, he vowed to cook her the best meal she'd ever had.

"Trent will be out to get you shortly," she informed him. "Stay in the car where it's warm. It's frostbite weather out there."

"Yes, ma'am, and thanks."

Their call ended, and he settled in to wait.

Forty minutes later a tow truck came into view and caught his attention. When it reached him, Trent July, one of the men he'd met briefly during his first trip to Henry Adams, got out. Tall and dark-skinned, he had on a heavy parka and a KU ball cap. With him was a man he hadn't met before. His height matched July's. He had gold-colored skin and was dressed just as warmly. Thorn got out to greet them. "Thanks for the rescue," he said.

"No problem," July replied. "This is our town fire chief, Luis Acosta."

"Pleased to meet you," Thorn said, shaking his gloved hand.

"Same here," the chief stated in a voice tinged with Spanish.

The two men surveyed his car's predicament.

"You're stuck all right," Acosta said, stating the obvious while viewing the snow-packed wheel wells.

July took a walk around it and cracked, "Nice vehicle, but Matchbox cars don't do good out here."

Amused, Thorn hung his head. "You got jokes."

They grinned. July added, "The snow has the best jokes, that's why most of us drive good old Detroit trucks."

Thorn had noticed all the pickups on I-80. Back in Oakland, the young people drove trucks as a status thing, but on the plains it seemed trucks were less about status and more about necessity and good sense.

"Okay," Trent said as if coming to a decision. "The snow's this deep all the way into town, so it doesn't make sense to pull you out only to have you get stuck again. Luis and I will get your car hooked up and we'll tow it in. You can ride in the wrecker with us."

Thorn agreed. Although he didn't want to think about the damage his Matchbox might incur from the tow, he was thankful his ordeal of a journey was almost over.

Getting to town took just a bit under an hour and as they rode down Main Street with his car attached to the back, he took in the snow-covered surroundings and the buildings lining the way. He wondered how he'd view the town a year from now. Presently it was all new and he was admittedly excited. Over time he'd come to know the various personalities, have a feel for the everyday rhythms of Henry Adams, and learn how things worked. Hopefully, he'd also learn more about its fabled history and why he felt so called by it. He couldn't wait to begin filling in the holes.

"We'll drop you off at the Power Plant," Trent told him. "Ms. Brown will take over from there."

"Sounds good." And before Thorn could say more, the wrecker turned into the parking lot of the distinctive brick red building. It was round and had a distinctive flat top. How such a cutting-edge design wound up on the plains of Kansas was something else that piqued his curiosity. It seemed more suited for a big city zip code.

With Trent working the winch, Thorn's car was eased down to a horizontal position and Luis released the large hook from the front end. To Thorn's relief, it looked none the worse for wear. "Thanks so much for everything."

"Anytime," Luis said walking back to the front of the wrecker. "I'm sure I'll see you around. And welcome to Henry Adams."

Trent added, "Let us know if you need anything."

"Will do!"

As his rescuers drove away, Thorn gave them a wave and went inside to find Ms. Brown.

"You made it," she said.

"No thanks to the weather," Thorn replied, dropping wearily into one the chairs.

"Mother Nature here and Mother Nature in Cali are two very different women."

"No kidding," he said, grimacing. "I'm beat. Is there a hotel or a B&B nearby where I can stay?"

"There are a couple of chain hotels in Franklin, the next town over, but we thought you might prefer one of the town double-wides on Tamar's land. You'll have a lot more space."

He wasn't sure about trailer living.

As if sensing his doubt, she further explained, "It's fully furnished, has two bedrooms, and the stove is gas."

The chef in him perked up at the mention of a gas stove. "How soon can I see it?"

"We can run out there now, if you'd like. Let me send

Tamar July a text and make sure she's been plowed out. We don't want you to get stuck again."

He didn't, either; he'd had enough drama.

The reply was prompt.

"She said Trent plowed her out early this morning. We should be good."

"Buying a truck is at the top of my to-do list."

"What do you drive now?"

He told her.

"Those aren't much use out here. Let me know when you're ready to look for one. There's a dealership over in Franklin and I can get you a discount."

"Good to know."

"Are you ready to roll?"

He was and hoped not to have to get back behind the wheel of a car again anytime soon.

The trailer turned out to be spacious and well furnished. There was even artwork on the neutral-colored walls. To his delight the fridge was fully stocked.

"Our local grocer will deliver anything else you might need. Just give them a call. They don't carry anything real fancy, but they have a good selection."

Inside the fridge he took in the eggs, bacon, milk, and the fresh veggies and fruit: like asparagus, blueberries, and navel oranges. "Do you always stock the fridges of visitors?"

"We do. Especially for those we want to entice to stick around."

"Are the other trailers we passed occupied?"

"Yes. Bobby Douglas, his wife, Kelly, and their toddler twins are in the blue one. They spent Thanksgiving in Texas where they're from. They'll be home soon. Our priest, Reverend Paula

Grant, and her teen cousin, Robyn, are in the gray one. Robyn's in Atlanta and Paula drove over to Topeka for a meeting. She'll be back in a day or so."

"I don't think I met the Douglases when I was here. I do remember the priest. We spoke about the partnership my restaurant had with one of the local Episcopal churches in Oakland." He also remembered being intrigued by her cowgirl boots and her eyes that were the color of sandalwood.

"I'll make sure they all stop by and introduce themselves if that's okay."

"I'd like that."

"And they won't mind you hitching a ride into town if it snows again and you haven't purchased your truck."

He kept staring around at the fine accommodations.

"Do you think this place will be okay for the short term?" she asked.

"More than okay."

"Good. I'm going to head back. Tamar will probably be by shortly to check on you. You met her on your first trip."

"I remember her." The older woman had told him something about Henry Adams being a place he needed to be. She'd come off as pretty mystical but not in a scary way. He was interested in finding out what she'd meant. "Thanks again for sending the rescue party and for taking care of my living arrangements."

"You're welcome. Here's a list of phone numbers just in case you need anything."

He took the small piece of paper from her hand. "Thanks, I'm going to get my stuff out of my trunk then fix myself a meal and probably crash for a few hours."

"Sounds good."

Thorn walked out with her, and while she climbed into her blue truck, he used his clicker to raise the lid on his trunk that was packed to within an inch of its life with clothes, cookware, pots, books, tech gear, and everything else he deemed essential. Nonessential items were being shipped. Anything else he needed he'd purchase as part of his new Henry Adams life.

She drove away with a wave, and he began hauling his possessions inside the trailer. He was making his last trip out to the car when an old green truck pulled in behind his car. Out stepped Tamar July.

"Afternoon, Chef."

"Hello, Ms. July. Ms. Brown said you might stop by. How are you?"

"I'm well. Do you need help?"

"No, ma'am, but you're welcome to come in if you care to."

"Okay. I won't stay but a few minutes, though. You're probably dead from driving, but I want to make sure you have everything you need."

Inside, she asked, "How was the trip?"

"Long and snowy."

"That time of year. I stocked the fridge. Wasn't sure what else you needed besides the basics."

"Everything is fine. Thanks so much for the food. How much do I owe you?"

She waved him off. "Don't worry about it."

The town matriarch's silver-haired presence was even more impressive than Thorn remembered. In spite of the old, battered peacoat she was wearing with her equally battered heavy wool skirt and combat boots, she exuded a majestic aura that was regal and commanding. He felt like he should be bowing.

"Did Bernadine tell you about your neighbors?"

"Yes, and she gave me a list of phone numbers in case I need anything."

"Good. Then I'll let you get settled. I'm up the road a short piece. Just so you know. Monthly town meeting is tomorrow evening. You can ride into town with me if you want. Be nice for folks to meet you and for you to meet them."

"I agree. Look forward to it. Thanks for everything."

"You're welcome. Get some rest."

"Yes, ma'am."

Once alone, the chef took a slow tour of his new home. He'd no idea trailers could be so elegant. He was impressed by everything he viewed, from the kitchen to the bedrooms, to the bathroom with its walk-in shower and high-end, cream-colored tile. The place offered more in terms of flexibility, space, and comfort than a hotel suite ever would. He returned to the living room to retrieve his suitcase so he could take a shower, settle in, and begin his residency, but first he called his sister, June, to let her know he'd arrived safely.

"You made it," she said. "How was the drive?"

"Scary. Ran into a blizzard."

"That's what you get for relocating to Nowheresville, America."

He smiled. "Going to buy a truck. The Benz wasn't happy."

"I'll bet. Have you checked in with the lovebirds?" That was her nickname for their parents.

"Not yet. They're next. Wanted to touch base with you first."

They spent a few more minutes talking about his trip, the completed sale of the restaurant, and his house in Oakland. She brought him up to speed on the latest doings of his niece, nephews, and brother-in-law. As the conversation came to an end, she said, "Glad you made it. Get some rest."

"Will do. Talk to you soon. Love you, sis."

"You better."

His call to his parents went straight to voice mail. He left a quick message and vowed to catch up with them later.

BRIGHT AND EARLY the following morning the big burlap-wrapped spruce that would be the town's Christmas tree arrived on an eighteen-wheeler flatbed. As word spread everyone came out to see it: Bernadine and Lily, Tamar, the staff and diners at the Dog, and the students at the school. With the help of the Dads, Warren Kelly's construction crew, and members of Luis's volunteer firefighters, the tree was hoisted into the air by a crane and guided into a large predug hole in front of the rec center. While the crane held it in position the workers used a backhoe to fill the hole with enough topsoil to help the tree stand on its own. It was then watered well. To ensure it wouldn't topple, the trunk had been fit with metal collars and lengths of chain connected to stakes, which the men firmly pounded into the ground. Once that was accomplished, Trent sent all the onlookers to the far side of the street for safety in case the tree fell. The burlap was cut away and the branches slowly unfurled like the wings of a mammoth green butter-fly. Loud oohs and ahhs rose from the onlookers. The crane backed away, leaving the tree standing tall and proud. Cheers and applause followed.

Bernadine was awed. "Look at that thing!" It was healthy, perfectly symmetrical, and huge.

"It's gorgeous, Sheila," Lily said to Sheila standing with them.

"That's definitely a big to-do tree," Bernadine pointed out.

Standing with the kids from the school, Preston yelled, "Great job, Mom."

"Thank you!"

And the crowd gave their approval by chanting her name. "Sheila! Sheila! Sheila!"

Embarrassed by the praise she dropped her head for a moment, then raised it and smiled.

THAT EVENING, A tired and hungry Reverend Paula returned to Henry Adams after her meeting in Topeka and drove to the Dog for the December town meeting. By the time she arrived the place was already packed. After looking around for a seat and seeing no empty ones, she'd resigned herself to standing along the wall when she saw Tamar waving her over. Thankful, she made her way through the crush to the booth where the matriarch was seated with Kyrie, and a tall man who looked vaguely familiar, but she couldn't place him.

"Glad you made it back," Tamar told her. "We neighbors have to look out for each other so I saved you a seat."

"Bless you." She removed her parka and sat next to Kyrie.

"Hey, Rev."

"Hey." She wanted to ask him if he'd had his conversation with Jack but thought maybe now was not the time. She saw the stranger watching her and suddenly remembered where she'd seen him before. "You're the chef."

"I am. And you're Reverend Grant."

"Yes. We met so briefly when you were here a few months ago and we talked about your restaurant partnering with a local Episcopal church. It took me a moment to place your face. I'm sorry."

"Not a problem."

Tamar asked, "Have you eaten, Reverend?"

"No, ma'am."

"Then go before it's all gone. Everyone and their mother's here tonight to hear about Sheila's Christmas plan. The buffet may run out."

As hungry as Paula was, finding the buffet empty was the last thing she wanted so she stood. "Can I get anyone anything?"

The chef asked Tamar, "Are we allowed seconds?"

"You're allowed as many trips as you want until the food runs out, so if you want more, now's the time."

He glanced up at Paula. "Mind if I go with you?"

"No. Come on." She'd be the first to admit he was the finest man she'd seen in quite some time. His marital status was unknown, but if he was single, women would be crawling through glass to get his attention. She'd not be one of them, though. He appeared a few years younger, and though she had many names, *cougar* wasn't one.

Her journey to the buffet was slowed by people wanting to say hello, share news about neighbors needing pastoral care, and ask about upcoming Advent events at the church, but once there she piled a bit of everything on her plate. "I'm so hungry."

"Ms. James and her crew put on quite a spread."

She agreed. There were wings, sliders, dumplings, and tiny quiches. The salad bar caught her attention as did the foil-wrapped baked potatoes and the nachos with all the fixings.

Bing walked up, looked the chef up and down, and asked, "This your new fella, Reverend?"

Paula almost dropped her plate. "No, Bing. This is—"

Appalled, she didn't remember his name. He offered her a smile filled with kindness.

"Name's Thornton Webb, sir. Just moved here. I'm going to be the chef at the Three Spinsters once Ms. Brown and her group get it built. And your name?"

"Bing Shepard. Good to meet you. You married?"

"No."

"Bing!" Paula was appalled all over again.

"Just curious, Rev. He could be your fella. I'd give you a run for your money myself if I was thirty years younger. You're a godly, good-looking lady."

She glanced around for Mal or Clay to come get their outrageous friend. As he leaned on his cane, the mischief gleaming in his dark eyes showed he was just stirring the pot, which was his well-documented superpower.

"Bing, you're one of my flock and I love you, but I'm going to ignore you."

"That's okay. Meeting's about to start and I need to get to my seat. Nice meeting you, Chef."

"Same here, Mr. Shepard."

"You take care of her now. She's a town jewel."

Caught between snarling and chuckling, Paula added another two pieces of raw broccoli to her plate and took a deep breath. She could only imagine what Webb was thinking.

"I'm sorry if he embarrassed you," Webb said to her.

The sincerity in his tone caught her off guard. In spite of the cacophony of noise, she'd heard the softly spoken words as if they were alone. Looking up into his blindingly fine face, something touched her too, and she shook it off because she had no idea what else to do. Turning away, she picked up a napkin from the pile. "Sorry, if he embarrassed you as well.

He has a way of joking you'll get used to. Let's head back before Tamar gives away our seats."

"After you."

A bit breathless and unsure of what just happened, she led the way.

While Paula took her seat and began in on the food on her plate, Sheila brought the meeting to order, silencing all the visiting and laughter. Former mayor Trent July hadn't waited for the new year to turn over the gavel and mayor's title. He'd given Sheila both the morning after she won the election last month, and he was now seated contentedly with his dad, Bing, and Clay. Chairing the meeting for the first time, Mayor Payne was at the long table in the front of the room with Bernadine and the recording secretary, Lily July.

Sheila began by introducing Chef Webb. At her invitation he stood and was greeted with smiles and applause. "Thank you for the welcome. I'm looking forward to being a member of this community and preparing great food."

More applause.

Sheila then thanked the crew who'd put up the big tree Paula passed on her drive into town. Because of the fading light, she hadn't been able to get a real good look at it but could see how huge it was. She was sorry to have missed the raising.

"Would you gentlemen please stand."

The room broke into much louder cheers and applause. The men, looking a bit embarrassed at the praise, acknowledged the love with nods before retaking their seats. Paula glanced over at Webb and wondered what he might be thinking of all this. She remembered how taken she'd been by Henry Adams at her first town meeting and the warmth she was shown.

Was he enjoying it as well? He'd stated his desire to be a member of the community, but was that the truth or did he think they were a bunch of country rubes? Although knowing next to nothing about him, she doubted a man of his reputation and stature would choose to live on the plains of Kansas if he thought poorly of the town or its citizens. Granted, she could be wrong, so she'd have to wait and see. As if sensing her thoughts, he looked her way, held her gaze just long enough to speed up her heartbeat, before she turned her attention back to the meeting. She wanted to blame her reaction on needing an adjustment to her blood pressure meds, knowing that wasn't the truth. The truth? She was attracted to him, a man she knew zip about. And because handsome hot men and middle-aged lady priests was so not a thing, she was determined to ignore it.

Up at the head table, Sheila was detailing the schedule for Saturday's townwide Christmas decorating event. While she detailed where all the garland and wreaths would be hung, Lily sent around sign-up sheets for those who wanted to help. The tree's topper would be placed on the tree Saturday evening, and after they plugged in its lights, there'd be a short community sing-along. Sheila then talked about the ornaments she'd purchased and held up a clear, glasslike sphere.

"I want everyone to take one of these home and make an ornament for the tree. You can use permanent markers or paint or decals, or anything else that won't be ruined if it snows. Your ornament can represent your family, individuals, whomever, or whatever. Make sure you put your name or initials on it somewhere so we'll know who it belongs to when the tree comes down after New Year's Day."

A buzz of interest rose in the room.

"There's no rush to do them tonight, we can add them to the tree whenever you're done. Any questions?"

There weren't any, but those gathered were smiling and talking excitedly. Community-inclusive events like this always filled Paula's heart.

While conversation temporarily paused the meeting, Kyrie asked, "Rev, what are you going to put on yours?"

"I don't know. I'll have to think about it. What about you?"

"My fraternity's Greek letters."

She chuckled. "Really?"

He nodded proudly. "It'll be purple and gold and say: Omega Psi Phi."

Chef Webb appeared amused by the young teacher's prideful boast as well.

She put the same question to him. "And yours?"

"Hmm. Not sure. Like you, I'll have to think about it."

Kyrie turned to Tamar. "What about you, Tamar?"

"It's a surprise."

"Uh-oh." Paula laughed. "Be afraid. Be very afraid."

Tamar's only response was a serene smile.

Sheila refocused the meeting and asked Paula to talk briefly about the church's Advent program. Paula stood. "As most of you know, Advent is the first season on the church calendar and is celebrated during the four Sundays before Christmas. The children will lead the worship and I hope everyone will join us. Service starts at ten as usual." That said, she retook her seat, carefully avoiding the interest in the chef's eyes.

Next up was Anna Ruiz. She stood and spoke about the Las Posadas celebration slated to begin the evening of December sixteenth. She then showed off Eli's beautiful piñata and everyone gasped at its beauty. "As I told Bernadine, we'll not be smashing this. It's too gorgeous. We'll hang it here in the Dog. The children and I will make three piñatas we'll be breaking instead. Anyone wanting to help, sign the sheet going around or see me after the meeting."

Anna sat down and Sheila asked, "Is there anything else?" She looked around. Jack James raised his hand. Sheila gave him the floor and he offered details on the viewing of the Jupiter and Saturn conjunction, and everyone seemed excited by the idea. "It'll be cold, so dress warmly. I'll send out emails and post further details on the rec's community board as we get closer to the date."

Sheila thanked him and continued, "Last thing. Riley's leaving town—"

Cheers rattled the windows before she could add more, and an amused Paula shook her head at the reaction from her flock.

The chef leaned over. "Who's Riley?"

Tamar replied, "How much time do you have?"

Paula laughed softly.

Tamar continued, "Let's just say the cheering is justified. Somebody will fill you in, don't worry."

Sheila's gavel restored order. "I know he's not the most favorite person here, but he's throwing himself a farewell parade."

Stunned silence followed that, then laughter.

"He's hired the Franklin High School Marching Band and their cheerleaders. It's scheduled for nine in the morning on Saturday right before we start decorating, so if you want to be a part of the send-off—"

"Or the kick out!" Riley's ex-wife, Genevieve, yelled.

More laughter.

"Or that," Sheila said. "Be on Main Street at nine."

The meeting ended and people lingered over goodbyes. Some of the older kids, like Preston, Leah, and Amari, joined the waitstaff to help with cleanup and were carrying the now empty buffet dishes into the kitchen. The tired Paula was ready to go home and crawl into bed. She'd had a long day. She shrugged into her coat just as Tamar said, "Paula, I have to talk to Rocky about some of the details for Saturday. Can Chef Webb ride back with you? I don't know how long I'll be."

"Sure," she said, hoping she sounded nonchalant even as her hands on the zipper shook a tiny bit.

Then came, "Reverend, I don't want you to be uncomfortable riding in the dark with a strange man, so I'll sit and wait for Tamar."

Fine and considerate. "Are you a serial killer?"

He paused. "No."

"Any outstanding warrants?"

"No."

"Grits. Sugar or no?"

He gave her an amused look she found contagious.

"No."

"You got the first two right, so you can ride with me. I'll overlook the wrong answer to the last one."

"I'm a chef and the cook's bible says, no sugar in grits."

"Wrong again. Are you ready?"

Tamar said, "I'll see you two tomorrow. And for the record, I'm with you, Chef."

Kyrie put on his coat. "I'm on Team Chef, too. Grits, shrimp, cheese, butter, salt and pepper. That's it. No sugar."

"I'm putting you all in my prayers. Are you ready, Chef?"

"I am."

Outside, they shivered on the short walk to her truck. He came around to the driver's side and she stopped. "What are you doing?"

"Getting your door."

"Ah." She added gentleman to the mix while trying to make out his features in the shadowy light. Was he playing her? "I appreciate the chivalry, but since I'm driving, totally unnecessary." She pointed her clicker at the lock.

"Just trying to be the gentleman my parents raised me to be."

"They did well. Get in before you freeze to death."

He hurried around to the passenger side.

While they waited for the defrosters to clear the front and back windshields, she said, "Sorry, I should've started the engine while we were inside." She was way more aware of him than she needed to be. Mentally taking in a deep breath, she strove to relax.

"It's okay. I'm originally from Chicago so I've been trying to convince myself I'm used to this freezing weather."

"How's it going?"

"Failing badly. I've been bone cold every time I've stepped outside."

"Layers are your friend."

"I know. Did some online shopping this morning. My haul should be here in a couple of days. Where are you from originally?"

"A little town in Oklahoma called Blackbird."

"My grandparents are from Tulsa. They moved to Chicago after the massacre in 1921."

That got her attention. "I hear many people left afterward."

"Yes, those who were lucky enough to live through it. That was a terrible time."

His eyes were focused out of the window and she wondered if his grandparents had related the events of those deadly days, and he was remembering.

"Is your family still in Chicago?"

"No. My parents are retired and living in Savanah. My sister and her family are in Oakland. They all want to come visit me but not until the weather warms up."

"Smart folks." The windshields cleared and Paula steered out of the parking lot and onto Main.

"How long have you lived here?" he asked.

"Three years. I was in Miami when I first met Bernadine and Lily. My church there was slated for demolition. To make a long story short, Bernadine offered to build me a church here, so I came."

"Just like that?"

"Just like that. She's a very persuasive and amazing lady."

"I got that impression when I interviewed with her, Rocky, and Tina Craig. She actually owns the town?"

"Yes. Purchased it off eBay. Won't take long for you to know all there is to know. There are no secrets here." She turned onto July Road. "Henry Adams is very special in many ways. The adults, the children, the town events. I wouldn't want to live anywhere else. Did you sign up for anything on Saturday?"

"I did but I talked to Rocky this morning, and she said she may need my help in the kitchen. We'll see where I wind up. Willing to help out where I can, though."

Paula liked that he seemingly wanted to be a part of the community. Not that Tamar would allow anything less. Fancy chef or not.

As they drove onto Tamar's property, the headlights of

Paula's truck played over the piles of snow lining the drive. He lived in the trailer that once belonged to Rocky before she and Jack tied the knot. It was a short distance from her own. Once there, she slowed to a stop. "Well, here you are."

"Thanks. I appreciate you bringing me back."

"You're welcome. If you need a ride into town, let me know. I usually leave here around nine, sometimes earlier if I want to get breakfast at the Dog."

"Will do." He opened his door and the cold air mingled with the cab's warm interior. "Once I get settled, I'd like to invite you over for a meal. If that's okay?"

"As long as I'm allowed to put sugar in my grits."

"We're going to work on you, Reverend."

"And I'm going to pray for you, Chef."

Their gazes held in the shadows and the silence lengthened until he finally said quietly, "Have a good evening."

"You, too."

Paula waited for him to go inside before driving on. It occurred to her that accepting an invitation to dine was not the way to stomp out her budding attraction. Agreeing to the invite was less problematic when she viewed it as just being neighborly, which was a component of her function as town pastor. Once she got to know him better, she was certain her feelings would fade. No way would a man like him be interested in a woman like herself. Yes, she'd asked God to send her someone, but she felt confident that Chef Thorn, fine as a sunrise, Webb, wasn't the person the Lord had in mind. Or was he?

Amari woke up to the smell of bacon. Smiling, he washed up, dressed, and went down to the kitchen. Standing at the stove was his mom, Lily, and in the skillet, big fat pieces of Mr. Bing's best bacon. "Morning, Mom."

"Morning, babe. How'd you sleep?"

"Pretty good."

"No visit from First Tamar?"

"No, not lately, but saw a hawk on the way to school the other day and thought about her. I wonder if that means she's going to show up sometime soon."

"You never know."

First Tamar was the matriarch of the nineteenth-century July outlaws. She'd appeared to Amari in a series of dreams a few years ago, and he still thought about her a lot. The current Tamar, his great-grandmother, and her brother, Thad, were direct descendants, as were his OG, Malachi, and his dad, Trent.

"Is your brother up?" his mom asked, taking some of the

now done strips out of the skillet and laying them on a paper-towel-covered plate.

He shrugged. "His door was closed, so I'm not sure. He's still pouting about not being the star of the wedding reception. I wish he'd get over himself."

"I do too, but it doesn't make me love him any less. You have to remember that when he lost his grandmother, he lost everything. All his drama is him trying to find his place in the new world he's in."

"Zoey lost everything and was attacked by a pack of rats. You don't see her acting that way."

"We're all different, babe. Zoey may not show it but she's healing inside, too. As are you," she added gently.

He had to give it to his mom. It was a good point. Although his present life was galaxies better than the one he had in Detroit, the little kid who had nothing and no one was still inside. Being rejected so totally by his awful birth mother, Melody, on that terrible visit was still an unhealed gash in his heart, even though he hid it well.

Devon came in and took a seat at one of the barstools at the counter. He looked glum. "Morning, Mom."

"Morning, baby. Did you sleep well?"

"I guess."

He was dressed for school in jeans, a long-sleeved tee, and Timbs. Seeing the wig on his head made Amari sigh. "Morning, Devon."

"Morning, Amari."

Accompanying the bacon were waffles. The red light on the iron was glowing, signaling it was ready to get to work. Amari asked, "Can I put some batter in?"

"Sure."

He opened it, carefully poured the light brown batter over the hot bottom plate and closed the lid. He loved waffles. "Dad still asleep?"

His mom shook her head. "It snowed again last night. He left before the sun woke up to get the plowing started. He should be back soon."

One of the things Amari enjoyed most about his new life was having everyone at the table for meals. He knew the plowing was necessary, but he still missed his dad not being there. To his delight, Trent came into the kitchen through the garage. "Morning, gang. Lord, it's cold out there. I need a kiss to warm me up."

Lily complied.

Devon responded, "Eww!"

Amari enjoyed the way his parents interacted but turned away from the kiss because it was kind of embarrassing. However, they set a good example with their love for each other, and he felt safe in believing they didn't do stupid stuff like police each other's phone the way Tiffany tried to do with him. He hoped to mirror their easygoing relationship when he entered married life.

His waffle done, Amari took it to the table and drowned it in syrup. By the time everyone else sat down with theirs, he was up and pouring batter for round two.

"Bobby Douglas and I are going to open a car restoration business," Trent announced.

Amari looked up.

Lily said, "That's a great idea, Trent."

Amari agreed. Having worked with him, he knew his dad had awesome restoration skills. "When do you plan to open?"

"Probably in the spring. Now that I'm no longer mayor and

Bobby's almost done with his associate's degree, I figure it's the perfect time. Plan to enlarge the garage and, depending on the orders we get, maybe hire a couple of assistants."

"Can I still come and help?"

"Of course."

Lily asked, "Do you have a name picked out?"

"I'm thinking B&T Cars. Short and sweet. What do you think, Amari? You're good at naming things."

"I like that, Dad. Short and sweet, like you said."

"Does anybody care that I'm sad?" Devon interrupted, derailing the conversation.

"No," Amari said before he caught himself. His mom gave him a side-eye, but Devon was getting on his last nerve. "I'm sorry, Mom, but why does he always have to be the center of attention. Dad's telling us something he's excited about and he butts in whining." He turned to his brother. "It's rude, Devon. Not everything is about you."

Mad, Amari carried his now done waffle back to the table and sat, mumbling, "So sick of him."

Trent asked, "What are you sad about, Devon?"

"I want to sing at OG and Ms. Bernadine's wedding since I couldn't at Mr. Clark's."

Amari filled his mouth with waffles to keep his snarling from being heard.

Lily said, "We're sorry you're sad, Devon, but we've discussed this. You pouting isn't going to change things."

He huffed and folded his arms.

Amari glared and forced himself to remember what their mom said about Devon trying to find himself. However, it didn't erase the urge to reach over and smack him upside the head and snap, *Stop being a brat!* Not long ago, he and Devon had a heart-to-heart talk about being brothers. Devon confessed to being envious of the way Amari moved through life and wanting to be him. Amari appreciated the compliment but stressed the importance of Devon being himself. For a while Amari's advice appeared to sink in and Devon was fun to be around. Amari began teaching him to play chess, they got into watching videos of the old-school music groups like the Temptations and George Clinton and the Mothership and bingeing the Marvel movies. Lately though, it was as if all that had been a dream because Devon had reverted to being a spoiled, whiny pain in the behind.

Having addressed Devon's complaint, Trent went back to his plans for the new business. Amari wanted to talk to his parents about Morehouse but decided to wait until later. Devon had already tried to take over the conversation and he didn't want to be guilty of the same.

With breakfast done, they all helped with a quick cleanup, their dad went back to bed, and Amari and Devon caught a ride to school with their mom. After dropping them off, she drove on to the Power Plant and hurried inside to get out of the frigid wind.

THORN WEBB STARTED up his brand-new black Chevy Silverado, and with the help of the onboard GPS headed to town. He knew the journey was a short one, but being new to the area, he didn't want to get lost. He'd purchased the truck from the dealer in Franklin and after the completion of the paperwork, including the Bernadine Brown discount, he'd not only gotten a great price but the salesperson had been kind enough to deliver the vehicle to his door. Thorn decided he liked small-town living.

He pulled the truck into the lot behind the Dog and got out. His entrance into the kitchen from the door of the loading dock made the staff freeze and stare his way with surprise and what appeared to be a bit of fear. He'd met most of them during his interview visit, but he sensed they were intimidated by his status and reputation.

Randy Emerson stammered, "M-Morning, Chef."

"Randy," Thorn replied, acknowledging him with a nod. It was almost lunchtime, so they were in the middle of prepping. "Didn't mean to show up and scare everyone. How're you?"

They continued to view him warily and responded with a few mumbles of, "Fine."

He asked, "Is Ms. James around?"

"In her office."

"Okay, thanks."

As Thorn exited, he smiled inwardly at the sigh of relief he imagined they'd all exhaled. It was his hope that at some point they'd get to know him well enough to greet him with smiles instead of dread. He had a plan to make that a reality but needed to speak with Ms. James first. Her office door was open, so he knocked lightly. She was seated at her desk concentrating on whatever was on the screen of a laptop.

At his knock she looked up. "Hey. Come on in. Have a seat. Be with you in just a minute."

Unlike the kitchen staff, she didn't view Thorn with awe, and he liked that. He used the silence to view the small clutter-free office, and to again note just how drop-dead gorgeous she was. Undoubtedly, it was something every man noticed, but she didn't give off the vibe that her looks were all she valued, unlike his ex-wife. Rocky James was part owner of the diner.

That it was so well run was a testament to her top-notch business acumen and showed that she was more than just a pretty face.

"So how are things?" she asked once she turned her attention his way. "Everything okay with the trailer?"

"All good. Had my truck delivered this morning, so I came to see if you needed help with anything here at the diner or tied to the Three Spinsters."

She eyed him for a moment. "Okay, I'm going to be nosy. Why'd you move from California now? We can't do anything with the new restaurant until spring."

He shrugged. It was a question he'd asked himself, especially on the harrowing drive across the country from Oakland to Kansas. "Was just ready to leave Oakland, I guess, especially once the sale of my restaurant and home were finalized."

She looked skeptical so he tried explaining further. "I want to learn about this place and the people living here. When we open the restaurant, I want to feel like a citizen as opposed to someone just dropping in. Does that make sense?"

"Yes. Henry Adams does grow on you. When I moved away a few years ago, it drew me back big-time."

"I want to stay busy too, so I'm wondering if I can work a few shifts in the kitchen."

"When?"

"Four, five days a week."

She looked surprised. "Really? Why?"

"Another good way to learn this place."

She went silent again before saying, "It's Randy's kitchen. He's earned his manager's spot. I'm not going to disrespect him by letting you come in and take over."

His admiration and respect for her grew. "I don't want to

disrespect him either, so put me on prep. I'll chop potatoes, onions, plate, wait tables. Help out with whatever he needs."

"You're serious?" she asked.

"I am. I don't want to lose touch with why I went into this business in the first place. Being at the bottom of the food chain will help that and keep me humble."

"You're an odd duck, Thorn."

"I'll take that as a compliment."

She showed a smile. "Okay. When do you want to start?"

"Is today good?"

"Yes. A crew member is out with the flu. We can use an extra set of hands."

"Then I'm all yours for lunch and dinner."

He followed Rocky back into the kitchen and once there, she announced, "I want to introduce you to the newest member of our crew: Thorn Webb. He's here to chop veggies, wait tables, plate, and whatever else Randy needs doing."

The wide eyes returned, and Randy's were as wide as his home state of Texas.

Thorn assured him with as much sincerity as he could muster. "This is your kitchen, Randy. I'm here to be put to work. Period. So everybody please call me Webb, not Chef. Okay?"

Randy, still looking shocked, nodded.

Rocky said, "I have some things to finish up. Be back in a bit. Put the man to work, Texas."

Holding Thorn's eyes, he croaked, "Yes, ma'am."

After her exit, the kitchen was thick with silence. Thorn waited and as the silence continued, he asked, "What's the job no one wants to do?"

"Cleanup," one of the young women offered with a disgusted tone.

"May I volunteer for cleanup, Chef?" he asked Randy.

Randy appeared torn. Thorn figured he was struggling with the idea of having a seasoned chef under his command and relegating said chef to something as mundane as cleanup. "When you head up a kitchen, you're in charge, so I need you to be that now," Thorn told him gently.

Randy pulled himself together. "Vanessa, can you show Chef, I mean Webb, how we work cleanup?"

"Sure can. Over here, Webb. Grab an apron from that pile."

Thorn complied and began his first shift on cleanup at the Henry Adams Dog and Cow.

During the lunch rush, when Thorn wasn't scraping food from plates and rinsing glasses, coffee cups, and utensils before placing them in the kitchen's large dishwasher, he was wiping down counters, sweeping up broken glass from dropped plates, and mopping up spills. Three hours later when the last order was filled, he was exhausted, but it was a joyous feeling. He'd sold the restaurant thirty days ago and didn't realize how much he'd missed being in the center of the whirlwind until he removed his apron and took a seat on one of the kitchen's barstools. Rocky entered and took a seat beside him. "Thanks for your help today."

"You're welcome. I'm worn out."

"If you want to skip the dinner shift, that's fine."

He shook his head. "No. I'll be here. Have to get used to being on my feet again, but other than that, this was fun."

He noticed Randy across the kitchen putting on his parka and said to Rocky, "Randy's going to be an outstanding chef one day. He has the cooking chops and the right temperament for running a crew."

"Hopefully not too soon. I just lost the kid he replaced a few months ago. He's now in Miami at a big-time restaurant."

"Which one?"

She named it and Thorn smiled. "He's in good hands. I know the chef there. Treats his staff well. Doesn't coddle but doesn't cuss or berate the young ones for making reasonable mistakes."

"Good to know."

Randy walked over. "Be back for dinner, Rock. Thanks, Webb."

"You're welcome. Thanks for taking me on."

"No problem. Gotta go so I'm not late for class."

He departed and Thorn gave Rocky a questioning look.

"He's taking culinary classes at the community college. Most of the staff is enrolled there. Students in the program fight one another to work here."

"What do you mean?"

"We pay well and help with tuition in exchange for the time they put in."

"That's outstanding."

"No. That's Bernadine. It was her idea."

Thorn was again impressed by the people of the little town he now called home.

She said, "If you're hungry, help yourself. Most of the kids eat in the dining room after their shift. You're welcome to join them. Cleanup person takes care of their dishes, too."

He dropped his head and chuckled.

"You said you wanted to work," she joked. "Be careful what you ask for around here. I'll be in my office if you need anything. And since you'll be part of the crew here, call me Rocky, okay?"

He nodded.

After her exit, Thorn helped himself to a large bowl of chicken noodle soup and threw together an even larger turkey sandwich. Placing his dishes on a tray he went out to the dining room. The once noisy and filled-to-capacity space was now quiet and all but empty except for the kitchen staff, Mal and his buddies lingering over coffee, and to his surprise, Reverend Paula, seated at one of the booths lining the windows. She was writing on a yellow legal pad. He hadn't seen her since the night she drove them home from the town meeting, and she was one of the residents he wanted to know better. Tray in hand he walked over to say hello.

SEEING THORNTON WEBB approach, Paula's heart began to dance around like a girl in middle school. She pulled in a deep breath to calm herself all the while wondering when this uncharacteristic reaction to him would run its course and leave her be. Feigning nonchalance, she resumed working on her sermon, hoping to fool herself into believing she had herself under control.

"Afternoon, Reverend."

She glanced up. "Hello, Chef. How are you?"

"Doing well. Just wanted to say hello. Didn't want to disturb you."

"I'm just finishing up my sermon for Sunday." And then, out of her mouth before she could stop came, "Join me if you like and catch me up on how things are going." The inner Paula screamed in disbelief, but it was too late to rescind the invite without appearing rude.

He took in her notepad. "You're sure?"

"I am." She gestured. "Please. Sit."

He complied and removed the bowl and plate holding his sandwich from the tray. "Have you eaten?" he asked.

"I have. Some days I like to stick around once the crowd thins out and jot down notes for my sermon. Not sure why that is, but it's worked well since I moved here, and I'm not about to fix something that isn't broke."

"Gotcha."

"Did you just arrive?"

"No. Got here before lunch. Had Randy put me to work in the kitchen."

He apparently saw the curious look on her face, so he explained.

When he finished, she was impressed. "Volunteering like that is very kind."

"It's a way to keep my skills on point."

He took a bite of his sandwich. After swallowing and wiping his mouth, he asked, "What's your sermon about? If I'm not being too nosy."

"Advent and practicing patience."

"I never knew churches had seasons until you mentioned it at the town meeting."

"Not every religion observes them, so that's understandable. Are you a churchgoer?"

"No. I was raised Baptist, and I occasionally attended services at the Episcopal church in Oakland my restaurant partnered with, but only enough to know that you all don't mess around. Service is short."

She chuckled. "Compared to some of the other denominations, I suppose our service is brief. Churches might worship differently, but it's all about praising God."

Mal walked up with a carafe of coffee. He eyed Webb silently for a moment before asking, "You want a warm-up, Rev?"

She glanced at her half-filled cup. "No, I think I'm good for now, Mal, thanks."

"How about you, Webb?"

"I'm good too, thanks, though."

"He being respectful?" Mal asked Paula.

She stared in disbelief. "Mal? Yes. Can you mind your own business, please?"

"Just checking."

She dropped her head then raised it and sighed. She shooed him away with a hand and a smile. "Go away."

He grinned. "Yes, ma'am." And after giving Webb a final pointed look, he left them alone.

Embarrassed down to the toes of her boots, she said, "My apologies. Not sure what's gotten into these folks around here."

"No apology needed. They're obviously protective of you. I find that commendable. Shows they care."

"I suppose, but being a woman of a certain age comes with its own built-in force field. I'm past the age of needing protection."

He viewed her over his raised cup. "If you say so."

His tone and what she thought she saw in his eyes brought back the breathlessness she'd experienced with him before. Needing to change the subject, and fighting to keep her voice even, she asked, "Did you look into getting yourself a truck?"

"Yes, bought it online."

"Did you test-drive it?"

He shook his head.

That surprised her. "You bought it sight unseen?"

"I did."

"Brave man."

"I figured if I didn't like it, I could always take it back and pick out something else. On the website it looked tough enough to drive through an earthquake."

"What color is it?"

"Black. I named it Earthquake."

She laughed. "That's quite the name."

"Seemed to fit."

"Glad you got some wheels."

"Me, too. Now I just need to figure out what to do with my car."

"Talk to Trent. He can maybe store it at his garage for the rest of the winter."

"Thanks. I'll do that. May wind up selling it eventually, though. I don't really need it now that I'm rolling with Earthquake."

She chuckled. He was easy to talk to and she was enjoying his company.

"The lights get strung on the big town Christmas tree this evening, right?" he asked.

"Yes. Did you sign up to help?"

"I did, but it was before volunteering for the dinner shift."

"Don't worry. They'll have plenty of help, so if you're too worn out after your kitchen shift, just go on home. There will be tons of things to do in the morning."

"Okay, I'll see how I feel once we clean up." He'd finished his lunch and began placing his dishes back on the tray. "I need to return this to the kitchen. Thanks for letting me interrupt you."

"You're welcome. Thanks for the company."

He stood and studied her silently for a long moment before saying quietly, "Enjoy the rest of your day."

She nodded and watched him make his way over to the kitchen's double doors. He was both gorgeous and charming. Her force field was going to need way more power.

AFTER LEAVING THE Dog, Paula walked the short distance back to the church. It was a brisk day, but she found the winter cold invigorating. When she reached the church, she went downstairs to her office, hung up her coat, and sat at her desk. Her calendar showed an after-school session with Preston. In addition to her theology degree, she held a doctorate in child psychology. Most of the town's children had been victims of trauma. Counseling them was one of her duties. She checked her phone for the time. School was due to let out in less than an hour, so while she waited, she reviewed her sermon again, made a few changes, and tried not to think about Chef Thornton Webb.

As always, Preston arrived on time. She appreciated his promptness. Some of the other kids, like Tiff and Devon, were habitually late, but not Brain. As he entered and closed the door behind him, she silently observed how different he was physically compared to when they first met three years ago. He was taller, thinner, and fit from working out. According to him he'd had fewer asthma attacks and rarely had to break out his inhaler. He attributed it to all the vegetables, fruit, and the exercise regimen his parents encouraged.

"How are you, Preston?" she asked as he took a seat.

"I'm okay, Reverend Paula. Got some things I want to run by you, if that's okay."

"Of course. Shoot."

He began by telling her about the contact he'd made with the family of his birth father and finished up by saying, "I really want to talk with them."

"Understandable. What's holding you back?"

"Not sure. I think I'm scared they won't like me, so I'm having trouble deciding whether to have a conversation with them right away or wait a little while."

"I don't think they'd have a reason not to like you. You said your birth mom says they're good people. And you're a very impressive young man. I'd think they'd be proud to know you."

"That's basically what my mom said."

"What's your dad saying about all this?"

"He's being okay."

Paula was glad to hear that. The colonel sometimes had difficulty dealing with personal issues tied to the sometimes rigid way he viewed life and his own trauma growing up with an abusive parent. In an earlier conversation, Preston revealed that the colonel had been less than supportive during his earlier search for his bio parents.

"So you think I should just go ahead and email them so we can FaceTime?"

"If you feel comfortable with that, yes. If not, give yourself a few more days, but the longer you put it off, the more you're going to question yourself. Sometimes it's better to jump in the pool and start swimming."

He nodded.

They spent a few moments discussing how his prep was

progressing for attending MIT in the fall, and then he asked, "Would it be possible for you to talk to me and Leah about our relationship?"

That surprised her. "Are you two at odds?"

"Yeah. She wants to break up."

She replied gently, "You can't force someone to stay in a relationship if they no longer want to be in it."

"I know, but she's being really illogical and that's not like her."

"Explain."

So he did and when he was done, she had to agree that something might be going on with Leah. Gary Clark's oldest was as smart as she was straightforward. Although she'd been doing well since her parents' divorce, Paula knew from their sessions that Leah hadn't come through the crisis as unscarred as she led everyone to believe. "If you can get her to agree to come in as a couple, we can try and sort through it. No guarantee it will be resolved to your satisfaction, though."

"I know, but I need help convincing her that I'm not going to dump her because of some mythical person she's sure I'm going to meet. She means so much to me, Reverend Paula, and I want us to be together. If we break up, let it be over something I did, not just because she thinks we might."

Her heart went out to him. "As I said, if she'll agree, we can try, but if she brings this conflict up in any of my sessions with her, I can't share what she tells me."

"I know," he replied glumly. "Ethics and privacy and all that."

"Exactly."

He looked so miserable, Paula wanted to give him a reassuring hug, but it was her job to be truthful with him. "And honestly, Preston, Leah may be right about your future as a couple. The potential for you both meeting someone else once you leave home is probably pretty high."

He blew out a breath that mirrored how bleak he felt inside. Her voice gentle, she asked, "Anything else on your mind today?"

"No," he replied softly. "Thanks for listening."

"You're very welcome."

She watched him put on his coat. Exiting, he turned her way. "Thanks again, Reverend Paula."

"Bye, Preston."

Sitting in the silence, she sighed. *Young love.*

"Giving Sheila that bullhorn might have been a bad idea," Bernadine said to Mal that evening. Because the temperature was in the single digits, they were sitting in his warm truck watching the yards of lights being woven onto the big Henry Adams Christmas tree.

"You may be right," he replied with a laugh. "Tell me again why we're doing this after dark?"

"She said it was the only time that fit everyone's schedule and there'll be too many other things to do tomorrow morning."

The chore was being handled by Dads Inc., whose members were on the ground, on ladders, and in the cherry pickers of the two trucks donated for the evening by the local utility company. All the workers were wearing Santa hats, and the entire operation was being directed by the Santa-hat-wearing mayor and her bullhorn. "Jack! Trent! Move that strand on the left up a bit higher. No, Jack, your other left!"

Both men glared her way before complying.

The event had drawn quite a few spectators. They were all parked across the street from the rec with their headlights facing the tree so the workers could see.

Watching Sheila marching around like her drill sergeant husband, Mal said, "Who knew Sheila would grow up to be so bossy?"

"She is all that, isn't she?"

Mal added, "Must be something in the water because from Tamar on down, every woman in this town is bossy as hell."

"But you love us just the same."

"Yes. Give me a kiss, bossy lady."

Bernadine leaned over. The kiss filled her so sweetly, she forgot where they were for a moment until a sharp rap on the window brought her back to reality. It was Lily. Bernadine lowered the window.

"Get a room. There are kids here." She walked away.

"See?" Mal said pointedly. "Bossy. Every last one of you."

Laughing, Bernadine had to agree.

An hour later, a half-mile string of lights encircled the huge tree, and the store-ordered ornaments hung from the branches. Bernadine looked forward to seeing it lit up tomorrow evening.

"Thank you for your help, everybody," Mayor Bullhorn called out. "See you in the morning at the parade."

Mal said, "I hope she doesn't believe folks are really going to show up."

"I'll be there just to make sure Riley and that hog actually leave town."

"Hmm. Never thought about it like that. That is a good reason to go. And once they do, maybe we can get Paula to say a prayer that they never return."

"You know Paula's not going to do that, but I like the way you think." Bernadine couldn't wait to see the last of Riley Curry and his awful hog. Since she'd moved to Henry Adams every kindness sent Riley's way by her and others had been repaid with foolishness. If there was anyone in the world more underhanded, she had yet to meet them.

ON SATURDAY MORNING, the people of Henry Adams and neighboring communities lined Main Street for Riley's going-away parade as if waiting for one put on by Macy's. Bernadine saw her neighbors and their kids, Clark's Grocery cashiers, men and women from the construction crews, and even Sheriff Will Dalton and Deputy Sheriff Davida Ransom among the onlookers. No one appeared particularly excited though, especially not Genevieve Barbour standing with her husband, TC, to her right, and Marie Jefferson on her left. Gen was wearing the angry face she always showed when it came to Riley. Bernadine hoped Gen wouldn't pelt her ex-husband with a hail of icy snowballs as a going-away gift. There was also a television news crew standing off to the side reporting into their station as if the parade was something their viewers wanted to see.

But there was no sight of Tamar. The town matriarch made no secret of how she felt about Curry, especially after he impersonated Trent to buy a car and Trent wound up arrested for car theft.

Truthfully, no one looked excited, so Bernadine assumed that like her, most had shown up to make sure this really was the end of Curry and his hog, Cletus.

While the crowd waited they helped themselves to the

cups of hot chocolate Mal and Chef Webb were passing out from a table set up outside the Dog. The coffee shop was doing big business too, selling coffees, donuts, and pastries. Pickup trucks, their beds piled high with garlands and wreaths for the postparade decorating were waiting in the parking lot at the rec.

Bernadine had no idea how long Riley's parade was due to last, but anything over five minutes would be too long. She didn't care if that made her petty. The sooner she saw the last of Riley and Cletus, the better.

"He's late," Lily groused, standing beside her and checking the time on her phone.

"Of course he is."

The parade was supposed to begin at nine. It was presently twenty minutes past.

Across the street, Bernadine saw Mayor Sheila checking her watch. The town decorating event was scheduled to begin at ten. Sheila was not going to be happy if the parade's late start impacted the carefully laid out schedule on her ever-present clipboard. Seeing Sheila's bullhorn hanging from a lanyard around her neck, Bernadine chuckled inwardly. *Girl-friend is not playing.*

Soon the rhythmic sounds of a drum line could be heard off in the distance.

"Finally," Lily declared.

A few minutes later, up the street came the Franklin High School cheerleaders dressed for the season in white parkas, short red skirts, and white tights. They were led by two girls holding a long white banner with "Good Luck Riley and Cletus" printed across the front. Behind the cheerleaders, the marching band, also wearing red and white, played "Jingle Bells."

As the groups neared, Bernadine's eyes widened at the pink masks covering the faces of the students.

Voice filled with disbelief, Lily asked, "Are those the stupid FUFA pig masks!"

Bernadine was caught between laughing and being appalled. "Yes."

When the county tried to have Cletus put down for the death of the old con man Morton Prell, Folks United for Animals, aka FUFA, and their president, Heather Quinn, helped Riley get the judgment dismissed. FUFA's piggy-masked, crackpot supporters descended upon Henry Adams like locusts and turned the town upside down. Riley must have had masks left over, or maybe he'd ordered them with his lottery money. Either way, as the cheerleaders and the band passed by, the stunned crowd could only stare.

Next came a vintage red Cadillac convertible with its top down. There were pictures of Cletus in his Hawaiian outfit attached to the doors. Inside the slowly driven vehicle stood Franklin mayor Lyman Proctor. Unlike the role politicians usually played in parades, he was neither smiling nor waving. He was just looking sullen.

"How much do you think Riley paid him to participate in this craziness?" Mal asked, walking up.

"Apparently not enough to smile."

"Or wave," Lily added.

There had to be a story behind the mayor's presence, but since it was probably tied to Riley having paid Franklin to hold the parade, Bernadine decided she didn't want to know.

Last but not least, a big, shiny, silver RV rolled slowly into view. The side of the vehicle sported a large picture of Cletus in his tuxedo and Ray-Bans. Above his likeness were the words "Cletus—World's Most Famous Award-Winning Hog." Beside the RV walked the smiling and waving Riley wearing his signature black suit with the fake red rose in the lapel. Next to him, Cletus strutted decked out in a Santa suit, complete with a white beard, black belt, and hat.

"Lord," Bernadine whispered.

The television reporter ran out into the street and stuck a mic in Riley's face. Before he could ask his question, Riley snatched the mic from the young reporter's hand and opened his mouth to say who knows what, only to have Gen yell out, "Just get out of town, Riley Curry, and take that damned hog with you!"

The crowd cheered for the first time.

Undeterred, Riley opened his mouth again, and this time, Sheila on her bullhorn called out, "Thank you for the parade, Mr. Curry. Let's give him a good send-off. Hip! Hip! Hooray!"

"Go Away!" Gen shouted.

"Hip! Hip! Hooray."

Others took up Gen's chant, "Go Away!"

Sheila tried one more time. "Hip! Hip! Hooray!"

"GO AWAY!" roared the crowd in full voice.

The reporter looked confused. Riley looked mad.

Sheila said, "Okay, everyone. Meet me at the rec." Clipboard in hand, she marched off. Many fell in behind her while others went to their cars. The angry Riley pushed his hog up a short ramp and into the RV, and whoever was behind the wheel headed the vehicle up Main Street. Two minutes later it disappeared from sight.

Lily cracked, "Well, that was nice."

Mal's smile lifted his mustache. "I thought it was a great send-off."

Bernadine chuckled and they joined the crowd streaming to the rec.

CHAPTER
7

By midafternoon, strings of lights and lengths of lush green garlands were draped across building fronts and around the poles of all the streetlamps on Main Street. Windows in places like the Dog, the coffee shop, the Power Plant, Roni Garland's recording studio, and the Sutton Hotel showed off evergreen wreaths centered by velvety red bows. Residents and area friends hung their brightly decorated, homemade ornaments on the branches of the big tree, along with cellophane-covered candy canes, and strings of popcorn and pine cones. Crystal's gift to the town was a beautiful star-shaped topper made of crystals and reflective glass beads designed to catch the glow of the lights and the moon. It would be placed atop the tree later that evening when the tree was plugged in for the first time.

After the decorating was completed, many people headed home. They'd be returning after dark to watch the tree lighting. Most of the kids stuck around to help Anna make the piñatas for Las Posadas and to lace on their ice skates now that the town's rink behind the school was finally open.

As Bernadine stood taking in Main Street she thought the decorations made Henry Adams resemble a beautiful Christmas card. Sheila had done an outstanding job of pulling everything together. Bernadine hoped that the day's efforts, without Riley's parade, of course, would become an annual tradition. Her phone buzzed with a text. It was from Tina. She and Bernadine's friends had run into travel delays but were on their way, so Bernadine and Mal set out for the Dog to warm up, get something to eat, and await their arrival.

As they entered, Brenda Lee was on the jukebox singing "Jingle Bell Rock." Bernadine asked, "Do you think 'Jingle Bell Rock' will be still playing at Christmas in the year 2525?"

"Probably in 3535, too."

She laughed and followed the hostess through the nearly empty dining room to the booth they always shared. Once they were seated, the hostess brought hot tea for Bernadine and coffee for Mal. "Your waitress will be right over."

Still shivering from the cold, Bernadine placed her tea bag into the small teapot to let it steep while Mal stirred sweetener into his brew.

"I've had so much coffee trying to stay warm today if I start twitching just ignore me," he told her.

"I understand. It'll probably be tomorrow before I get warm again."

When the waitress came to take their order, Bernadine ordered a bowl of chowder and a grilled chicken sandwich. Mal ordered a burger and fries. After the young woman's departure, Mal asked, "Wonder how soon Riley will be back? You know he's going to run through that money like a hot knife through butter."

"Don't say that. Repeat after me, 'Riley will never return.'"

His amusement showed in his smile. "Riley will never return."

"Good. Now let's talk about something else."

Still smiling, Mal sipped. After setting his cup down, he asked, "So tell me about the two friends Tina's bringing with her for your shower."

Bernadine wanted to pout like Devon because no one cared about her not wanting the shower. "Gwen Baker and Patty Hamilton."

"Americans?"

"Gwen is. She's from Chicago but lives mostly in Costa Rica now because the weather's better and her telecom empire is based there."

"Empire?"

"Yes. Television and radio stations all over South and Central America. Owns a dozen newspapers, a couple of publishing companies, and lord knows what else. She's always on the lookout for another company to put in her purse."

"And Ms. Hamilton?"

"Patty's from the UK. Her ex-husband owns a ton of hotels in Europe. He claimed to be able to trace his line back to Charlemagne. He's like fifty-fifth in line to the throne of England."

"That close?"

Bernadine paused to smile and pour her steeped tea into the cup. "Yes. She says when they were married, he was so far back in the royal line, they needed a satellite to even see Windsor Castle."

"Does she own an empire, too?"

She shook her head. "Patty's a retired pediatric neurosurgeon. Spends a lot of time these days treating children in villages around the world that don't have access to specialized health care. One month she may be in Peru and the next in Ethiopia. She volunteers at clinics sponsored by the United Nations."

"That's amazing. She's probably saved a lot of lives."

"She has. It's one of the things I like most about our group, the women give back when they could be spending their time doing nothing but being rich and useless."

Nat King Cole was now crooning the always lovely "Christmas Song" when the waitress returned with their food. After her departure, Mal asked, "Will the rich lady society kick you out when we get married?"

Bernadine cut her sandwich in half as was her custom. "No. Once a Bottom Woman always a Bottom Woman. We have members who've remarried."

"Would you still marry me if you had to give up your membership?"

She stopped. "Is that a trick question?"

He eyed her, and she could tell he was wondering if he'd overstepped. "Just asking."

"Do we need to go back to Paula for more counseling? Because we may need to if you're having issues."

"No."

"Would you still marry me if you had to give up playing bid whist with Clay and Bing?"

He chuckled.

"What's so funny?"

"Clay basically asked that same thing the other night:

whether you'd be okay with me playing cards after we got married."

Bernadine shook her head. "Clay's an idiot. Why would I ask you to give up something you enjoy?"

"That's what I asked him."

"And he said?"

"Something about that's how women are."

"Like he knows anything about how women are. If he did, he'd still be with Genevieve."

"You sound like Bing." Mal chuckled. "He said the same thing."

"If Gen, as sweet and kind as she is couldn't put up with him, no woman with sense is going to, either. Who wants to wade through all his baggage?"

"It's not all his fault. Nam killed who he used to be. He's finally talking to one of the therapists at the VA, though."

"Good for him. Is it helping?"

"A bit, but he needs joy in his life. A good woman would help with that."

"I'm not sure God put women here to fix men."

"You fixed me," he countered quietly, "and bring me joy every day. Just the thought of you does that."

His words were moving. No man had ever spoken anything like that to her before. Leo had loved her during the early years of their marriage, but he'd never professed it on a regular basis the way Mal did, or so tenderly. Was it any wonder she loved him? "You're just trying to sweet-talk your way out of that dumb question you asked me about the Bottom Women."

He chuckled then added in a serious tone, "Maybe, but loving you, and the joy you bring me is truth, baby. The whole truth and nothing but."

Emotion filled her heart. Their past issues aside, how could she not want to spend the rest of her life with a man who brought her joy as well? "You're a real smooth talker, Malachi July."

"Also, the truth. Runs in the blood." He reached out and gently stroked his thumb over her hand resting on the table. "I'm looking forward to being with you for however many more years the Good Lord grants an old man like me."

"Hoping it'll be a long time. And you aren't that old."

"You lie really well, missy."

"Eat," she ordered with mock severity.

He gave her that saucy July smile and they went back to their meal.

BERNADINE'S FRIENDS ARRIVED so late that she and Mal had just enough time to pick them up from the chopper landing spot behind the rec before the tree-lighting ceremony started. After quickly introducing Mal to Patty with her red hair and English accent, and to short, curvy, dark-skinned Gwen, Bernadine shared a hug with Tina and they all piled into Mal's truck for the drive to the festivities. He parked behind the Dog, and they hurried to Main Street to join the large crowd gathered for the event.

Sheila, using a wireless mic and standing in the big floodlights illuminating the darkness, began by welcoming everyone, before adding, "The kids are passing out the song sheets you'll need for the one song sing-along of 'O Tannenbaum.' You can use the flashlights on your phones to see the words. Please raise your hand if you need a sheet."

Bernadine raised her hand and it brought Tiffany to her

side. "We don't have enough for everyone, Ms. Bernadine, so you'll have to share. Sorry."

"That's okay. Sharing works."

Tiff smiled and moved on. Seeing Roni Garland standing near Sheila, Bernadine assumed their resident songstress would be overseeing the singing part of the program. Zoey, Maria, and Devon stood with her.

Sheila called out, "Jasmine? Would you make your way up here, please?"

Ten-year-old Jasmine Herman, wearing her red Santa hat, came out of the crowd to stand by Sheila.

Patty whispered to Bernadine, "Do you all do these kinds of extravaganzas often?"

"Yes, but this Christmas tree lighting is a first timer."

Patty said, "I feel like we've stepped into a Hallmark Christmas movie."

Mal and Tina chuckled.

Sheila announced, "Trent and Barrett are in charge of turning on the juice, so if we're ready let's start the countdown. Ten, nine . . ."

The crowd picked up the count. When it arrived at one, the tree and the festive, multicolored holiday lights came to life all over town. Cheers and thunderous applause erupted in response. And there was Jasmine standing in the cherry picker as it slowly carried her up to affix Crystal's gorgeous star to the top of the tree.

It was all so beautiful Bernadine got teary. Then Roni and the kids began to sing, "O Christmas Tree, O Christmas tree, how evergreen your branches . . ."

The crowd joined in, and for the next little while the Henry

Adams's frosty night air resonated with voices raised in song. They sang two verses, and when the last notes faded away, Sheila thanked everyone for coming and wished them all a merry holiday season.

The official program was over, but people stayed to marvel at the lights and take pictures of family and friends in front of the massive tree. While Bernadine and her friends lingered, Gwen said to Bernadine, "Tina didn't tell me you'd purchased Whoville."

Bernadine laughed so hard she almost fell down.

THE FOUR FRIENDS entered Bernadine's home and plopped down onto the couch and chairs with relief. Everyone was exhausted: Tina, Patty, and Gwen from a day of travel, and Bernadine from the all-day Henry Adams Christmas big to-do.

"How about some coffee?" Bernadine asked.

"Make mine wine," Tina countered.

The others agreed, so Bernadine broke out a bottle and some crystal tumblers.

Once they were all comfortable, Patty said, "I had a good time, B. I love your town."

Bernadine saluted her with her rosé. "Thanks, I do, too."

Gwen added, "Lots of fine-looking men around here, too. Is that a prerequisite for residency? Mal. His son. The fire chief. And don't get me started on that chef. Wow, girl."

Bernadine grinned as she sipped.

Patty asked, "So you're really going to marry him? After all the drama?"

"I am." She studied their faces for disapproval but saw none.

Gwen asked, "You're sure?"

"Sure as I can be."

"The embezzlement drama aside, no other concerns?"

These women had been in Bernadine's life for almost two decades. She could be truthful. "My only concern is will we be able to merge our lives. He's never been married, and I haven't lived with a man since Leo. Oh, speaking of Leo—he left me everything in his will."

Tina cracked, "The man never stopped loving you. Too bad he was such an asshole."

"Hear! Hear!"

Patty said, "I wonder if hell has that dishwashing liquid the environmentalists use to remove oil from ducks after a spill? Leo will probably need some."

They howled. Leo's corpse had been discovered inside an oil drum.

"You're going to hell for that, Pat," Bernadine declared.

"Probably, so be sure to put some of it in my casket in case Leo needs more."

Bernadine couldn't've asked for better or crazier friends. They could be so inappropriate.

Laughing, Tina said, "Back to your concerns."

Bernadine thought for a moment before continuing. "I'm probably making a mountain out of a molehill. No question about how much I love him. The whole embezzlement madness broke my heart, but we got through that and he's so good for me in so many ways. I just worry about us being up under each other all the time."

Gwen tossed out, "If this was a romance novel, being up under each other would be a good thing."

"Not that kind of up under each other, woman!"

More hoots of laughter.

Gwen came to her own defense. "I'm sorry but it was just lying there. One of us was destined to pick it up."

Glasses were raised in another silent salute.

Gwen continued, "But seriously, I understand your concern. Who's to say being around each other twenty-four seven doesn't cause issues? He probably enjoys his private space, and I know you do. Love doesn't always run smoothly. I've been divorced three times. I know."

"Have you given up?" Tina asked.

"On love, no. On men and marriage? Absolutely."

Patty raised her glass. "Hear! Hear! Me too, unless Whoville has someone I can toss over my shoulder and take back to the UK."

The friends spent the rest of the evening talking, laughing, catching up on the latest Bottom Women's gossip, and enjoying the camaraderie.

At one a.m., Bernadine declared, "I need to go to bed. I'm a reader at church tomorrow. Anybody wanting to go with me is welcome to come along."

She received no firm commitments but that was okay.

Tina asked, "What time is the bridal shower?"

"Three. At Tamar's. I'll be back here way before then, though. I don't want a shower but of course no one listened."

"Why don't you want the shower?" Patty asked.

"Because I'm not some dewy-eyed bride walking down the aisle for the first time. I don't need anything old, borrowed, or blue."

Gwen replied, "You are so hard to love sometimes. Do you know that?"

Bernadine cut her a look. "Meaning?"

"You give but you don't know how to receive."

Patty drained the last of her wine. Backing up Gwen, she said, "This isn't about what you need. This is about a gift."

Tina weighed in, "Granted, I don't know everything that's happened here since you bought the town, but I do know you've made some great friends who love you, and from what I've seen you love them, too. Lily. Genevieve. Tamar. Sheila. Right?"

Bernadine nodded tersely.

"Do you think they're grateful for all you've done here?"

"I'm sure they are."

"Then let them show you how much they love and appreciate you. Unlike us, they can't buy you jets or islands or mountains, but they can give you an afternoon filled with joy."

"Which is priceless, by the way, girlfriend," Gwen pointed out.

"This is Whoville," Tina stated and followed that with her best imitation of a radio announcer. "The part of the Grinch will be played by Bernadine Edwards Brown."

Bernadine dropped her head. The truth-filled words made her chastise herself for being ungrateful instead of thankful for all the intangibles her new friends had provided. Turning Henry Adams into a jewel would never have been possible without them. Not to mention their positive influence on her health and well-being. "You're right. I need to be grateful. They didn't have to embrace me or my vision for what I believed the town needed."

"No kidding," Tina replied with gentle sarcasm. She drained the last of her wine. "Now that that's settled, let's get these glasses washed up and go to bed."

Once that was done, they tiredly trooped up to the second floor.

A few minutes later, as Bernadine climbed into bed and turned off her bedside lamp, the house was plunged into quiet darkness. She turned over and got comfortable only to hear Tina call out, "Good night, John-Boy!"

A puzzled-sounding Patty called back, "Who's John-Boy?"

Laughing, Gwen replied, "I'll explain in the morning, Tina. Go to sleep."

"Yes, Mama."

Bernadine laughed, too. Silently acknowledging how much she loved her friends, she closed her eyes and slipped into sleep.

CHAPTER
8

Paula enjoyed the hum of activity that accompanied the start of Sunday service: the smiles on faces of the well-dressed congregation as they entered the building and greeted her and their neighbors; the chatter and laughter of the choir members and acolytes as they put on their robes; and the exuberance of the teens and tweens heading to their worship classes. She viewed her enjoyment as affirmation that being a priest was what she'd been born to do.

As always before the beginning of service, she placed the readings for the day on the lectern and checked the altar to make sure everything was ready. Another one of her jobs as priest was to keep an eye out for visitors or people who hadn't attended in a while for whatever reason. She made a special point of introducing herself to the new faces and offering them a welcome to the church. This was the first Sunday in Advent. The altar guild members Sheila Payne, Roni Garland, and Gemma Dahl had placed the traditional Advent wreath on a small table inside the altar rail. The wreath was made of greenery and encased four candles: three purple and one rose colored. A candle would be lit each of Advent's four Sundays by one of the children.

Pleased by the preparations, she left the altar and made her way back down the center aisle intent upon joining the procession, but the sight of Chef Webb seated in a pew with Rocky, Jack, and Tamar threw her for a moment. Gathering herself, she walked over to welcome him. After nodding a greeting to Tamar, Rock, and Jack, she said, "Welcome, Chef Webb. Good to see you."

"Morning, Reverend. Thank you and please call me Thorn."

"Okay. Enjoy the service."

"I'm sure I will."

Her job done and pleased that he'd come to worship with the congregation, she stopped and said hello to a few of the regulars before moving on.

At ten o'clock, she took her place at the back of the church and raised her voice for all to hear. "This is the first Sunday in Advent, a season of quiet and stillness, so we will process in silently."

Leah, the day's crucifer, raised the cross high and looked to Paula whose replying nod was the signal for her to begin the walk to the altar. Flanking Leah were torchbearers Wyatt, Gemma's grandson, and Lucas Herman, one of her foster children.

As Leah began down the aisle, the congregation stood. Many bowed their heads as the cross passed by. Behind the cross came the choir, and behind them, the solemn-faced Reverend Paula dressed in her purple robe, the traditional color for the season. Upon reaching the altar, Leah and her torchbearers stood with their backs to the congregation and waited for the choir to move to the choir box before placing the cross and torches in their spots on the wall and taking their seats.

Thorn had never seen a silent procession before, and he was both intrigued and moved by the dignified, understated pageantry. He'd made the decision to attend to further assess and understand the town, its citizens, and where he might fit into the scheme of things, and to learn more about Reverend Paula Grant.

He was still no expert on which child belonged to which family, though. Two tweens Paula introduced as Devon and Zoey read short explanations about the colors of the candles on the Advent wreath, and what each one stood for. The purple candle for the first Sunday represented Hope. It was also called the Prophecy Candle as a reminder of prophets like Isaiah who foretold the coming of the Messiah. Glad for the information, Thorn filed it away.

As the worship continued, Paula said to the congregation, "I usually have the youngest child in the congregation light the first candle, so Jasmine, you get to do the honors."

Thorn remembered her as the same girl who'd ridden in the cherry picker the night of the tree lighting. She lit the purple candle with a long white wick Paula handed her. After the candle flared to life, she gave the priest a shy smile and returned to her seat next to a White woman with blond hair. Thorn wondered how long it would take him to fully connect all the family ties.

Over the course of the next ninety minutes, he listened as Bernadine did the readings of the Scripture and led the congregation in a psalm. Paula's sermon reminded her flock that Advent was a contemplative season—a time of silence and quiet, reflection and self-assessment.

"Slow down your life," she said in a gentle tone. "The reason for the season is not to fight someone in the mall over a big-screen TV, be rude to the tired, underpaid cashiers because the lines are long, or to put yourself in so much debt you can't breathe when the credit card statement shows up in January. The season is about that baby in the manger and the love and blessings ushered in with his birth."

Thorn nodded inwardly at her wise counsel. Maybe coming to Henry Adams was his own personal version of Advent. He'd definitely slowed down his life and been doing a lot of self-assessment and reflecting. Once again, the feeling that he was supposed to be in this town with these people resonated deeply.

Even though Paula encouraged everyone to take Communion, Thorn felt he didn't know enough about what it meant to participate, so he stayed seated and observed. Twenty minutes later the service was over. His attendance had made him more knowledgeable about the season, and the sermon had given him food for thought. He'd be back.

PAULA WAS HANGING up her robes when she heard a knock on the door. It was Leah. "Hey, Leah. Thanks for serving today."

"You're welcome. Do you have a few minutes to talk to me. I know my usual appointments are Wednesdays, but I don't think this can wait."

"Sure, come on in. Close the door."

They both took seats. "What's up?" Paula asked.

"Has Preston talked to you about what's going on with us?"

"You know I can't divulge that, so how about you tell me what's bothering you?"

"Okay. I've broken up with him and he refuses to accept it.

He keeps wanting to talk about it, hoping I'll change my mind and I'm just not feeling it."

Paula studied her for a moment while pondering how best to approach this. "Do you no longer care for him?"

"I do. I probably care more about him than anybody else in the world besides my dad."

"Then why break up with him?"

"So I won't get hurt when he finds another girl at MIT."

"Why do you think he will?"

"Percentages, and I saw some of the girls at Stanford during orientation and a lot of them are really pretty. Way prettier than me, so I'm assuming the ones he'll meet at MIT will be, too."

Paula now had more pieces of the puzzle.

Leah added, "He says he won't be looking for someone else, but life is cruel and I'm tired of pretending it isn't, so I'm protecting myself."

"I see. So what do you need my help with?"

"Convincing Preston that I'm right. I don't want to hurt him, but I don't want to be hurt either, especially when we'll be on opposite sides of the country."

"Okay, let's back up for a moment. Why do you think Preston liked you in the first place?"

"Because we're both science geeks. I play chess and I love sports. There aren't any other girls here his age who like the same things he does."

"So you think you're just a placeholder until he finds someone else?"

"Yes."

"Has he ever said that or given you that impression?"

"No," she said. "But I'm not pretty, Reverend Paula, and

everyone knows boys like girls who are. He'll find someone at MIT who likes all the things I just talked about and she'll be a babe, and he'll drop me quick."

Paula knew today was Sunday, that she was a priest and should never have unkind thoughts about anyone, but she wanted to find Leah's mom, Colleen, and shake her until her teeth rattled. Paula learned from earlier sessions and from talks with Leah's father, Gary, that his ex-wife, Colleen, seemed to take great pleasure in telling Leah her entire life that she wasn't pretty and never would be. That cruel message had wormed its way into Leah's psyche like a virus and was now festering. Inwardly, Paula was furious. Asking God for forgiveness, she calmed herself and studied this amazing young woman destined for greatness. "Would you be willing to have a sit-down with me and Preston so the three of us can try and work this out?"

"I guess so."

"I'll need to talk to your parents first, though. Are you comfortable with that?"

"Why do you have to talk to my dad?"

"To get his permission. I'm supposed to help you individually, not as couples and I'd feel better if they know why we're meeting."

"I suppose. He's going to ask me a bunch of questions."

"As he should. He loves you and cares about you. And didn't you just say you care about him more than anyone else?"

"I did," she admitted.

"I don't think your dad will pry too much and who knows, he may have some sound advice to offer."

Leah stared off into the distance, exuding a raw sadness Paula felt able to touch. "Do you really want to break up?"

She whispered, "No."

"Then let me talk to your dad and Preston's parents. If they approve, the three of us will get together and see if we can't find a solution."

Unshed tears showed in her eyes. "Okay."

"Things will work out, honey. No matter how it's resolved."

Leah nodded and stood. "Thanks, Reverend Paula."

"You're welcome. I'll see you for our regular get-together on Wednesday."

"Yes, ma'am."

She left the office and Paula let out a sigh. Both Leah and Preston were hurting, and she had no idea if she could help. She vowed to do her best, though. After a short prayer asking for guidance, she put the two teens in her heart and went to catch what was left of the after-service coffee hour. She also wanted to get an up-close look at the decorated Christmas tree to see how the townspeople had decorated their ornaments. It had been difficult last night due to the darkness.

THORN SPENT THE coffee hour meeting the members of the congregation. Although he'd been introduced at the town meeting, he'd not had a chance to meet the majority or know their stories. However, thanks to Tamar, Rocky, and her husband, Jack, by the time the coffee hour began winding down, the chef had connected with quite a few new faces who asked where he was from, how he liked the weather, and how soon the restaurant would be opening. He answered the questions readily and referred the restaurant questions to Rock. Tamar and Jack helped him with which kids belonged to which family and offered a few details about their backgrounds. He was surprised to learn most had been in the foster care system and that Ms. Brown had been instrumental in finding them adoptive parents. The overall friendliness of everyone he met and spoke with went a long way toward making Thorn feel less of a stranger. He'd yet to see the reverend, however. "Does Reverend Paula attend coffee hour?"

Rocky, putting on her coat, said, "Usually yes. Someone probably has her pinned down in her office. She makes herself available whenever people need her, especially after church if it's an emergency."

"I wanted to let her know how much I enjoyed the service."

"She'll like hearing that, but you can probably catch up with her anytime. Henry Adams is so small we can't help but stumble over each other no matter where we go."

That amused him.

Jack said, "We're going to check out the ornaments on the tree before heading home. You're welcome to come along. Did you make one?"

"I did. It's in my truck." He'd picked up some markers at Clark's Grocery but hadn't come up with anything really imaginative for his contribution. His creative talents were better suited for a kitchen, he supposed. As he walked with Rock and her husband to the exit, Thorn felt good about his decision to attend church. He'd met a bunch of people and enjoyed the service but was admittedly disappointed by not having the opportunity to speak with the reverend.

When they reached the rec, a small crowd already gathered around the tree was searching high and low for the ornaments hung on its branches by their friends and neighbors. Thorn added his. He'd drawn an apron on it and written "CHEF" across the front. As noted, not very creative. Rocky pointed out hers.

"Why a motorcycle?" he asked.

"Not just any motorcycle. That's a Black Shadow. It's a picture of the one I own. Cut it out of an article I found on the internet."

He stared. "You ride bikes?"

"Yes, sir. Shadows are some of the baddest bikes ever made."

He looked to Jack, who chuckled. "Close your mouth, Chef, before your tonsils freeze. I felt the same way when she and I began dating. Women here are something else. Nothing small-town about any of them at all."

"I see," Thorn replied.

Rocky asked Tamar, "Where's yours?"

Thorn remembered Tamar saying on the evening of the town meeting her design would be a secret.

Tamar pointed. "There, beside the big candy cane." She reached up and took it down so Rocky could get a better look at it.

Rocky eyed it and laughed. "Is this real?"

"Yes. I copied the original and had Preston shrink it down so it would fit."

Rocky held it up so others could see, too. However, Thorn wasn't sure what it was, let alone what to make of it. He saw the word *WANTED* and below that the face of a young dark-skinned woman.

Tamar explained. "It's a wanted poster for my aunt Teresa July."

Thorn's jaw dropped again.

Tamar viewed his surprise and explained. "She and her brothers were outlaws. Train robbers to be exact. I think she'd get a kick out of having one of her posters on the town tree."

Jack said, "See what I mean, Thorn? Even a hundred years ago this town's women were a force to be reckoned with."

"I do." He took in Tamar's small smile. "And your aunt robbed trains, too?"

"Had as many wanted posters as her four brothers. Served time in the penitentiary, too. Ended up marrying a Philadelphia banker of all things. The two had quite the grand romance."

Thorn was so taken aback by the revelation he didn't know what to say.

They continued to check out the ornaments. Chief Acosta's fire truck hung beside one made by his mother-in-law, Anna Ruiz, that featured the multicolored flag of Mexico. Zoey's sported a taped-on picture of the Korean boy group BTS, while Devon's was a selfie in his wig. Tamar cracked, "Looks like James Brown's middle-school yearbook pic."

Thorn remembered Devon reading the Advent introduction during church and the teen's interesting-looking pompadour wig but knew nothing about the story behind it. He couldn't wait to learn enough about the town to get the jokes.

Paula walked up. "Hey, everyone. I came to see the ornaments, too."

Thorn turned from the mini James Brown to the calm serenity of Reverend Paula Grant. "I enjoyed the service," he said to her.

"I'm glad. Join us as often as you care to."

He couldn't seem to look away from her, and she appeared to be having the same problem. He thought back to Tamar's talking about her outlaw aunt's grand romance and he won-

dered whether the reverend had ever been in such a relationship. From her auburn highlighted twists to her soft angular
face she was a beautiful woman. In his mind, single men
should be filling the church's pews every Sunday to hear her
words while hoping to catch her interest.

Rocky broke the moment. "Paula, did you make an ornament?"

She reached into her parka's pocket. "Sure did. It has a
cross and the Christmas star."

Rocky said, "Hand it to Thorn. He's tall. He can hang it
high where people can get a good look at it."

As if unsure, she hesitated for a moment but complied, and
he placed it on a branch above their heads.

"Thanks," she said to him.

"You're welcome."

Their eyes met. For a long moment a rising sense of something he couldn't name gently arched between them before
she quickly looked away. "I need to get back to the church,"
she said. "Rocky, Tamar, I'll see you at the shower. Thorn and
Jack, have a good afternoon."

She hurried off. Thorn watched her walk away and wished
he knew if her seemingly hasty departure was tied to her having sensed the same thing. When he turned back, all eyes
were directed at him. Tamar's were assessing. Rocky wore
a slightly raised eyebrow. Jack was poker-faced. Wondering
if his budding interest was that obvious, he waited for some
type of response. They remained silent, however, so he used
that to make a graceful exit. "I'm going back to my truck and
head home. Thanks for taking me under your wings today. I
appreciate it."

"We're all parked at the church," Jack said. "We'll walk with you."

A few minutes later Thorn was driving back to his trailer thinking about lady outlaws, grand romances, and the woman known as Reverend Paula Grant.

CHAPTER
9

"Didn't you all hear me say no gifts?" Bernadine fussed mockingly as the guests began arriving at Tamar's place for the bridal shower.

Genevieve shot back, "You're not the boss of us," and placed her gaily wrapped small box on the table with the other gifts.

The festivities were soon under way. There was lunch, laughter, and stories, punch for the young ladies, and Bernadine's fine wines for the adults. The Henry Adams crew knew Tina, and they seamlessly integrated Gwen and Patty into the fun.

Crystal arrived last, carrying something small and square wrapped in brown craft paper. Bernadine guessed it was artwork and looked forward to the gift opening portion of the gathering to see if she was correct.

When the time came, they all took seats to watch. Genevieve's small box held a set of crystal shot glasses. One lettered Hers, the other His. Lily's contribution was an Idris Elba coloring book and a box of sixty-four crayons. It drew laughter and some envy. Roni cracked, "Don't be surprised if that comes up missing, Bernadine."

To which Reverend Paula responded, "Though shall not covet thy neighbor's Idris."

They howled.

Zoey gave her a BTS CD. Bernadine was familiar with the hype surrounding the boy band but had never heard their music. "I'll play this on the way home, Zoe. Thanks."

Her Bottom Women friends gifted her with a week's stay at the Body Holiday spa in St. Lucia. Tina told the group, "To me, it's one of the best spas in the world."

Bernadine, who'd stayed there in the past, agreed.

Sheila, the fountain pen aficionado, gave Bernadine a gorgeous indigo-and-gold version. From her spot by the fireplace, Sheila said, "Every woman of power should own a fountain pen."

Lily cracked, "And a bullhorn."

That drew lots of laughter.

The gift from the Clark girls was a wall calendar for the upcoming new year. Each month featured an iconic African American woman and an affirming quote. Flipping through the glossy pages, she saw Cicely Tyson, Toni Morrison, Michelle Obama, and others. Bernadine looked to Leah and Tiff, and said, "Thank you. This will keep me inspired all year."

From Tamar she received a snow globe with a model of the earth inside. "So you can keep turning your own world and ours," she explained affectionately.

Reverend Paula's gift was a beautiful daily devotional. "Thanks, Reverend. It'll be a daily reminder to stay focused on the spiritual."

Jasmine handed Bernadine a large, festively wrapped flat

box. "Mama Gem had to work, so she told me to give you this. It's from all of us."

The curious Bernadine removed the paper and inside found a beautiful blue-and-gold quilt that displayed the buildings of Henry Adams. There was the Dog and the Power Plant, the rec center, Paula's church, and the Marie Jefferson Academy lined up on Main Street. Also included was Roni's recording studio, the Sutton Hotel, the fire station, and the coffee shop. Gemma was the town's unofficial seamstress, and the quilt reflected her stellar skills. The border was lined with sunflowers. There was a ribbon of blue water flowing in the creek behind Tamar's place, and a group of kids dressed in winter gear were skating on the ice rink. "This is gorgeous, Jaz. I'll call your mom later and tell her how much I love this."

Jasmine smiled. "Look down in the right-hand corner."

Bernadine did and then laughed. "I'm going to get her for this." Almost unnoticeable was a very small applique of Cletus wearing his sunglasses. She handed the quilt to Lily to pass around. Everyone loved it, even Genevieve.

Marie Jefferson was next. "When Olivia July ran for mayor back in 1882, the women of Henry Adams wore little handmade ribbon roses to show their support. They were called Olivia roses and a few were passed down our family line from Cara Lee Jefferson to my mother, Agnes, and then to me. You're supposed to have something old and blue, so here. Add it to your keepsakes."

Bernadine stared at the faded blue ribbon in its tiny frame and tears stung her eyes. "Marie, this is an heirloom. I can't accept this."

"You're going to be a July, Bernadine. Olivia was a July. She and my great-great-grandmother were close friends. I'd like to think that after a few bumps in the beginning, you and I have become friends as well. I want you to have it."

Moved, Bernadine gave her a big hug, which an emotional Marie generously returned. They'd butted heads in the past, but now? Yes, they were friends. "Thank you," Bernadine whispered.

"You're welcome."

Tissues were passed around, eyes were dabbed, and noses were blown.

Roni's gift was an invite to an appearance she'd be making next year in Detroit. "It's the Detroit Jazz Festival. The largest free jazz fest in the world. I know it's your hometown and I know how much Mal loves his jazz."

Bernadine hadn't been home in ages. As a teen she'd gone downtown to the jazz weekend with her father and sisters every year. Back then it had been known as the Montreux-Detroit Jazz Festival. She knew Mal would enjoy it, and she would, too. "It's a date."

Bernadine then opened the small box from Anna Ruiz and her granddaughter, Maria. Her jaw dropped and her laughter filled the room. It was a bobblehead of Bernadine in a white wedding gown standing next to Mal in a little black tux! Holding it high for the others to see, she asked in a wondrous voice, "Where on earth did you get this?"

Over the excited glee of the others, the giggling Anna replied, "Google is my friend."

Totally amazed, Bernadine shook the little couple. The heads wobbled and she grinned as she handed it Rocky to pass it around. "Thank you, Anna and Maria!" And to think, she hadn't wanted a bridal shower. *Silly girl!*

Crystal's gift was equally amazing, but instead of laughter, it evoked another teary-eyed moment. As Bernadine had predicted, it was indeed an art piece. A small framed watercolor featuring two soaring dragon kites. The trailing strings were gracefully entwined in a heart. "Oh, Crys," she whispered emotionally. "This is beautiful." One kite was teal with highlights of burgundy and gold just like her kite, Mimi. The other dragon, black with red accents, was a twin of Mal's. He'd taught her kiteflying and it was an activity they enjoyed as a couple.

"Hoped you'd like it," Crystal replied.

"I do." She couldn't get over its beauty, its significance to her relationship with the man she loved, and Crystal's talented insightfulness. Bernadine took the tissue handed to her by Tamar and dabbed at her eyes. Moved by the happiness and joy on the faces of the women and girls surrounding her, she said, "I love you all, so much."

"We love you, too," Lily replied. "So, before we flood this place with tears, how about some cake?"

Cheers soared like kites.

WHEN THE SHOWER ended, Bernadine shared goodbye hugs with everyone, and Patty, Tina, and Gwen helped her carry the gifts out to the truck. On the drive home, Tina riding shotgun turned to Gwen and Patty in the backseat. "See why I'm so captivated by this place?"

"I do," Patty answered. "What a lovely group of people."

Gwen added, "I may want to build here just so I can visit. It's so peaceful."

"Not all the time," Bernadine countered. "We've had our

share of drama, and something is always jumping off, but you'd be welcome to move in. In fact, I'd love to have you close even if for only a few days at a time."

"I'll bet you're glad you had the shower now, aren't you?" Tina cracked as they pulled into Bernadine's driveway

"Smart-ass. Go in the house!"

Everyone laughed.

They had an hour before they were due to meet Tina's chopper at the rec, so Bernadine's friends spent the time packing, checking emails, and making calls to prepare themselves for stepping back into their busy, high-powered lives.

"I HAD A marvelous time," Gwen said as they all sat in Baby waiting for the chopper to arrive.

Patty said, "I did, too, and I will be back. I'm anxious to see Tina's bed-and-breakfast when it opens.

The B&B, like the restaurant, was slated to be constructed and opened in the spring.

"So am I. We'll keep you posted on the progress," Tina promised. She peered through the windshield. "There's Mike." The chopper came into view.

It landed, and the women exited the truck. Buffeted by the noise of the rotors, they all shared one last love-filled hug with Bernadine, grabbed their luggage, and hurried to the helicopter to board. A few minutes later, they were in the air. A teary-eyed Bernadine waved and watched her friends fly away.

Before heading home, she sent Mal a text to see if he was home. Texting back that he was, she let him know she was on the way and drove the short distance to the Dog.

"How was the shower?" he asked as he stepped back to let her come in.

"We had such a good time." Bernadine always enjoyed being at his place. It was so cozy and welcoming. From the soft gray paint on the walls, to his lush green plants, music room, and books, his personality could be felt everywhere. Entering was like being given a Mal hug. *Would he resent giving this place up when they married?* She set the thought aside. "I have something for you." She reached into her tote and handed him the small box.

"What is it?"

"I thought the groom should get a shower gift, too."

They sat side by side on his nice navy-blue couch and he opened the box. When he withdrew the bobblehead, his laugh filled the space. "This is the bomb! It's us! Where'd you get it?"

"Anna Ruiz."

He leaned in and viewed it closely. "He even has my mustache!"

"Yes, he does."

"Oh, this is great."

"Thought you'd like it. It's yours. There's a little suction cup you can use to attach it to your dash if you want."

He reached into the box and withdrew the small plastic oval. "Bernadine, I love this. Give me a kiss." When it ended, he shook the figures, the heads wobbled, and he laughed again.

"I have something else." She withdrew Crystal's small painting.

"Oh my," he said quietly, eyeing it. "I love this, too."

"I cried when I first saw it."

"I see why. She has such a great heart. When she first came to town, who knew she had all this talent hidden underneath that awful gold weave."

Bernadine smiled at the memory of the original Crystal. "I know. She's come a long way."

"All due to your love."

"And the people of this town."

He kissed her again, then handed her the painting.

"No. You keep it for now. Hang it in here somewhere."

He paused. "Why? I'll be moving in with you soon."

She shrugged. "I know, but I just think it belongs here, at least for now," and she tried to explain. "One of my Bottom Women sisters is a painter, and she firmly believes art will let you know where it wants to be hung. And I have the feeling that it should be here."

"Are you sure?"

"Positive, but you don't have to hang it now."

He glanced around for a moment as if looking for the perfect spot. "Okay. I'll let you know where it winds up."

"Good. Now. It's been a long day, and I'm pooped."

He placed an arm over her shoulders and eased them closer. "Did you get a chance to check out the ornaments on the tree?"

"I did. I saw yours with your truck, and your aunt Teresa's wanted poster on Tamar's."

"That blew me away. "

"I saw Trent's, too." It was covered with lilies.

"He's so tenderhearted about that girl of his."

"I know. You have a tender heart, too."

He kissed the edge of her hair. "Don't tell anybody."

She chuckled. "Let me get up from here and go home so I can fall out."

Bernadine stood and Mal enfolded her in a hug that filled her heart. She looked into his eyes and whispered, "I love you, Malachi July."

"And you are my life, Sweet Bernadine."

She rested her cheek against his chest and savored the way he made her feel. She finally stepped away and put on her coat. After sharing one last kiss, she left his place and drove home.

On the way, she once again wrestled with the question of whether their being together would ruin the near perfect lives they seemed to have living apart. As it stood now, she called her own shots and he called his. At their ages, were they too set in their ways to give up that independence and freedom? It worried her that they might be. She had no clear answer, though, and wished the question would go away and leave her be, but she also knew it was something they'd need to discuss sometime soon before saying "I do."

PRESTON WAS UPSTAIRS in his bedroom. He'd decided to connect with his birth dad's family because the anxiety of putting it off was keeping him awake at night. Throw in the problem with Leah and the stress was way too much for a kid his age. He took the short walk down the hallway to his mom's office. "I'm going to call Aunt Cecily."

Sheila looked up from her laptop. "Do you want me and Barrett to sit with you?"

"Would you, please?"

"Absolutely. Be right there."

While he waited for his parents, Preston emailed Cecily to see if they could chat. He received a prompt one-word reply, "Yes!"

He sent her a Zoom link and waited for her to join him on-screen. His parents stood off to the side out of view of the camera just as Cecily appeared. She was brown skinned, had a coiled crown of braids, and there was a smile on her face. "Preston?"

"Hi."

"I'm Cecily." Tears filled her eyes. Her voice thick with emotion she whispered, "You look so much like your father." She drew in a visibly deep breath and wiped her eyes with her fingertips. "I told my husband I wouldn't cry. I'm sorry for blubbering."

"It's okay." He was attempting to keep his emotions under control, too. He'd waited so long for this. "I want you to meet my parents." They stepped into view. "This is Sheila and Barrett Payne."

"Pleased to meet you," she said.

"Same here," the Paynes replied.

"My mother's going to be mad she missed you all. She's at the Sunday night church service."

"I'll call again so I can talk to her, if that's okay."

She nodded. "Perfectly okay."

Preston wondered if she felt as awkward and uncertain as he did.

Cicely said, "So you all live in Kansas?"

"Yes, town called Henry Adams. It was founded by Black people in 1879."

"Really?"

He nodded. "Google it when you get a chance. The lady who owns it brought me and some other foster kids here and that's how I met the Paynes." He looked up at them. "They've been real good to me."

Cecily said, "Thank you, Mr. and Mrs. Payne, for watching over him. He's been a missing part of our hearts since Margaret put him up for adoption. Had we known she wasn't going to keep him, we might have made arrangements to raise him our-selves. She didn't even bother coming to Lawrence's funeral."

Preston got the impression that the Mays family weren't happy with his birth mom and he came to her defense. "I didn't go into the system because she didn't want me. Her mom and dad made her give me away. She stopped talking to them afterward and went to live with her aunt."

Cecily went still. "I didn't know that."

Preston added, "I met her mom. She's not a nice person."

Sheila weighed in. "Preston's correct. I hope you haven't been harboring any ill will against Margaret. She was young and scared and had no way to counter her parents' demands. Having to give up her son became a missing piece in her heart, too. She lost both Lawrence and their child."

"We weren't aware of the circumstances. We just thought—" She stopped and wiped more tears. "Never mind. I'll let my mother know that what we believed was wrong."

Barrett said, "Please do, and so you'll know, she spoke very highly of your family."

Cecily looked away as if embarrassed by her unfounded opinions of Margaret.

Sheila added, "And she didn't come to the funeral because her family wouldn't allow it. She was a student, pregnant, and they provided her income. I get the impression that she had no money of her own. She had no way of getting to Phila-delphia. It had to have been a terrible time for her."

Cecily nodded solemnly. "Agreed." She asked Preston, "Do you see her often?"

"We email and text pretty regularly. The last two sum-mers, she's gotten me an internship with her at NASA."

"That had to be exciting. So you like science?"

"I do. Very much. She said Lawrence did, too."

"Lived it and breathed it." Cecily quieted for a long moment before saying, "I still miss him. A lot."

"I wish I had known him."

"You two would have gotten along so well. He'd be proud that you love science. And like I said, you favor him so much, seeing you is like seeing him."

Preston felt emotion clogging his throat.

"I'd love to see you in person," Cecily continued. "I know my mother would, too. Maybe at some point you could come and visit."

Sheila said, "Or you could come here. We have room."

Preston was glad his mom had made the offer. If things didn't work out, he'd rather be at home than unhappy a thousand miles away.

Cecily said, "If I tell my mother that, she'll want to be on a plane first thing in the morning."

Barrett said, "She'd be welcome. Maybe come a few days during the Christmas holiday."

Preston liked that idea and asked his parents, "Do you think Ms. Bernadine could fly them here in the jet?"

Cecily looked confused. "You know someone with a jet?"

He nodded. "Yes. The lady who brought all us kids here. She has a private jet."

Sheila said, "I can ask her."

Cecily said, "Whoa. Wait. You're talking about having a jet come and get us?"

Barrett said, "Buying a ticket at this late date will cost an arm and a leg. This way you can maybe fly with no cost."

Preston saw his mom raise her phone to her ear and walk

out into the hall. She returned less than a minute later. "Bernadine's pretty excited about this and said as long as you all come and do the round trip before Christmas, she'll send Katie to Philly to fly you here and back. She'll need the jet Christmas day for her honeymoon."

Cecily asked, "Who's Katie?"

Preston answered, "Her pilot."

"Are you all punking me?"

"No."

Sheila said, "I can call you tomorrow and we can finalize the arrangements. We have two bedrooms and a pullout sofa. How many people will be coming?"

"Just me, my mother, my husband, and my son, JR. How many passengers will the jet hold?"

Preston thought back to his first flight. There were five kids, Ms. Bernadine, and Ms. Lily. "Seven, for sure."

Cecily said, "My husband isn't going to believe this. Let me see if I can take some time off and we'll talk tomorrow evening. Will that work?"

"Sounds perfect," Sheila said.

Preston asked, "How old is your son?"

"Fourteen. He's been pretty excited about meeting you."

Preston smiled. He had a cousin.

They spent a few more minutes discussing the possibilities of them traveling to Henry Adams and then Cecily had to go. "I drive a city bus, and my shift starts at five in the morning. Preston, thanks so much for reaching out. This has been wonderful."

"You're welcome."

"Mr. and Mrs. Payne—"

Sheila interrupted her. "Please call us Sheila and Barrett."

"Okay, thanks for your generosity. I'll be in touch. Take care."

The meeting ended.

Preston looked up at his parents. "Thank you."

Sheila and Barrett nodded, and his mom said, "This was important for you. That makes it important for us, too. Text me her email when you get the chance so I can touch base with her tomorrow."

"Will do."

His pops squeezed his shoulder on his way out of the room. His mom leaned down to give him a hug and a kiss on his cheek. "Love you."

"Love you, too."

Preston smiled. All in all, this turned out well. His phone chimed. He picked it up and his eyes widened at the name on the caller ID. He accepted the call. "Leah?"

"Hey. I talked to Reverend Paula and she wants to help us work this out. She has to get our parents' permission, though."

"Okay. I—"

"She'll let us know when."

Before he could respond, the call ended. He dropped his head, slowly raised it, and sighed.

AFTER CHURCH AND Sunday dinner Amari and Trent spent the rest of the day at Trent's garage putting the finishing touches on a 1965 Chevy Impala owned by a lady librarian in Franklin who wanted to show it at car shows in the spring. It hadn't been driven in decades and had needed a lot of work. Although Trent hadn't restored one before, and finding the right parts had been a pain in the butt, he and Amari were enjoying the restoration.

Amari glanced up at the old clock on the wall. It was almost 8:00 p.m. He knew his dad would work until sunrise if he weren't stopped. "Getting late, Dad. I have school in the morning."

His dad looked up from the carburetor they'd been installing. "Okay. One more minute and I should have this right."

The one more minute turned into twenty, but they finally called it quits. They put the tools away and left the bay to remove their old overalls and wash their hands. Afterward, Amari pulled a juice box out of the small fridge and took a seat on the bench. He thought it might be a good time to talk about his college choice. "I think I want to go to Morehouse for college, Dad."

Drinking a can of orange soda, his dad smiled, "Really?"

"Yeah."

He sat down next to Amari. "Why Morehouse?"

"One, it's got a good reputation. Two, it's an HBCU and all about Black male excellence. And three, I think it would be nice to be in that kind of an environment."

"Dr. King went to school there."

"I know. So did Spike Lee, Samuel L, and a bunch of other important people. Just not sure if I can get in."

"What's your GPA now?"

"About a 2.8. Makes me real close to a 3.0, which isn't bad for a kid who a few years back couldn't read."

"True. Your mom and I are so incredibly proud of you. I think your GPA will get you a good look at being accepted, especially if you do well on the SAT."

"I'm worried about that part and how much it's going to cost. I know private schools are expensive."

"Your mom and I have your back on the tuition. We'll order some SAT practice books you can study from."

Amari felt some of the weight he'd been carrying lift a bit. "I also miss being in a big city. I love Henry Adams but it's kind of slow, Dad."

"Which I find perfect, but you weren't born here. Atlanta will have a lot more action."

"You think I can take my car?" He could already see himself cruising like a boss in his restored midnight blue 1969 Camaro.

"No."

He couldn't ever remember his dad giving him such an emphatic no before. "Why not?"

"One, you don't want to have to deal with maybe being pulled over every time you get behind the wheel, and two, we didn't put in all that work restoring it just to have it stolen. Both are strong possibilities in a place like Atlanta."

"But—"

"No, son. If you need wheels, I'll gladly get you something to drive that has a lot less flash."

Amari sighed. He understood what his dad was saying. The world could be dangerous for kids who looked like him, but still. Never one to give up, he'd ask again soon.

But as always, his dad was two steps ahead. "And I won't be changing my mind just in case you're planning to ask me again in the future."

Amari laughed. "Damn, Dad, I thought Mom was the only mind reader in the family."

His dad's phone chimed. He checked the screen. "Speaking of Mom. This is her now. Hey, babe."

Amari couldn't hear what his mom was saying, but the look on his dad's face and tone of voice as he replied "Why?" made Amari think he might be the subject of their conversation.

His dad said, "Okay. We'll be leaving in a few minutes. Stop cussing, Lil."

"Am I in trouble?" Amari asked warily.

"No, but Melody just called."

"My birth mother, Melody? What's she want?"

"Your phone number apparently. She wants to speak to you."

"Mom refused to give it up, right?"

"Right. And I guess Melody got snippy."

"And Mom's cussing."

"Bingo."

Amari smiled. He loved his Lily Mom. "Whatever Melody wants the answer is no. If I don't have to speak to her ever again in life, I'm good." The visit with her two years ago in Detroit left him crushed and heartbroken. All he'd wanted was for her to like him. She'd given him raw pain instead.

When he and his dad got home, Lily was sitting on the couch watching the Sunday night game and from her tight-set jaw and the fire in her eyes, Amari could tell she was still angry. "Thanks for not giving her my number."

"After the way she treated you? She should be glad she was on the phone and not within snatching range."

"What did she want to talk to me about? Did she say?"

"Something about another visit."

"Does Reverend Congressman know his wife is smoking crack?"

"Then she had the nerve to accuse me of trying to keep her away from her son. Her son? I lost it!"

His dad sat beside her and with an arm draped over her shoulder eased her close. He gave her a kiss on the forehead. "I'm glad she was on the phone, too. Otherwise, I'd be passing the hat for bail money."

That made her smile. "No doubt." Amari always looked upon his dad's ability to smooth out her temper as one of his superpowers.

Amari asked, "Why would she think I'd want another visit?"

Lily looked his way. "Smoking crack."

After the visit two years ago, Amari returned home so broken inside Lily came up to his bedroom and held him while he cried. It was a moment he would never forget. "If she calls back and needs to hear me tell her to beat it, I will." He walked over and gave her a kiss on the cheek. "You're such an awesome mom. I want to grow up and be a great parent just like you, but taller, though."

She playfully punched him in the ribs. "Go to your room."

Amari headed up the stairs, reminded again how wonderful it was having family that loved him.

CHAPTER
10

Monday morning, Paula placed a box holding some personal items Robyn asked to be shipped to her on the backseat of her truck, then took her spot behind the steering wheel. Thanks to the remote starter, the cab's interior was nice and warm, a sharp contrast to the frigid fourteen-degree temperature outside. Dressed for the weather in a sable-colored down parka and her hair tied up in a red scarf beneath her black Stetson to keep her ears covered, she used the control on the wipers to clear the windshield of the moisture left by the defroster. With that done, she put the truck in drive and set out for the shipping outlet in Franklin.

There was minimal snow on the short strip leading to the main road, but it was still icy, so she drove slowly over the bumpy, uneven ground. Passing the Douglas place, she spotted Bobby's truck parked out front and was glad to know they'd made it back from Texas. Passing Chef Webb's Earthquake brought up memories of their brief encounter at church the day before. She continued to hope the more they got to know each other, the sooner her silly attraction would cease. She was entirely too old to be crushing like a middle-school teenager over him. Although he'd been respectful and kind, she doubted his interest was rooted in anything other than being neighborly—at least that's what she told herself, even if whatever was rising between them had sent her running for cover yesterday.

Reaching July Road, she steered out onto the plowed two-lane blacktop and headed west. When she arrived at the mailing outlet, the clerk at the counter typed in the who, what, where, and when of what Paula was shipping. Once everything was in order, Paula pocketed the receipt and returned to her truck. Before leaving the parking lot and while the Brooklyn Tabernacle choir sang the moving "Who Will Go?" through her truck's speakers, she took a moment to send Robyn a short text about when the box would arrive. Receiving a prompt thumbs-up emoji in reply, she set out for Henry Adams. Items at the church needed her attention, but first she wanted to make a quick stop at the Power Plant to talk with Sheila about the counseling idea for Brain and Leah. She was pretty confident Sheila would be supportive; she'd always wanted what was best for her adopted son. She was a bit concerned about the colonel, though. Even though his sessions with Paula over the past few weeks had broadened his approach to life, there was no guarantee he'd see the value in what she was proposing.

Entering the Power Plant, she walked past the beautiful plants lining the path through the atrium. Bernadine's door was closed. A quick glance through the glass framing showed Bernadine and Lily inside, no doubt turning the world. She didn't want to disturb them so she continued on to Sheila's office farther down the hall.

The door to the outer office was open. Paula knocked on it and heard Sheila call out, "Come in. I'm coming."

Paula entered the nicely furnished sitting-room-like space, which was decorated in tans, rich browns, and cream. Sheila, dressed in a gray twin set with a matching skirt and black boots, walked out of the inner office and greeted Paula with a smile. "Morning, Reverend. How are you?"

"Doing well. Do you have a moment to talk? Promise not to keep you."

"Sure. What's up?" She gestured Paula to a seat and settled herself on the brown leather sofa.

"Want to talk to you and the colonel about Brain and Leah. Can we meet this evening sometime?"

Sheila stilled and studied her for a moment. "Is something wrong?"

"There is, but it's nothing major like pregnancy or—"

"Who's pregnant?"

They turned to see Barrett Payne standing in the doorway. His stern eyes swept them both.

"No one's pregnant," Paula replied reassuringly, "and I'm glad you're here, now I can speak to you both. Leah and Preston are having issues."

His voice hardened. "Leah's pregnant?"

"Barrett, no one is pregnant. Please come in and sit down so Paula can tell us what she wants to talk about."

He offered a tight nod and sat beside his wife on the rounded arm of the sofa.

Paula laid out the issues, and when she finished, Sheila

said, "Poor Leah. This is all that awful Colleen's fault. I've been wondering why Leah hasn't been to the house lately. I didn't want to ask Preston and be all up in his business. Kids resent that most times."

Paula agreed.

Barrett added, "Sorry to hear this. I like Leah a lot. She and Preston have been good for each other."

"I agree. Your son suggested couples counseling."

Sheila showed a small smile. "He's always so mature. What do you think, Barrett?"

"I think it's a great idea."

Paula was pleased by their responses. "Then I have your permission to counsel them as a couple?"

They nodded.

"I've told both kids that this may not resolve their problem, but getting them to discuss it face-to-face may be helpful. I still need to talk to Leah's dad and get his permission before we can start though." She questioned Barrett. "Do you know if he and Nori are back from the honeymoon?"

"They are. They got back late last night he told me. He's at the store now. When will you be talking to him?"

"Probably later this afternoon or this evening. First day back after taking time off can be hectic. I'll give him some time to settle into his routine."

"Then I won't say anything to him about this for now and let you ride point."

"I appreciate that."

"I'm on my way to an all-day meeting in Franklin, so I won't see him until tomorrow anyway. Only reason I stopped by here was to have Mrs. Mayor sign off on some paperwork

I'm taking with me. Glad I did. Quite the coincidence that we're all here."

"Einstein once said, 'Coincidence is God's way of remaining anonymous,'" Sheila informed them.

The impressed Paula said, "Go 'head, Ms. Mayor. I never knew that."

Barrett eyed Sheila affectionately. "You never cease to amaze me."

"Have to keep you on your toes."

Paula was pleased by the love Barrett directed toward his wife. Everyone in town knew it hadn't always been that way. "Once Gary and I talk, I'll let you know if he's agreed to let his daughter participate. If he does, I'll set up my meets with Leah and Preston."

"Sounds good," Sheila replied.

"Any questions?"

"Should we talk to Preston about this?" Barrett asked.

"If you don't put him under the lights. Be gentle and let him guide the conversation. Sometimes just listening and being supportive goes a long way when teens are trying to figure things out."

They nodded agreeingly.

Paula stood. "Okay, thanks, you two. On to my next stop. We'll get this settled one way or the other. I'll be in touch."

"Oh, Paula, before you go."

She turned back to Sheila.

"I don't know if Preston told you about being contacted by his bio family in Philly."

"He did."

"Well, he reached out to them last night, and his aunt is a

lovely woman. We've invited them to spend some time with us as soon as it can be arranged."

"That's outstanding." Paula was happy for Preston. "I'd love to meet them if that's okay."

"Our kids are well loved by everyone around so I think the entire town's going to want the same thing, but I don't want them or Preston to be overwhelmed. We'll play it by ear."

Paula asked Barrett, "Are you okay with them visiting?"

"Truthfully, I was initially skeptical but once we talked to his aunt and to Preston, I realized how important it was for both sides. So, yes, I'm okay and looking forward to meeting the family in person."

She liked the way Sheila smiled up at him and squeezed his hand approvingly. "Excellent. Enjoy the day."

Buoyed by the Paynes' good news, she exited.

On Mondays Paula usually checked on the sick and shut-in. There were only a few under her wing, but she made it a point to keep the appointments because they looked forward to her pastoral visits, even if some, like the always cranky Mrs. Georgia Head, pretended not to. When she first moved to Henry Adams, Tamar would accompany her to make sure everything went well, and to ensure Paula didn't get lost on the back roads. Eventually, her charges became comfortable enough for Paula not to need Tamar's assistance with them or getting around.

Now, driving away from town, the wide open, snow-covered fields glistened in the sunlight. The landscape, dotted here and there by farms set back from the road, rusted-out silos, and the occasional abandoned barn, reminded her of rural Oklahoma. Thinking of Oklahoma made her mind drift to her aunt Ardella and how she might be handling incarceration. The one time Paula and Robyn visited her, she'd made it clear she never wanted to see either of them again in life or in death. "Leave my body to the state," she'd snarled. The disquieting memories of that day always filled Paula with pain so she sent up a prayer for her aunt's well-being, then set the thoughts aside to prevent them from clouding her day.

The two rusting red Cadillacs positioned like chained guard dogs on either side of James Redding's olive green farmhouse hadn't been driven in thirty years but served as useful landmarks when Paula was first learning her way around. Seeing them up ahead, she smiled. Mr. Redding was ninety-five years young. Spending time with him was always a joy.

She stepped up onto the porch and gave the house a quick visual inspection to make sure it hadn't incurred any visible damage since she'd seen him last. The assessment was something Tamar requested she do because sometimes the elderly didn't leave their homes for long stretches, especially during winter, and might not notice until spring that a storm had blown shingles off the roof or a gutter was hanging loose. Noticing nothing amiss, she pressed the doorbell.

Mr. Redding responded almost immediately. As always, he was wearing a nice blue sports coat and perfectly pressed gray pants. Add to that, freshly polished shoes, a pale blue shirt, and black bolo tie and you had a picture of a man bound for a date or headed to church instead of an hour-long chat with a priest.

"Ah, my favorite lady pastor," he said, showing a smile. "Come on in." As he took her coat and she removed her boots, he called out, "Reverend Paula is here, boys."

His two cats appeared. The ginger's name was Levon, and the calico went by Benny. Mr. Redding was a huge Elton John fan. The felines purred soft welcoming meows and wound themselves around her jeans as a further greeting. She reached down to stroke their soft furry backs and smiled. "How is everyone?" she asked before slipping her feet in the pair of red bunny slippers she kept there for her winter visits.

"The boys and I are fine. Let's go into the living room."

For a man of his advanced age, he didn't use a walker or a cane. He did move slowly, however, and his thin six-foot frame was a bit bent, but there was nothing bent about his mental acumen. His mind was as sharp as his attire. In the small living room, the gray sofa and matching upholstered chairs were old but clean, and the wood end tables gleamed from years of polishing. On the walls were paintings of flowers done by his late wife, Muriel. They didn't show much skill, but the colors were bold and bright.

Mr. Redding gestured Paula to the sofa while he sat in one of the chairs. Levon and Benny joined her on the couch, cuddling close and framing her much like the old Cadillacs outside. She enjoyed their company as much as she did their human.

The reading of Morning Prayer from the *Book of Common Prayer* always began their time together. He read the lessons and a few of the psalms, and they took turns with the rest. The service was short, so half an hour later they recited the last prayer and closed their books. Next came tea. Accompanied by the cats, Paula followed him into the kitchen with its faded sunflower wallpaper. Once the tea was ready, they carried their cups back out to their seats.

"So how have you been, Mr. Redding?"

"Not bad for a ninety-five-year-old former hog man. I hear the town's got a fancy new chef who's got his eye on you."

Paula choked on her tea. After recovering and using her napkin to wipe her mouth, she spied a familiar twinkle of mischief in his green eyes. "And you heard this from whom?"

"Bing, of course. He keeps me up to date on everything that goes on in Hankville."

Hankville? "I've never heard it called that before."

"Henry. Hank. Hankville."

"Ah. But you shouldn't be listening to Bing. He loves to gossip."

"Yes, he does but never known his gossip to be a lie."

"Then let's say Bing is misconstruing things."

"If you say so," and he smiled her way over his cup. "I hear the fruitcake and his hog left town."

She chuckled softly, "You are a mess, Mr. Redding."

"The fruitcake is a mess. I'd've turned that hog into bacon years ago, but it probably wouldn't be very good considering his diet. And do you believe Curry had the audacity to run for mayor? No one with a lick of sense would want him to run anything, let alone a town. Glad the colonel's lady won. I've been friends with Thad July since we were kids. Wasn't giving him my vote, either. Tricksters have no business running a town."

The mayoral election with all its shenanigans would make a great *Movie of the Week*. "How're your daughters?"

"They're fine."

Like most Americans during the fifties and early sixties Mr. Redding and his wife were devoted fans of the *Lawrence Welk Show* and named their three daughters Kathy, Peggy, and Dianne after the then popular Lennon Sisters, a fact he'd shared with Paula during one of her first visits. Kathy lived in Topeka; Peggy in Austin, Texas; and Dianne in Syracuse, New York. They were all retired and faithfully checked on him often.

"And how's Tamar doing?" he asked. "I haven't seen her recently."

"She's doing well. She was in church yesterday."

A wistful look came over him, and he stared off into the distance at something only he could see. He was silent for so long, Paula asked quietly, "Are you okay?"

The cats left her and went to his side. He smiled down fondly and gave them both a gentle scratch behind their ears. "The first time I saw Tammy July, I was maybe eight years old. She walked into our classroom and I thought she was the prettiest girl God had ever put on this earth."

Paula was surprised by that. She'd had no idea.

"Fell in love with her there and then. Went home and told my father I was going to marry her when I grew up. He dragged me into the barn and whipped me until my back bled. Told me if I even looked at her again I was going to hell. Being a good Catholic boy, I was more afraid of hell than I was of him, and he scared me half to death until the day he died." He turned her way. "Why are some people so filled with hate, Reverend?"

"I wish I knew," she whispered. The pain in his voice put tears in her heart.

"I loved my wife, Muriel, so I put my feelings for Tamar aside, but they never dulled. Still love her after all these years. Never said anything to her about it though, so please don't tell her."

"I won't. Promise."

He nodded. "After the beating, I asked my mother why my father didn't like Tamar, and she gave me my first lesson on race. How do you hate someone just because their skin's a different color? To this day, I still don't get it."

"I don't, either."

"I could've maybe understood if the Julys had been bad

people, but they weren't. They didn't have the wealth my family had, but Tammy's father owned his own land, worked for the railroad, and she and Thad were the smartest children in our classroom. The teacher didn't like that though, nor did some of the parents. You can't have two Black children who could outspell and outread all the White ones, so they talked to the school board and Tam and Thad and the rest of the Black students, like Bing Shepard and Agnes Jefferson, were no longer allowed to attend."

"That's shameful."

"Those were the times we lived in." He went quiet again for a few moments before continuing, "When I got old enough to have my own place, I tried to help make things better. Bing raised some of the best hogs in the county, everyone knew it, but the slaughterhouse people always paid him less than those who looked like me. One year, he and I mixed some of his stock in with mine. We didn't tell anyone, of course, and when I was given top dollar for the quality of those hogs, we split the profits. He and I ran that ruse for forty years. I'm glad he and the other Black farmers sued the government for cheating them, because it just wasn't right."

She'd always thought highly of Mr. Redding. This conversation raised him even higher.

Levon climbed into his lap, and Mr. Redding stroked him absently. "Times are changing now. Blacks and Whites are marrying. Men are marrying men. Women can vote and marry each other, too. Were I a young man today, maybe I'd get up the courage to ask Tamar if I could court her. No guarantee she'd say yes. Knowing her, she'd more than likely fill my backside with buckshot like her father and his brothers did the day the local Klan members tried to run the Julys off their land."

"What?"

"Yes, but those potato-sack-wearing bigots, my father and uncle included, made the mistake of choosing the same day the Julys from Oklahoma and Texas were in town to celebrate Tammy's daddy's birthday." He smiled. "I'm sure none of those cowards had ever seen so many Black men with guns firing their way, and they rode out of there like their saddles were on fire. Needless to say, Tammy's people weren't run off and the Klan left her family and the rest of Hankville alone after that."

"That's quite a story."

"A true one, though."

"Were there repercussions from the local sheriff afterward?"

"Supposedly the sheriff arrived the next day to arrest the men involved but they'd ridden out the night before and not a July could be found. Not even Tammy's father."

"Wow." It was a Henry Adams story Paula had never heard before, but she was glad the Julys had defended themselves and been smart enough to put themselves in the wind to escape arrest.

They spent a few more minutes discussing his plans for Christmas. One of his daughters would be coming to visit. Paula was glad knowing he wouldn't be spending the holiday alone.

"I should let you get on with your day, Reverend, instead of rambling like the old man that I am. It's always a pleasure when you visit."

"I enjoy our times together as well. Do you want me to wash these cups before I go?"

"No."

"Anything else you need help with?"

He shook his head. "But thanks for asking. Your kindness means a lot." He walked her to the front door and handed her her coat. She dragged on her boots. Her red bunny slippers went back into the box and were placed on the shelf in the closet.

When she was ready, she gave Levon and Benny a few strokes of goodbye and said to Mr. Redding, "You know to call me or Tamar if you need anything."

"I do. Please tell her hello when you see her next."

"Will do. Take care. See you next week."

"I look forward to it."

Paula stepped outside and walked the short distance to her parked truck. Giving Mr. Redding a wave as he stood in the door, she waited for him to close it and checked her phone. There was a text from the daughter of Georgia Head, who was also on her list to visit today. Georgia had the flu and would see Paula next time. The woman was not the nicest person and always tap-danced on Paula's last nerve by constantly complaining about everything from her saint of a daughter caregiver, to the state of the world, to the many doctors in her life—all of whom were guilty of malpractice, according to her. Paula knew she shouldn't be relieved by the text, but she was. She did offer up a prayer for a full and speedy recovery then backed out of Mr. Redding's driveway.

Driving back to Henry Adams, she mused over Mr. Redding's stories and revelations. Did Tamar know he'd been in love with her all these years? She couldn't ask the town matriarch because of the pledge she'd made. It was an interesting question, however. Paula also wondered what if anything she should do about Bing and his gossiping about her and Thorn

Webb. Ignoring the matter was probably best. Knowing Bing, confronting him would only make things worse, but she wished he'd hush up about it.

BECAUSE IT WAS still early, the Dog wasn't very crowded when Reverend Paula arrived. In another hour or so seating would be at a premium, but at the moment she had a choice. Hearing Atlantic Starr's "Secret Lovers" playing sweetly via the jukebox made her think about Mr. Redding again and wonder if the music system was somehow psychic. In the back of the dining room, she saw Gary Clark eating alone. She didn't want to disturb him but thought it might be a good time to talk to him about his daughter and Preston. It would only take a moment and he could go back to his meal.

Rocky appeared beside her. "Can I get you a seat, Paula?"

"Yes. I'll take a booth by the window, but I want to talk to Gary for a minute first."

"Sounds good. Go ahead and put your coat in the booth so it's not stolen out from under you. Place is going to fill up shortly. I'll send one of the waitstaff over when you're ready."

"Thanks, Rock."

Taking Rocky's advice, Paula claimed her booth then walked over to speak to Gary.

"Sorry to bother you, Gary, but can I speak to you for a moment?"

"Hey, Paula. Sure. How are you?" He gestured her to the open seat at the table.

"Doing good. Welcome home. Hope you and Nori enjoyed your honeymoon."

"Enjoyed it so much I had to come back to work to get

some rest." His eyes behind his black-rimmed glasses sparkled with humor.

"Want to talk to you about Leah."

He paused and studied her for a moment. "Something going on?"

"Nothing earth-shattering, but she wants to break up with Preston and he's been trying to change her mind."

"I need him to honor her decision."

Paula was pleased to hear him back his daughter. "In a way he's doing that, but Leah doesn't want to break up either, not really." She related the conversation she'd had with Leah and her emotional confession that breaking up wasn't what she really wanted.

His shoulders slumped, and after a moment, he sighed softy. "Colleen's done so much damage to Leah. How can my brilliant, beautiful girl think she's not enough?"

Gary's pain touched her. "I know, but Preston has an idea." She explained what she meant.

He seemed to brighten. "I think that's a wonderful idea. Do I need to sign anything or do anything to make this happen?"

She shook her head. "I just need your approval."

"You have it."

Like the Paynes, he asked if talking to Leah would help or hinder. She offered him the same advice. "Be gentle."

He nodded.

"So sorry for cutting into your lunchtime."

"No apology needed. I want to know what's going on with my girls, especially when they're hurting. Thanks for being there for them. You're a godsend."

Paula pushed back her chair and stood. "Once I set up a schedule, I'll be in touch."

"Okay."

Pleased to have him on board, Paula walked to her booth.

BECAUSE TWO OF the Dog waitstaff were out with the flu, Thorn was filling in. It had been years since he'd waited tables, but he was enjoying himself. He looked upon the assignment as a way to help out the shorthanded crew, and as an opportunity to further familiarize himself with the Dog's customers. He was carrying an order to two businessmen seated up front when he spotted Paula seated with a man near the back of the room. Thorn had never seen the man before so he didn't know the man's name or if he had a connection to the town. Forcing himself to stop gawking and concentrate on setting the plates on the table so they wouldn't wind up in the diners' laps, he stepped back and asked if they needed anything else. They didn't. He told them to enjoy their meal and, with his eyes on Paula, left them to their lunch. When he reached the kitchen's double doors, Rocky was exiting with a tray holding an order. He stopped her. "Who's that guy the reverend is sitting with?"

She looked over at Paula then up at him. As if needing to explain, he added, "I've just never seen him before."

"Ah," she said, still studying him. There was a hint of amusement in her gaze. "That's Gary Clark. He manages the grocery store."

Thorn watched Paula stand and leave the grocery man's table to take a seat in a booth.

"Gary just got back from his honeymoon. Paula married him and his high school sweetheart right after Thanksgiving."

Thorn's gaze moved to hers.

"So he's not a threat to whatever your intentions are."

He dropped his head. *Busted.*

"We'll discuss your intentions later. For now, you have tables to take care of, so get to work," and she left him standing there.

Feeling as if he'd just had a session with the principal, Thorn gathered himself and got to work. Although Paula wasn't seated in the section of the diner he was assigned to, he paid close attention to the kitchen's incoming orders. When hers was ready to go out, he nonchalantly picked up her plates, told the young man who'd waited on her that he'd take it. The kid didn't mind. The dining room was filling up and there were tons of other orders to oversee.

While jazz saxophonist Kirk Whalum's "All I Do" floated through the room's speakers, Thorn wound his way over to her booth. "Hey there, Reverend."

She glanced up from her tablet and startled at the sight of him.

"Sorry. Didn't mean to scare you. Brought your lunch." He placed the steaming bowl of tomato soup in front of her and added the small plate holding her grilled turkey sandwich.

"Thanks. I didn't know you were working the floor. How are you?"

"I'm well. You?"

"No complaints."

"Do you need anything else?" he asked. "More coffee?" *When can I cook for you so we can share a meal? What makes you smile—brings you joy?*

"No. I'm good for now."

"Okay. Enjoy your lunch." Thorn wanted to take a seat and spend the rest of his day in her company. In his peripheral vision he saw Rocky watching him. He cleared his throat. "I should get going. Lots to do. Take care."

"You, too."

The smile she gave him felt like a gift.

Rocky stopped him on his way back into the kitchen. "Come see me in my office at the end of your shift."

He felt like a kid with the principal again. He didn't care for it but didn't argue. "Okay."

When his shift was over, and the kitchen sparkling and ready for the evening's dinner customers, Thorn hung up his apron and made the short walk to Rocky's office. The door was open. She was at her desk viewing the screen on her laptop. "Knock, knock."

"Come on in," she said. "Give me a minute."

He used the moment to take a seat and wondered how best to respond if she grilled him about his interest in Paula Grant. He and Paula were grown. They didn't need anyone's permission to interact. It wasn't as if Rocky was the reverend's mama.

She finally swung her chair his way. "So how are things with you? Are you settling in okay?"

"I am. I like the crew, the kitchen, and the setup here. Love where I'm living."

"Good."

She handed him a folder. "Here are the latest blueprints for the Three Spinsters. Thought you might want to give them a look."

A bit surprised that he wasn't there to be interrogated, he pulled out the drawings and gave them a quick once-over. "Can you send a copy to my email, too?" He wanted to take his time poring over them.

"Sending to you now."

"Thanks."

"Second thing. I don't know if you know but Mal and Bernadine are getting married Christmas Day."

That was a surprise. "No, I didn't know."

"The Dog's catering the reception. Will you be around?"

"Sorry, no. Promised my parents I'd spend the time with them in Savannah. I'm flying out on the twenty-third, but I can help with the early prep if you need me. What's the menu look like?"

She handed him another folder. He leafed through the papers until he found the answer to his question. What he read confused him. "Hot dogs?"

She smiled. "Bernadine said their first date was a picnic in his truck. And I guess they've had a few more since then, so they're having a picnic-themed reception."

He read down the list: potato salad, baked beans, coleslaw, fried chicken, corn on the cob, ribs. "Definitely different."

"And pretty surprising, to tell you the truth. Lily and I had to almost lock Bernadine in a closet to keep her from going completely overboard during the planning for our weddings. None of us ever thought hers would be this simple."

"If I can help before I fly out, I'm your guy."

"Thanks." She quieted for a moment before saying, "So tell me about you and Paula."

He shrugged. "Nothing to tell at the moment. Yes, I'm interested in knowing her better, but she and I are grown. She doesn't need a duenna."

"Understood, but she's revered here. She's our healer, our source of faith, our everything. From the kids to the adults, we believe she walks on water. And frankly, you'd much rather have this conversation with me than with Tamar."

Thorn stiffened.

Rocky raised an eyebrow.

He admitted, "True." He'd yet to have a serious interaction

with the town's formidable matriarch, but from the little bit he knew it seemed better to stay on her good side, especially after learning she was descended from outlaws.

"You've shown yourself to be a very kind person in the short time you've been here, and honestly, I'd be rooting for you if you two got together. Knowing Paula though, she'd be real unhappy with me saying this, but she needs someone in her life. She spends so much time carrying everybody else's weight, there's no one to help her carry hers."

He appreciated her positive words about his character, so he wanted to be truthful. "I was drawn to her from the very first time we were introduced. I wanted to ask you and Ms. Brown then if she was married but figured that might come off as creepy, so I didn't."

"I'm glad you didn't. Probably wouldn't have gone over well."

"I have no idea why she's grabbed me the way she has, but I'm not the type to hit it and quit it. I'm not a player. Never have been."

"Good to know because if you treat Paula like trash, Tamar will morph into a lammergeier, drop you from a mountaintop, and eat your bones."

He stared. "Into a what?"

"A lammergeier. It's a bearded vulture. Lives in the mountains of Africa and Europe. Eats bones instead of flesh."

His eyes widened further. He was at once appalled and fascinated. What in the world was this place he wanted to make his home? Thorn took out his phone. "Can you spell it?" He'd google it later. She spelled and he typed the letters into his Note app. And no, he didn't want Tamar dining on his bones.

Mal stuck his head in the door. "Sorry to interrupt."

Rocky looked his way. "No problem, we're almost done."

"Thorn, Dads Inc. is meeting at Trent's tonight. We're hoping you can come."

"Dad's Inc.? I don't have any kids."

"Not a problem. It started as a group for the town's dads but now any man who wants to come hang out is welcome."

Thorn turned to Rocky.

"They're a good group. They do a lot for the community."

Mal added, "And try to keep these bossy women from taking over the world."

Thorn chuckled. "What time?"

"Eight. You can ride over with me if you'd like."

"Okay. If I'm not too wiped out after the dinner shift. I'll let you know."

Mal gave him a thumbs-up and left.

He turned to Rocky. "So my intentions toward Reverend Grant are honorable. Whether she's open to getting to know me is up to her. No means no. I can accept that."

"Good, but be aware that there are no secrets here. People are going to be in your business whether you want them there or not. And yes, it can be real annoying but it's because people care . . . and we don't have a lot of entertainment."

He smiled. "Got it."

Her voice took on a serious tone. "Paula helped me a lot when she moved here, and lord knows I was a mess. She holds a special place in my heart, and I just want her to be happy."

"Understood."

"Thanks for putting up with me on this. Some guys wouldn't have been as patient."

"As you said, better you than Tamar."

Rocky chuckled. "Happy courting."

"That's a word you don't hear these days, but thanks." Getting to his feet, he turned to leave.

"Thorn?"

He turned back.

"This conversation was just between us. I'm not going to say anything to Paula about what you've shared with me."

"I appreciate that. Thanks. See you later."

She nodded and he exited, wondering if Tamar could really turn into a bearded vulture.

"So is the Dads group a historic organization?" Thorn asked as Mal drove them to the meeting.

"No. It began about five years ago. I was the only dad in town before Bernadine rode in on her white jet, and I wasn't a very good one."

Thorn didn't know what to make of that. Yet another Henry Adams story he knew nothing about.

Mal continued, "We started Dads Inc. after the kids moved here. They'd all been in foster care before then."

"All from the same place?"

"No. They came from all over." He shared their names and where they were from. After a series of turns off Main Street, Mal drove them to a small group of homes decorated with Christmas lights. "Where are we?" Thorn asked. It was an area of Henry Adams he'd not seen before.

"Bernadine's subdivision. The kids and their parents live here."

He pulled into a driveway of one of the homes. "This is where my son, Trent, and his family live. We're meeting in his basement."

Mal turned off the ignition and he and Thorn got out. They

entered through the raised door of the garage. Inside was another door that opened onto a flight of stairs. "Basement is down these steps."

As they descended, sounds of male voices raised in animated conversations floated to Thorn's ears, along with Nas rapping "If I Ruled the World." Thorn found himself smiling. He certainly hadn't expected to hear that.

Trailing Mal, he entered a large space nicely furnished with couches and recliners. The walls painted a soft beige held multiple flat screens positioned above a pool table and a Ping-Pong table. He was greeted warmly with calls of welcome, raised bottles of beer, and handshakes from those he hadn't met before, like Colonel Barrett Payne, Clay Dobbs, the doctor Reg Garland, and the two youngest men in the room, Bobby Douglas and teacher Kyrie Abbott. Pot-stirring Bing Shepard shot him a smile. He shot one back. Mal encouraged Thorn to help himself to the bevy of snacks spread out on the counter of the small kitchen area. There were also cans of soft drinks and bottles of beer in a cooler.

Once he and his snacks were settled in, the meeting began.

Trent said, "Glad everybody could make it. Gary just got back from his honeymoon and wanted to spend the evening with his girls, so he'll join us next time."

The reference to Clark reminded Thorn of his lunchtime encounter with Reverend Paula, and he wondered if he'd get the third degree from these men about his interest in her, too.

Trent continued by saying, "We want to welcome Thorn to our meeting and to Henry Adams. Are you settling in?"

"Thanks for the invite. I am. Still figuring out who's who and their relationship to each other but I know that will come with time."

Luis said, "I googled you. You played football for the Raiders."

"Only a year. After the opening game of my second season, got injured in a car accident and that was that. Career over. Turned out to be okay, though."

Barrett asked, "What position?"

"Tight end."

Bing asked, "Have you asked Reverend Paula out yet?"

Thorn ran his hands down his face. "No, sir."

"What're you waiting on?"

A confused Reg held up a hand. "Question. What?"

Bing replied, "He's interested in our good reverend. She seems interested, too. Just trying to get things moving."

Now all eyes were on him, and Thorn waited for what might follow. Rocky warned him folks would be in his business and wouldn't care if he approved or not. He'd always been a private person, though.

Barrett asked, "Is Bing right?"

He replied without hesitation. "Yes."

Mal said, "Other than suggesting he take our good reverend to Movie Night on Friday, I vote we stay out of his and Paula's business."

Trent added, "I second that. All in favor?"

Ayes filled the room.

Thorn decided he liked the men of Dads Inc.

CHAPTER
11

D id you know Chef Webb is sweet on Reverend Paula?"
Unsure if she'd heard Lily right, Bernadine turned
from her laptop to view Lily standing in front of her desk.
"What?"

"Thorn is sweet on Paula," she repeated.

Bernadine decided it was too early in the morning for this
level of Henry Adams breaking news. She'd started the work-
day less than thirty minutes before and hadn't had nearly
enough coffee. "Where in the world did you hear that?"

"Trent. Apparently, Bing let the cat out of the bag last night
at the Dads meeting and Thorn verified it."

Bernadine's jaw dropped.

"The Dads voted to stay out of their business, which isn't
going to happen, of course, but who knew?"

"I certainly didn't," Bernadine replied, "and I'm the one
supposedly turning the world. We're failing at our jobs, Lil,
if we have to find out the gossip from the men. It should be

the other way around. Does Paula know?" She made a mental note to quiz Mal during dinner at his place this evening.

"According to Bing, yes, maybe?"

"How about Rocky?"

"No idea."

Truthfully, Bernadine had no problem with Paula and Thorn getting together, not that she had a say in the matter. She'd always hoped Paula would find someone to share her life with. However, she hadn't expected the candidate to be a man fine enough to make women weep. Usually reverends aren't paired with hotties. "Paula is old enough to know her own mind and handle her own business, so I'm just going to get a bag of popcorn and watch from the bleachers."

"I'll join you."

"Anything else going on we need to know?"

Lily shrugged. "Stay tuned, though. See you later." And she left for her office to begin her day.

What an interesting turn of events, Bernadine thought to herself, while wondering where Paula really stood on this. "Guess we'll find out," she said aloud and returned to her screen.

She was poring over a proposal by a tractor company wanting to build a fulfillment warehouse on a portion of the vacant land between Henry Adams and Franklin. Sheila and Franklin mayor Lyman Proctor were handling the negotiations. Always wanting to have her hand on the wheel, Bernadine was doing her best not to muscle in on the matter so the two elected officials could do their jobs, but it was hard. Her need to be in charge was both a gift and a flaw of her sometimes type A personality. As a result, few people had the balls to tell her to back off and take a seat when she wanted to take control. Mayor Sheila Payne had no such problem. The citizenry of Henry Adams had made the right decision voting her into office. Sheila and her clipboard took no prisoners, and if she had to step on Bernadine's toes in her Jimmy Choo pumps to get things done, so be it.

"Knock, knock."

The aforementioned mayor of Franklin, Lyman Proctor, stood framed in her doorway. "Lyman, good morning. How are you?"

"I'm well. I don't want to interrupt you, but do you have a minute?"

"I do. Please come in and have a seat."

He was a short, balding man, but unlike his predecessor, the bigoted Astrid Wiggins, Proctor was honest, fair-minded, and easy to partner with on issues that affected his town and hers.

"What can I do for you?"

"Hoping you know how I can get in touch with Riley Curry."

Warning bells clanged in Bernadine's head. "I don't. Is there a problem?"

His lips thinned. "The check he gave us for the parade bounced."

Of course it did. "I'm sorry, but I don't."

"I figured as much, but I had to ask." His anger showed itself. "That little snake."

It was an apt description.

He sighed. "Guess I'll have to involve law enforcement. Our budget can't handle a ten thousand dollar loss, not to mention the fees tacked on by the bank for insufficient funds. We were going to use that money to raise the salaries of our two librarians but now . . ." His words trailed off.

She honestly felt bad for him. "I'll ask Bing and Clay if he left a forwarding address. Maybe his ex-wife knows something. I don't have a current number, but her name is Eustacia Pennymaker. There can't be that many women with that name in Texas, can there?"

Lyman shrugged. "I'll see if I can find her." He got to his feet. "I'm on my way to a meeting with Mayor Payne. If anyone hears from him or knows where he is, will you let me know?"

"Definitely."

"Thanks for your time."

"You're welcome."

After his departure, Bernadine shook her head. Everywhere Riley went he left a mess in his wake. While in California he somehow managed to steal a car from a dealership. The employee he bamboozled was fired and Trent was jailed because Riley used Trent's name on the paperwork. Cletus's Hollywood trainer suffered a broken shoulder, a heart attack, and was banned from the movie industry for life after the Animal Academy Awards debacle this past Halloween. And poor Genevieve. Not only did Riley steal a ton of money from the estate set up for her by her late father, her lovely little home was declared a hazmat site thanks to his killer hog. Bernadine hoped Mayor Proctor would be able to track him down, and that Riley had enough of the lotto money left to cover the bounced check, but there was no guarantee. As Mal predicted, Riley would probably go through that money like a hot knife through butter.

Returning to the proposal, she studied the warehouse blueprints and then the company's estimated number of jobs the enterprise could bring to the area. According to Sheila, one of the reasons the company hadn't made a firm decision on the Franklin–Henry Adams area was the lack of available housing. Most of the potential employees would be local but there could be as many as fifty transferring in from other facilities. Presently, there was no place for that many new people to live. Granted, new residences, be they homes, condos, or apartments, could be built but it would probably take more time than the company would be willing to wait.

And therein lay the problem. For the past two years, Bernadine had been set on ignoring the need to grow her tiny town for fear of losing the camaraderie and familylike feel that pervaded everything from the Dog, to the Friday night movies, to celebrations like the August First parades. During the mayoral debates last month all the candidates, except Riley, emphasized the necessity of expanding Henry Adams's footprint to ensure its future. Failure to do so could result in it slowly reverting to the near death state it had been in when she initially purchased it. She didn't want the successes they'd achieved since then to go down the drain, but she didn't want to lose what made the town unique. As a businesswoman, Bernadine knew there was no way to do both. She was going to have to face reality and get on the growth bandwagon whether she liked it or not.

A text chimed on her phone. She looked at the screen. It was from Marie Jefferson. *Do you have a minute for me to stop by? Need to talk to you.*

Bernadine typed back *Yes.*

Marie arrived a short time later and she appeared upset. After the news about Paula and Riley, Bernadine wasn't sure she was ready for whatever Marie wanted to discuss.

"We're losing Kyrie Abbott."

Bernadine froze. "What do you mean?"

"He's moving back east."

"When?" She was definitely not ready for this turn of events.

"After Christmas."

"This Christmas?"

A tight-lipped Marie nodded.

"Did he say why?"

"The isolation and lack of things to do."

"How can we get him to stay?"

"We can't. His mind's made up."

Bernadine whispered, "Lord."

Marie said, "He stopped by last night after the Dads meeting and told me. He's heartbroken because he knows the lengths we went to bring him here and the great salary and benefits we provided. He doesn't want us to think he's ungrateful but he said he's withering here, Bernadine. There's no one here his age. No places for him to go and socialize. There's nothing here for him on any level outside of his love for teaching."

"Has he talked to Jack about this?"

"Yes, last night privately at the meeting. Jack FaceTimed me this morning before school. He's not happy, but understands Kyrie's decision, and frankly so do I."

Bernadine exhaled a heavy sigh. She wanted to be angry or to blame someone. However, the only person she could point a finger at was maybe herself for being so resistant to growth and change. Honestly, were she a millennial living in an isolated town inhabited by nothing but school-age kids, their parents, and senior citizens, she'd probably wither, too.

Marie said, "I hate that we're losing him. He's such an outstanding teacher."

Bernadine agreed. He hadn't even been in town long enough for Tamar to hold a welcoming ceremony for him. "So what do we do with his students? Is Jack prepared to go back to teaching the entire school again?"

"You know Jack. He'll make a way out of no way. In the meantime, he and I will start beating the bushes for Kyrie's replacement. Maybe we can find someone who's older and won't mind being in our little one-horse town. If all else fails, I can step back into the classroom if that will help lighten Jack's load."

A thought occurred to Bernadine. "Maybe we can ask Nori. Isn't she a retired teacher?"

Marie's face brightened. "Now that's a great idea. Hadn't even thought of her. See, that's why you turn the world, Bernadine. She might say no but we won't know if we don't ask."

"True." Bernadine vowed to be understanding if Nori did say no. She'd retired from teaching and was enjoying hiking and climbing mountains all over the world. Being married might alter the frequency of her trips but sometimes retirees didn't want to return to their former working personas.

Marie got to her feet. "I'll talk to her right now and get back to you."

"Good luck," Bernadine called as Marie hurried out.

Bernadine picked up her phone to text Bing to see if he knew anything about Riley's whereabouts for Lyman Proctor when a young man wearing winter gear asked from the doorway, "Bernadine Brown?"

Wary, she replied, "Yes."

He walked in, handed her an envelope. "You've been served. Have a nice day."

Her mouth dropped, and before she could question him, he disappeared. She opened the envelope, read the contents, and said, "Oh hell!" She was being sued by Leo's two other ex-wives for alienation of affection and embezzlement. Both of which were crap.

She put in a call to her personal lawyer, Jim Edison.

He asked, "How can an ex-wife sue another ex-wife for alienation of affection?"

"You're the lawyer, you tell me."

"It's frivolous and stupid. Give me the name of the law firm."

She did.

He told her, "Thanks. You go on with your day. I'll handle this and be in touch. These women must be on drugs."

Bernadine checked her watch. It was lunchtime. After the morning she'd had, she needed not only food, but a drink.

OVER AT THE school, Amari and Preston found seats and removed their lunches from their backpacks. Kids were sitting with their cliques. Zoey and her crew were seated across the room laughing and talking. Leah was still avoiding Preston. Devon wandered over to where Amari and Preston were, but before he could sit down and join them, Amari said to him, "Find someplace else to sit."

Ever the little brother, Devon replied, "It's a free country. I can sit here if I want."

"Go away, Devon."

"Fine, but I'm telling Mom."

"I don't care. I have to put up with you at home, I don't have to do it at school, too."

Devon left and Preston chuckled. "Getting on your nerves again?"

"On my nerves, my retina, my DNA, all of the above. I want to give him away as a parting gift like on one of those old-school game shows Tamar watches, but they'd probably send him back like in 'The Ransom of Red Chief.' He's still whining twenty-four seven about wanting to sing at OG and Ms. Bernadine's wedding. My dad was telling us about the car-detailing business he and Bobby are going to start, and Mr. Wig Head busts into the convo and asks does anyone care that he's sad. I wanted to punt him into next week. Just real tired of him."

"I get it. When is your dad going to open the business?"

"Not sure. He didn't get to finish telling us thanks to Devon butting in." Amari shook his head. "Be nice if I had a brother I didn't want to Hulk smash every time I see him." He looked over at Brain. "Glad I have you in my life, though. Makes up for having to deal with him."

"Glad I have you to roll with, too."

"Thanks."

"That being said, I should probably tell you what's going on with me and Leah."

"Up to you, man."

Preston went silent for a moment before saying, "She wants to break up."

That was the last thing Amari expected to hear. "She say why?"

Brain explained, and when he finished, Amari said, "That doesn't make sense. I mean, yeah, you both might meet somebody else but it won't be like the first day you're on campus. At least I wouldn't think so."

"And I'm not going to MIT looking to get with somebody else. I really want Leah to stay in my life. She and I are going to be talking to Reverend Paula about it."

"Sort of like marriage counseling?"

"Yeah."

"If anybody can fix this, Reverend Paula can."

"I hope so."

Amari felt bad for him and for Leah being so insecure. She obviously didn't see herself the way he and her other friends did. She was all that and more as far as he was concerned. "I'm sorry, man."

"Me, too. But something great has happened, too." And he told Amari about the upcoming visit from his bio relatives.

"That is great! How long are they going to stay?"

"Just overnight. My aunt drives a city bus and doesn't get a lot of time off for vacation and stuff."

"Think I'll get to meet them?"

"Of course. She has a son who's fourteen. He's coming, too. Ms. Bernadine is going to send the jet for them."

"Sweet. That ought to impress the hell out of them."

"It did us."

"Sure did." Amari thought back to that first flight. He, Preston, Zoey, Devon, and Crystal had come a long way since that day. "And I might as well share my news, which is way less awesome than yours."

"What is it?"

"Melody called my mom and wanted to talk to me."

"Your bio mom, Melody?"

Amari sipped at the straw in his juice box and nodded.

"What did she want to talk about?"

He set the box down. "Don't know. Don't care. But she made Mom mad enough to want to snatch her through the phone."

"That's not good."

"No, it's not. Of course, Mom didn't give up my digits. After the way Melody treated me when I did that visit? Not a chance I want to hear anything she has to say in this life or the next."

"I hear you. Let's hope she got the message and will leave you alone now."

"Let's hope."

The conversation switched to their beloved Kansas City Chiefs and the run-up to the NFL playoffs, and then to the latest episode of *Reservation Dogs*, a streaming show about a crew of Native American teens, which they both enjoyed. Soon Mr. Jack's voice came over the speaker announcing the end of lunch. As they gathered up their trash and belongings, Amari said seriously, "I hope Reverend Paula can fix things with you and Leah because regardless of what happens, I want us three to still be friends when we get old like OG, Ms. Marie, and Ms. Gen are still friends."

"Me, too."

Amari spent the rest of the school day thinking about Preston and Leah, as well as Preston hooking up with his bio family. He was happy for him. Personally, he was grateful for his connection to his ton of July cousins and Harley-riding Lakota grandmother on his bio dad Griffin's side. However, a part of him quietly wished Melody had embraced him instead of making it clear she hadn't wanted anything to do with him. It still hurt and probably always would.

REVEREND PAULA CLOSED her laptop with a pleased sigh. She'd been watching a symposium on the role played by the Black church during the abolitionist era of the nineteenth century, sponsored by the Smithsonian's National Museum of African American History and Culture in Washington, DC. The

Blacksonian, as it was affectionately called, was on her bucket list of places to visit, but for now she had to be content with enjoying their historical content virtually. Before watching the day's presentation, she'd known a little about the contributions of the church during that time and some of its leaders like Richard Allen who'd founded the African Methodist Episcopal Church. Being an Episcopalian she of course knew about Absalom Jones, a friend of Allen's and the man behind the establishment of St. Thomas's African Episcopal Church in Philadelphia, the nation's first Black Episcopal church. She hadn't known that Samuel Cornish who'd helped start *Freedom's Journal*, one of the first Black newspapers, had been a man of the cloth or that the women of Allen's Bethel AME Church, and other free Black women had rallied around the Free Produce Movement, which boycotted products made by slave labor such as sugar and cotton. The objective was to deprive slave owners of the profits made from the unpaid labor of the three million people enslaved in the South. Paula, with her sweet tooth, couldn't imagine going without sugar but knew it would've been a movement to support had it helped bring about the demise of slavery.

Her stomach grumbled from hunger. She'd been so engrossed in the lecture, she'd forgotten lunch. Looking up at the clock on her office wall, she realized the Dog would only be serving lunch a short while longer. Picking up her phone, she called and got Mal on the other end of the line. "Hey, Mal. Can I order lunch to go?"

"Hey, Rev. You sure can. What can we get you? Sandwich of the day is a Reuben with all the fixings. Soup is chicken noodle."

"Not a big fan of sauerkraut, and although I like cheese, it doesn't like me, so can I have the Reuben without them?"

"However you want it is fine."

"Okay and let me have the chicken noodle."

"Yes, ma'am. Are you at the church?"

"Yes."

"Got a crew member on their way home. They'll drop it off."

"I can come and get it, Mal."

"Not necessary. They'll be there in about fifteen minutes."

And before she could protest further, he was gone.

Fifteen minutes later, Paula heard footsteps coming down the stairs. Getting up to greet the person, she walked to the doorway and froze at the sight of Thorn Webb coming toward her.

"Hey there, Reverend. Special delivery."

Gathering herself while wondering if she'd ever get used to how big and handsome he was, her smile met his. "Hey, Thorn. I told Mal I'd come and get it. You didn't have to go out of your way."

"Not a problem. Was heading home to eat my own lunch." He raised the large paper bag in his hand. "Mal put everything in here, so let me take yours out. Where do you want me to set it?"

"Let's put it on the table. Come on in."

He followed Paula into her office and she was aware of him behind her as she was of her swiftly beating heart. "How's your day going?" he asked.

"Going well."

He set the bag on the table and began unpacking the contents. "I don't know why he put your order beneath mine."

She watched while he placed a few foil-wrapped packets on the table, then withdrew more. "Your Reuben without the fixings." It was followed by a round short container with a top on it. "And your soup."

"Thank you."

"He sent utensils, and some oyster crackers."

"Great."

Watching him begin to place his order back in the bag, Paula heard herself ask, "How about you eat here? I'd hate for you to get home and your food's cold because you had to stop by here first."

He paused and held her eyes for so long her already heightened awareness of him ratcheted up into overdrive. He finally replied quietly, "I'd enjoy that."

As nervous as she could ever remember herself being, she swallowed in a dry throat. "Then sit, and let's eat."

He shrugged out of his parka and took a seat at the table.

"Let's bless the food first," she said and offered up a softly spoken prayer thanking God for their bounty. "Amen."

Paula removed the top from her soup and willed her hands to stop shaking. As Thorn unwrapped a large roast beef sandwich and a foil packet of fries, he asked, "So what does a reverend do when she's not leading a service?"

"Visit the sick and shut-in. I also have a degree in child psychology so I have standing weekly appointments with the kids. Some of them had pretty traumatic lives before moving here. I also make myself available to the adults when needed."

She bit into her still warm Reuben. "This is so good."

He looked her way and smiled. "Is there a church secretary?"

"No. The congregation is so small there's really no need for one, at least for now. So I handle administrative duties too, like the banking and putting together the Sunday bulletin."

He nodded while munching on a fry.

Paula was glad they were making small talk; it was helping deflate her nervousness. Somewhat. "So tell me about yourself. You said you grew up in Chicago."

"I did. Was born there, but my family moved to Oakland when I was eight."

"Siblings?"

"Just one. A sister. She's a year and a half older. Her name is June. What about you? Any brothers or sisters?"

She shook her head. "I'm an only. Was born in San Diego. Mom died when I was fourteen, so I wound up in Oklahoma until I graduated and went to Spelman. Did you go to college?"

"I did. The University of South Central."

"Where's that?"

He grinned. "Officially it's the University of Southern California, but it's in South Central, LA's hood."

"Gotcha. Did you get your culinary training there?"

"No. Went to culinary school after an injury canceled my NFL career."

She stiffened with surprise. "You played in the NFL? I love me some football."

He grinned. "Yep. Tight end for the Oakland Raiders. Got hurt after my rookie year. Career over."

"That had to be disappointing."

"It was at first, but I had a good agent. I was drafted high in the first round and my money was guaranteed, so after I convinced my parents to retire and bought them a place in Savannah, I had the world at my fingertips. Who are your favorite teams?"

"Sooners for college. Cowboys for the NFL. Neither are the behemoths they used to be when I was growing up. When I moved to Atlanta, the Falcons became my team." She paused and added, "I like that you looked out for your parents."

"They'd worked hard and raised my sister and I well. I owed them a life with no struggles. I send them on a cruise every year for their anniversary."

"You're a good son."

"I like to think so."

She was pleased with what he'd shared about his life. "So how long after retiring from the NFL did you start culinary school?"

"Took me almost a year to get back on my feet after the injury, and six months later I started school. After I got my certification, I decided to see the world, so I cooked my way across Europe, Africa, and South America. Took jobs on kitchen crews in Madrid, Barcelona, France, Rio, Kingston, Cairo, Kenya. Did that for about five years before coming back to the States."

"I've not traveled much, would love to do so, though."

"Where would you travel to if you could?"

She thought for a moment. "I'd go to Rome to see Michelangelo's *David*. Cambodia to see Angkor Wat. Victoria Falls in Africa, along with Mt. Kilimanjaro. Bahia in Brazil. I have a long list. The volcanoes in Hawaii."

"Why haven't you visited any of the places?"

"Work commitments and I'm not sure I'd enjoy traveling alone."

"I see."

Silence rose between them.

"So can I ask you a question?" he asked.

"Sure."

"How does a guy go about courting a lady reverend?"

She froze.

He added, "Asking for a friend."

She couldn't suppress her amusement. "A friend," she replied doubtfully.

"Yes." He sat back against his chair and folded his arms. "What should he know?"

She studied him for a long moment, wondering where this might lead. "First and foremost, he should know that she's not a bed bunny."

He laughed. "A bed bunny?"

"Yes. If your friend is looking for someone to hop around in bed with, she's not the one."

"I'm pretty sure he already knew that, and honestly it's nowhere near the top of his list."

She liked hearing that but had no idea how truthful it might be. Instead of worrying over it, she set it aside, gave him the benefit of the doubt, and framed her next response. "He should also know that he'll always have to bat second to her faith and commitment to Christ."

He nodded. "Understood. Is it okay if he calls her by her given name?"

"It is," she replied softly.

The connection between them rose with a gentle strength she could no longer deny or pretend not to feel, and she wondered what he'd ask next.

"What brings Paula joy? Not the reverend, but Paula the person."

"Your friend has some intriguing questions."

"He'll be glad you said that."

She was enjoying this gentle and yes, novel interrogation. "Well, let's see. That's a hard question to be honest. She's spent so much of her life focused on others. Can she come back to that one later?"

"Of course."

She honestly had to think on that one and wondered if not having a ready answer made her life seem lacking in some way. She didn't believe serving her faith made her less of a person, even if others might think it did. "Does that make her less interesting in your friend's eyes?"

He shook his head. "No. It just makes him want to help her discover what that personal joy might be if she's open to exploring it."

"She might be." A thought occurred to her. "She does love the Cuban and Haitian food of southern Florida and misses it big-time. Will that answer do?"

"More than do. Since it's tied to food, he'll think you're a woman after his own heart."

That left her so shaken, she forced herself to look away. "How old is this friend of yours?"

"Forty-eight."

"Does he know that she's fifty-four?"

"No, but a six-year difference doesn't matter to him. He's interested in her. Not her age."

She turned back and saw the honesty in his eyes. She again wondered what this fine gladiator of a man found in her, not that she didn't have value, but she was a small-town priest and he looked like a man who'd just stepped out of *GQ*.

"A french fry for your thoughts?"

He had a delightful sense of humor, too. "Why me, Thorn?"

"Why not you? You're wise, kind, focused, and if I may say so, gorgeous."

That brought heat to her cheeks.

He added, "And my friend wants her to know that when you're together he'll do everything in his power not to embarrass her, belittle her faith, or try to make himself first in her life. He also has been married once and is divorced. He'd want me to throw that in. His ex didn't like batting second to what he does for a living."

That he'd used her words to describe his failed marriage showed he understood what being committed to something like faith actually meant. His questions and responses were as intriguing as she found him to be.

"May I ask one last question?" he said to her.

She nodded.

"Will you go to the movies with me Friday night?"

She smiled and didn't hesitate. "Yes."

Driving home, Thorn was so ecstatic that were he in a Hollywood musical he would've burst into song. He liked that she'd played along with his questioning and hoped she recognized he'd taken her responses to heart. Taking that approach hadn't been something he'd planned in advance. After last night's Dads meeting, he'd been trying to figure out how and when to approach her about the movies. Mal to the rescue. Thorn had the sneaking suspicion that Mal sending him to deliver her lunch had been Mal playing matchmaker. So much for the vote on staying out of his business, but it had worked out. Perfectly in fact.

That she seemed to be passionate about the cuisine of southern Florida was perfect as well. He knew what he'd cook for her when the time came. But for now, he was content with her allowing him into her world. Remembering what she'd said about not being a bed bunny made him smile all over again. She'd get no pressure from him on that issue. He'd let her set the pace for wherever their interactions led because that's what a man was supposed to do. He now knew how to court a lady reverend and he didn't want to screw it up.

AFTER WORK, BERNADINE made a quick trip home to change into more casual attire before heading to Mal's place for dinner. He answered her knock on his door wearing a black apron that read: *Mr. Good Lookin' Is Cookin'*.

"Like the apron," she told him, taking off her coat and draping it on his sofa.

"Lily got it for me."

"Smells good in here," she told him.

"Hoping it tastes good, too. Give me a kiss."

She obliged and followed him through his cozy living room and into the kitchen. She loved his apartment with its dark blue walls accented by gray, and the way both hues were picked up in the furnishings. Pops of color were added by the artwork positioned around the room. She smiled seeing their bobbleheads on top of the bookcase. Once again, she was unsettled by the thought of Mal giving up his place after they married because of all the TLC he'd put into making it uniquely his own.

In the kitchen she took a seat at the table and ran her eyes approvingly over his small jungle of leafy green plants in front of the sliding door.

He opened the oven to check on whatever was smelling so heavenly

"How was your day?" he asked.

"Interesting. I'm being sued by Leo's two ex-wives."

He paused. "Really?"

"Yes. Alienation of affection or some such nonsense. Embezzlement, too."

He removed an emerald-green Dutch oven from inside the oven and set it on the stovetop. "That is interesting." They spent a few more minutes talking about it while he finished putting the finishings touches on his pots.

"Jim Edison is handling their lawyers. Said he'd keep me posted."

Mal removed the top of the saucepan on one of the burners and the sweet scent that floated out made her say, "Yum."

He grinned. "We're having pot roast, honeyed carrots, and some roasted Brussels sprouts that I cooked in the air fryer. Hope you're hungry."

"Always hungry for whatever you're offering."

He chuckled. "All right now, missy. We're going to wind up in the bedroom you keep talking like that."

"What did I say?" she teased with mock innocence.

"Grab you a plate."

Once their plates were filled and they began eating, she said, "You're such a good cook, Mr. Malachi July."

"I love good food. It makes up for living on cold, day-old pizza and Pop-Tarts when I was drinking."

Bernadine hadn't known Mal then but from what he'd openly shared about that time in his life, he'd been incredibly broken. She was glad he'd gotten help and remained committed to his sobriety.

Seated across from her, he asked, "Anything else happen on your interesting day?"

"Well, let's see," and she ran down the list of events and visits that made up her morning.

The Riley news made him shake his head. "One day, somebody's going to kick Riley's butt from sunrise to sunset. No need saying I can't believe his check bounced because I totally can. Being underhanded is his brand."

"I know. I'm hoping Bing or Clay might know how to run him down for Lyman."

"Don't count on it. The only person happier than Genevieve to see Riley leave town is Bing. Clay's not far behind."

"I told Lyman to see if he can maybe find Eustacia, but last I heard she didn't want anything to do with Riley or his hog."

"I still remember that hog wedding," he said, shaking his head at the memory of that foolishness.

"I'll never be able to unsee that hog in the wedding gown on the internet. Back then, Eustacia was as much of a hot mess as Riley. Had the sense to leave him, though. She gets points for that."

"Yeah, she does."

The conversation moved on to Kyrie.

Mal said seriously, "Sad to see him go."

"Me, too. I'm going to have to get off the fence on the growth thing though, otherwise the only people still here in ten years will be us oldies."

"If we aren't growing, we're dying."

"Sad, but true."

"Things will work out. How are you handling Sheila being in charge?"

"Honestly, not well."

"She's doing a great job, seems to me."

"She is, but I don't like being on the outside looking in. I'm used to being in the trenches."

"Stepping back is good for you."

"How so?"

"You get to relax. You've been running like a thorough-bred at the Derby for the past five years. It's time for you to slow your roll."

"And do what?" she asked, unable to keep the testiness out of her voice. "I'm not going to sit at home eating bonbons and watching the soaps for the rest of my life."

He simply eyed her and remained silent.

She got the message. "Sorry. Didn't mean to snap."

"No, you're good. I understand. Change is hard on a lot of levels. And not knowing what your future is going to look like is another reason for growing this place. A new and improved Henry Adams might offer you some opportunities to not have to sit home eating bonbons."

"Like what?"

He shrugged. "No idea but as Sam Cooke sang: A change is gonna come. Whether you want it to or not."

She sighed. "I suppose." She studied him. "You're good for me."

"We're good for each other."

And she agreed. He gave her the balance she sometimes needed, and she helped wean him off running the streets with girls young enough to be his great-granddaughters. "So how did you guys know about Thorn being sweet on Paula?"

He quirked an eyebrow and took a sip of his cola. "You ladies mad that we figured it out?"

She laughed. "I think we are. Since when did the Dads become romance aficionados?"

"Thorn's been pretty transparent to be honest. Every time I've seen him around her he's looked—what's a good word? Smitten."

"Smitten?" she echoed dubiously.

He nodded. "Yes. Smitten. Good Scrabble word. You might want to write it down so you can use it the next time I'm whipping your lovely little butt."

"Hush, braggart."

"Say my name."

She absolutely adored this man. Thanks to their counseling sessions with Paula they'd gotten past the issues that broke her heart and were in a much better place as a couple. "Do you think Paula and Thorn will actually hook up?"

"Time will tell, I suppose, but I did my part today."

"What do you mean?"

"When she called for her lunch, I knew Thorn was on his way home, so I had him deliver her order."

"I thought you all voted not to meddle."

"Nobody believed that except maybe Thorn."

"Do you think he stayed and talked?"

"I don't know but at the meeting we encouraged him to take her to the movies Friday night. We'll have to see if they show up together."

"This is like a live version of those romance novels Genevieve loves so much. And who'd ever thought a man would be playing the role of matchmaker."

"Last time I checked matchmaker wasn't gender specific." He added, "Specific. Another great Scrabble word. Lots of points. You should write that one down, too."

"I'm going to punch you. Keep it up."

They finished their meal and she helped him clean up. Once

the dishwasher was loaded and running, they retreated to the living room. Mal put on some soft jazz and joined Bernadine on the sofa. She cuddled into his side, he placed a kiss on her brow, and held her close. The atmosphere felt perfect. "What are you going to do with this place after we get married?"

He didn't reply for a long moment. She straightened up and asked, "Something wrong?"

He shrugged. "Not really, but I've been wondering about that myself."

"You don't want to give it up, do you?"

"Honestly, no."

"That's been bothering me, too."

"My giving it up?"

"Yes."

"Having this place, especially after the renovation, and doing the painting and finding just the right furniture. I have it just the way I want it. It's home, my home. I have my books and music, and art. I can walk around in my drawers if I want to, and now . . ."

"Marriage is making you live with me."

"It's not making me. I'm choosing to."

"Even though you'd rather not."

"Bingo," he replied quietly.

One of the things Paula stressed in their counseling sessions had been honest communication.

"Then let me be honest, too. I know there are going to be days I'm going to come home from work and love having you be there, and other days . . ."

"You'd want to be by yourself."

She nodded. "Are we too old and set in our ways to be doing this, Mal?"

"I don't know, doll, but if you want to call off the wedding—"

"No. I'm looking forward to being Bernadine Brown July. I'm like Amari. I want to be an official July, and go to the gatherings, and meet the relatives I haven't met, and hear the old stories. Not sure about your uncle Thad, though."

He smiled and looked down at her. "Sorry, but he comes with the package."

She smiled back. "I know. Just kidding." Her voice turned serious again. "I want to be your wife, Mal, very much. But I also like having my own private space as much as you like having yours."

"So how do we do that and still marry?"

"I don't know."

"Maybe we should talk to Paula and have her help us figure it out."

"I think that's a great idea."

"Thanks for speaking your truth."

"Same to you."

He gave her a squeeze.

The music filled the silence that followed. A few moments later he said, "I figured out where to hang Crystal's watercolor of our kites."

"Where?"

"Bedroom. Do you want to see?"

There was mischief in his eyes.

"Are you intending to seduce me, sir?"

"If I ain't trying, I ain't breathing."

She laughed. "Lead the way."

Preston came down to breakfast to the smells of bacon and the sight of his mom at the stove. "Morning," he said quietly.

"Morning, Preston. Did you sleep well?"

"Yes, I think so."

"Do you want eggs and grits or French toast, or both?"

"Just the grits and two eggs, please. Pops already gone?"

Sheila cracked his eggs into a bowl, scrambled them with some milk, and slid them into the hot skillet. "Yes. He had an early morning meeting with Gary."

"Oh."

"Something wrong?"

"No. Just wanted to tell him, and you, thanks for saying yes to Reverend Paula so she can help me and Leah figure out our problem. She sent me a text last night asking if we'd meet her after school today." He spooned some grits onto a plate and doctored them the way he liked.

"Was an easy thing to agree to. I was wondering why Leah

hadn't come by lately and why you were looking so blue. I thought maybe the two were related, but I didn't want to be one of those moms all up in your business. I'm still learning how to do this raising a man-child thing."

He smiled. "You're doing great. I really thought I could handle it on my own, but I guess not."

"I'm sorry things have gone sour with you two. I like Leah a lot."

When his eggs were done, Sheila added them to his plate.

"Thanks. I like her a lot, too. I just wish this wasn't so hard." Preston began eating and thought back on some of the good times he'd had with Leah: their homework competitions, chess matches, stargazing.

His mom said, "Being in a relationship can be challenging. Heartache is no fun. At least it sounds as if Leah is open to talking things out. That's a plus."

"But I don't understand why she'd think this way? She acts like the first thing I'm going to do when I go to MIT is dump her for someone else."

"We all have insecurities, and I think how she sees herself is one of hers."

"But she's a babe, and way smart, and funny, Mom."

"And I agree, but how we see her and what she sees are different. Society can put so much pressure on young women that they think they must look a certain way, act a certain way, wear the right clothes, be the right size, be the right skin tone, and be conscious of how they present themselves not only in everyday life, but to guys, too, or they won't be liked."

"I like her just the way she is."

"And that's great, but she's being constantly bombarded by what's online and by what's on TV and in magazines."

"And what she's been told about who she is by her mom."

He and his mom shared a look. Everyone in town knew how messed-up Leah's mom was. Preston didn't expect his mom to say anything bad about Leah's mom because she wasn't that type of person, and she didn't.

"How we're raised plays a big part, too. I spent my teen years being told to keep my math brain on the down-low or I wouldn't find a husband."

"That's dumb."

"I know, but many women my age believed that. Some still do. Navigating life can be difficult for women no matter their age."

He figured she must've sensed how glum he felt because she walked over and placed an arm across his shoulders and gave him an encouraging squeeze and a kiss on the forehead. "But you and Leah have someone on your side many young people don't have," she told him.

"Which is who?"

"Reverend Paula."

He offered a small smile.

"And if anybody can help you figure this out, I'm putting my money on her."

He glanced up and seeing her familiar kindness, he replied, "Like I said, you're really good at this raising a man-child thing. Thanks for helping me better understand what Leah might be dealing with. It kind of makes sense now."

"Then my job here is done. Finish your breakfast, I'm going to get ready for work. Be back in a bit."

As she left him alone, Preston was again reminded of how lucky he was to be in Henry Adams and to have the Paynes as his parents. When he set fire to that house in Milwaukee what seemed like a zillion years ago, no way did he imagine that this was where he'd wind up; in a magical place, having a magical life with people and friends who actually cared about him. He just wanted to get things straight with Leah so that magic could continue for them both because he missed her a lot.

AT SCHOOL, AFTER the morning ritual of the Negro national anthem and Maria playing the Mexican anthem on the piano, Mr. James surprised them by saying Mr. Abbott's class would be joining them for a few minutes to hear an announcement he had to make.

Preston leaned over to Amari, whispering, "Wonder what this is about?"

Amari shrugged. "Guess we'll find out."

Mr. Abbott and his ten students arrived. The kids stood in the back of the room while Mr. Abbott joined Mr. James up front. Mr. Kyrie said, "I want you to know that I'm leaving Henry Adams. I won't be back after the holiday break."

Gasps filled the room.

With sadness on his face, he continued, "Teaching here has been a wonderful experience and a big part of that has been you students. Every teacher would love to have students as bright and engaged and as committed to learning as you are. I'm going to miss you all very much."

His words ended with a sharp elongated wail of "Nooo!" from Tiffany.

Preston shared a look with Amari and they both shook their heads at her reaction. She called herself crushing on him since the new term began in the fall and, according to Leah, wanted him to stay at the school until she was eighteen so she could ask him out. Amari said she suffered from Tiff-Foolery and the CDC needed to develop a vaccine before it spread nationwide.

Mr. James said, "Ms. Jefferson and I are very pretty sad to see him go because he's been an excellent teacher and will be missed. We've already begun a search for his replacement, but no one will be able to replace him in our hearts."

As a buzz filled the room, he went on to say emails would be sent to parents to alert them of Mr. Abbott's departure and explain the steps being taken to find another teacher to take over his class. Preston was disappointed by the news. He liked Mr. Abbott. He hadn't been in town long enough to really know a lot about him, but he'd hung out with them occasionally on pizza Saturdays and showed off his video-game skills. He was also so good at chess not even Leah could beat him consistently. He had a style and personality any kid would want to match once they got older. Preston wished he'd be staying so they could get to know him better.

Amari leaned over. "I wonder why he's leaving?"

"Same here."

"Maybe he wants to escape Tiffany. I know I did. Free at last. Free at last. Thank God almighty, he's free at last."

The startled Preston snorted so loud Mr. James sent him a quelling look that made him hastily pull himself together. Moments like this was one of the thousands of reasons he'd miss Amari when he left for MIT.

A few minutes later, Mr. Abbott and his class trooped out, and the school day got under way.

For the rest of the morning, Preston did his best to stay focused on his work, but his mind kept drifting to the upcoming meeting with Reverend Paula and how it might turn out.

He also couldn't stop his eyes from sliding across the room to Leah. He caught her glancing back a couple of times but the contact was always brief, never long enough for him to figure out what she might be thinking. By lunchtime, the uncertainty had his stomach in knots, to the point where he wondered if he might be developing an ulcer. No matter how many times he told himself to calm down, the anxiety remained.

At the end of the day, he was gathering his belongings when Amari asked, "You on your way to the church?"

He shook his head. "Not yet. Leah has her weekly appointment first, and I'm supposed to go in in an hour."

Across the room, he saw Leah give him a quick look before she averted her eyes and headed out the door.

"Do you need me to hang with you until then? I can."

"No. I think I'm just going to sit here until it's time."

Amari studied him for a moment as if trying to determine what he might really be feeling inside. "It's going to be okay, man. Reverend Paula's got this."

"I hope so."

"I know so. Text me later if you need to."

"Will do."

A few minutes after Amari's departure, Mr. James came out of his office. He appeared surprised to find Preston sitting in the classroom alone. "You okay, Preston? Did you stay to talk to me about something?"

"No, sir. I'm seeing Reverend Paula in an hour. Thought I'd wait here."

Like Amari, Mr. James studied him closely before adding, "Okay. I'll be in my office if you need anything."

"Thanks." Alone again, Preston dug into his backpack for

the graphic novel he'd started a few days ago. He opened it to where he'd left off but found himself unable to concentrate on the words or the drawings. Exhaling a sigh, he put the novel away and sat in the silence to wait for the time to pass.

REVEREND PAULA'S OFFICE door was closed when he arrived. He didn't want to knock if she and Leah were still in the session, so he took a seat in one of the nearby chairs. Just as he got settled, the door opened, and Reverend Paula appeared. "Hi, Preston. Thanks for being so prompt. Come on in; Leah and I are done."

Filled with dread, his stomach in even tighter knots, he followed her inside. Leah was seated on the couch; beside her, a box of tissues. Her eyes were watery and red. He knew her well enough to know she'd been crying. Wondering if the tears were tied to her not wanting to speak to him made him feel even worse. His hands shook a bit as he removed his coat. He sat down on one of the chairs closest to the reverend's desk and waited to see what would happen next. To his surprise, Reverend Paula didn't take a seat but instead remained by the door. "I'll let you two talk and pop back in in a few."

Leah pulled a tissue and wiped lingering tears from her eyes. "Thank you, Reverend Paula."

The reverend offered them both a quiet smile and departed, closing the door behind her.

Inwardly, he panicked. *Wasn't she supposed to be the person guiding them?*

Leah met his eyes and said softly, "Hi, Preston."

Being addressed after being ignored for the past two weeks caught him off guard. It pleased him though, because she was talking to him again. "Hey, Leah."

"Do you remember when we first met, and I ended up apologizing to you for dragging you about your weight?"

"I do." They'd been at Reverend Paula's welcome reception.

"I owe you another apology."

"Why?"

"For being so scared of stuff that I broke us, and we ended up here."

"You don't have to apologize."

She nodded. "I do. You have never been anything but kind to me. Always. I had no reason to believe you'd up and dump me. You're my boyfriend and I let all the mess inside make me not kind to you. I hurt you, Preston, really bad, and I'm so sorry." Tears rolled slowly down her cheeks.

"Don't cry, Leah. Please don't cry."

"Reverend Paula has been helping me see that the past is the past. She wants me to try and face forward instead of always wanting to go backward and fix whatever my mom says is wrong with me."

"There's nothing wrong with you."

"In my brain I know that, but still. I guess I just want her to love me even though everything she's done and said says she doesn't. And it hurts so much," she whispered on a broken sob.

Preston went to her and took her into his arms and held her while she wept her heart out. His own heart broke. Having never dealt with anything like this before he didn't know what to offer, so he gave all he knew to give, the solace of his embrace. And as Leah continued to cry, he wanted to tell her how perfect and brilliant she was, and how proud he was that she'd chosen him to be with; there was so much he wanted her to know. Instead, he held her tight and whispered, "It's okay, Leah. It's okay."

After a little while, the depth of her pain seemed to lessen somewhat, and she eased back and looked up at him. Seeing his tears, she wiped them away with her fingertips. "Got you crying, too."

She handed him the box of tissues. He took a couple and dried his eyes. "I'm good. Guys can cry these days, you know. Just don't tell my pops." The colonel had come a long way in how he viewed people and life, but men shedding tears was still a no-no in his world. "He'll make me do push-ups until my shoulders catch on fire."

She smiled and it made him feel good to see it.

"Missed you smiling," he told her.

"You're so tenderhearted, Preston Mays Payne."

"Just with you."

He realized he could be content to spend the rest of his life just sitting there with her. "Are you better—at least a little bit?"

She nodded. "Reverend Paula helped me a lot. She told me about how hard it was for her when she had to go live with her grandfather in Oklahoma after her mother passed away. I can't tell you details, but her life was bad, Preston. Really bad. Still has her messed up in some ways, she said."

Preston found that hard to believe.

Leah stared out for a moment as if thinking before saying softly, "We look at the adults in our life and think they never had bad stuff to deal with growing up, but they did. Her telling me about what she went through made me look at my problems differently. She wants me to remember that in spite of what my mom says, God doesn't make junk. I am who I am and the way I am because this is who I'm supposed to be. Not whoever my mom decided I should be. I'm a perfect and unique Leah, and I should embrace that and not hate on myself."

Preston agreed. She was looking up at him again and even with her red puffy eyes and tear-swollen nose and face, he thought she was the finest babe in the world.

She asked, "Will you still be my boyfriend?"

"If you'll still be my girlfriend."

She gave him a shy smile. "I will."

He stuck out a hand. "Deal."

"Deal."

After a moment of looking into each other's eyes, the deal was further cemented with a kiss. The sweetness of it salved and healed all Preston's hurts and sorrows. When it ended, he held her close. They'd agreed on no sex until they were older because they couldn't even raise themselves, let alone a kid, and yes, they'd done some messing around, but they hadn't done *IT*. Even with protection they were too afraid of the consequences. "Are you ready for some good news?"

She nodded.

"My bio aunt is coming to visit this weekend."

"OMG, Preston. That's amazing. Can I meet her?"

"Yes."

They spent a few minutes talking details, and when he finished answering her questions, he paused for a moment before asking her in a serious voice, "So are you and I really good now?"

"Yes, and I want us to be together for as long as we want to be. I know I still have stuff to work through, probably maybe until I get to be my dad's age, but Reverend Paula's got my back while I'm here in town. She said she'll help me find a good therapist in California when I go away to school, and that she and I can always Zoom or FaceTime. I'm so glad she moved here."

"I am, too." Reverend Paula had helped Preston work through some of his own issues and as a result he understood what a difference therapy could make, and that it wasn't something to be afraid or ashamed of.

A quiet knock on the door drew their attention.

Leah said, "It's probably Reverend Paula," and she called out, "Come in."

She was right.

"Are you two better?" she asked.

They nodded.

Preston admitted, "I sorta panicked when you left because I thought we needed you to direct our conversation." He turned to Leah. "But we worked things out on our own."

"Yeah, we did." She looked to Paula. "You told me to be honest with him and everything would be okay. You were right."

"I'm so glad. Do you two need me for anything else?"

They shook their heads.

"Then my work here is done," she summed up with a smile.

Preston and Leah put on their coats and picked up their backpacks. After giving the reverend a hug each, they left her office.

Outside, Preston asked, "Are you going to the store?"

She nodded. "Yeah. Too cold to walk home so I'll wait there until Dad gets off and ride with him." The Clarks were the only family who didn't live in the subdivision.

Preston said, "Wish we had our regular driver's licenses and could drive without an adult so I could take you or you could take me."

"I know. I'll FaceTime you later."

"Okay, and I'm glad we're good."

"Me, too."

They shared a long hug. She took off toward the store and he stood there watching her and wanting to do so for the rest of his life. She turned back and laughed, calling, "Go home, Preston."

"Going." Feeling on top the world, he struck out for the Power Plant to catch a ride home with his mom.

That evening, just before bed, he sent Amari a text. *Leah and I are good.*

A grinning emoji and a thumbs-up came back in reply.

Preston put down his phone and heard a soft knock. "Come in."

It was his mom. At dinner, he'd told his parents that he and Leah had solved their problems and were back together and they were pleased with the news.

"Just came in to say good night," his mom said. "I'm glad you and Leah worked out your issues. Looking forward to her visiting again, too."

"So am I. Going to be nice being with her instead of without her until we go away to school next fall. I've really missed her."

"Sounds like she's missed you, too. Are you excited about seeing your family on Friday?"

"I am. Thanks for offering to go with me. If they turn out to be not-so-great people, I don't want to be stuck on the jet with them by myself."

"I'm sure they'll be fine. I'm anxious to meet them. Cecily said your grandmother is coming, too."

"Good. As long as she's not as evil as Doc's mom."

"Your grandmother Lenore Winthrop has many issues."

"Yes, she's evil like a villain in a Disney movie."

She laughed. "Okay, get some sleep. Don't be up too late talking to Leah. You both have school in the morning."

Busted. He grinned. "Yes, ma'am."

She left and he got into his pajamas, crawled into bed, and called Leah. They finally ended the conversation around midnight and Preston slept like a baby for the first time in days.

BERNADINE SPENT THURSDAY morning going over details for her wedding with the triumvirate Lily, Sheila, and Rocky. She tried to convince herself that it was a task she enjoyed, but failed badly. She didn't want to deal with the guest list, or menu, or the setup for the service, although she did agree to allow Devon and Zoey to sing "Ave Maria" as a duet so he'd stop pouting and getting on everybody's last nerve.

"How about I just elope?" That triggered some serious side-eye. "Guess not," she muttered.

"Don't even go there, Ms. Taj Mahal."

Bernadine stuck out her tongue at Lily, who shot back a smile.

Sheila explained, "This wedding is having all the trimmings because one, it's going to be at Christmas, and two, you turn the world here. Everyone will be expecting an all-out, no-holds-barred event."

Rocky cracked, "And because you deserve it after the foolery you made the rest of us deal with when we got married. Not that I'm being petty."

"How many times are you going to bring that up?"

Lily said, "As many times as we begged you to rein things in and you told us no."

Bernadine came to her own defense. "But you ended up getting the understated weddings you wanted."

"No thanks to you, lovely lady."

Bernadine mockingly huffed and folded her arms across her chest. "Be that way then."

Smiles showed and the discussion moved on to the rehearsal dinner. Rocky asked, "Since you're doing the picnic theme for the reception, any idea what you want for the rehearsal dinner?"

"Waffles."

"Waffles?" Rocky looked to Lily and Sheila as if seeking confirmation that she'd heard Bernadine correctly.

"Yes. Waffles. Not a whole lot of work for your kitchen staff, and since all the kids will be involved in the service, too, they'll probably enjoy waffles at the rehearsal dinner."

Rocky sighed and shook her head. Bernadine couldn't tell if it was from disbelief, surrender, or both.

"Waffles it is," Rocky replied. "Bacon, too?"

"Of course. This will be a wedding rehearsal to remember."

Sheila cracked, "You got that right."

Bernadine sang, "It's my wedding and I'll do what I want to . . ." to the tune of the old sixties' song, "It's My Party" by Lesley Gore.

They all laughed.

Sheila glanced at her clipboard. "Tina called and said your friend Nisha— She didn't give me a last name."

"Arthur."

Sheila wrote it down. "Nisha's yacht will meet you in Santa Barbara. You'll have a full crew and once you drop anchor in Hawaii, Letty— No last name again."

"McFarland."

Sheila added that name to her notes. "Will send her chauffeur to the marina to drive you to her place on Maui. Her staff is expecting you, and they and the chauffeur will be at your disposal for the ten days you and Mal will be there. Tina said your jet isn't large enough to fly to Maui without refueling along the way so she's chartered one that is to bring you back to LA. Katie will meet you there for the trip home."

"Sounds good." Bernadine was so grateful for the generosity of her Bottom Women sisters. She wasn't looking forward to all the hoopla surrounding the wedding but was looking forward to the ten-day honeymoon very much. She couldn't wait to trade the Kansas winter for Letty's luxurious oceanfront vacation home and the sun-warm beaches of Maui.

Sheila asked, "Status on your gown?"

"Done and shipped. Should arrive in a few days. I've spoken to Gemma and she'll take care of any last-minute adjustments. Letty's daughter, Cynthia, has created gowns for me before so her help may not be necessary." Cynthia McFarland was an award-winning designer and a darling of both Hollywood and the rich and famous.

Rocky asked, "Is Mal going to lease out his apartment?"

Bernadine debated how to respond but finally replied with the truth. "He hasn't decided. Our living arrangements are still up in the air."

Lily appeared confused. "I thought he was moving in with you?"

"That's the question we're wrestling with. We like the privacy living by ourselves brings but we do want to be with each other, so we're trying to figure out how to do that."

Her friends stared. She knew if the arrangement she and Mal settled on didn't meet traditional expectations, people were going to talk.

Sheila asked, "So . . . you two aren't going to live together?"

"Twenty-four seven, three, six, five? Maybe not, but we'll see."

Sheila sat back and studied her for a silent moment before replying, "That's so interesting. What a potentially novel idea. Barrett would stroke out if I even hinted at something like that, but there are days . . ." Her words trailed off, but everyone knew what she was saying.

Lily weighed in. "I don't know what I'd do if Trent hadn't built my she cave. When the testosterone gets to be too much, especially during the run-up to my period, I can go in, lock the door, and act like I've left the planet, so I get it, Bernadine. I just never knew any women who had the balls to actually make that a priority."

Bernadine was pleased with their words of support. She looked to Rocky.

"Jack knows when I need my space I put on my leathers, get on the bike, and let him know when I'm coming back. So far, he hasn't complained. In fact, I think he secretly enjoys the occasional breaks as much as I do."

Bernadine knew how much they loved their husbands and families but wondered how many other women would enjoy the option to just sit and breathe alone every now and again. After listening to her friends' takes on the matter, she decided she and Mal were on the right track. The tenets of traditional marriage could kick rocks. And if their plans fed the gossips, so be it. It wouldn't be the first time she and Mal were the talk of the town.

"I need to speak to Bernadine Brown."

They all turned to see a short Black woman swathed in burgundy fur, a ton of jewelry, and a waist-length weave the color of her coat standing in the doorway. Bernadine put her age at somewhere between twenty-five and forty because it was always difficult to guess a Black woman's age. The extralong nails were fake for sure, as were the eyelashes that curled out from her lids like the furry legs of a tarantula. In her arms she held a small dog wearing an animal print coat and a fake diamond choker.

The women were so taken by surprise by her sudden appearance, not to mention her rude entrance, that for a moment they stared her way in stunned silence. She introduced herself, "I'm Alizé Franks Brown, Leo Brown's wife."

Bernadine asked, "Are you ex number two or three?"

She raised her chin. "Number three." The dog bared its teeth at Bernadine and growled. Its owner said, "This is Roger."

Ignoring the animal, Bernadine introduced herself. "I'm Bernadine. How may I help you?"

"I need to speak to you about Leo's will."

"I've nothing to say. Didn't my lawyer contact yours?"

"Yes, but I wasn't satisfied with what he had to say."

"Because?"

"I have bills to pay. I figured if you and I talked we could come to some kind of agreement."

"Such as?"

"Continuing my alimony checks. I need to get my hair and nails done. Pay my housekeeper. Keep the lease paid up on the Benz, and I have a house note. I shouldn't have to move to a cheaper place just because Leo was murdered."

Bernadine wondered if Alizé had been this entitled her

entire life or just since marriage to a wealthy man. "Sounds like you need a job."

"My doctor says I have a delicate constitution and it can't handle the stress of a nine to five."

Bernadine said, "Sorry, I can't help you with your financial issues."

"You mean you won't."

Bernadine eyed her and her attitude. "That, too."

Another woman appeared. Older. Dressed for the weather in a parka and jeans. Normal eyelashes. "Excuse me, ladies. I'm Catherine Renner. Her aunt. So sorry to intrude on your day."

Bernadine said, "Hello, Ms. Renner. Bernadine Brown. Can I help you?"

"Yes, came to drive this one back to Topeka."

Her niece snapped, "I told you to stay in the car."

"You and Roger planning to walk back to Topeka?" she asked coolly. "Because I'm heading home as soon as I go back outside."

The tight-lipped niece looked away.

Catherine said, "When she flew out here from Orlando yesterday and told me about coming to see you, I told her she had no legal standing. Apparently, Leo's lawyer told her the same, but she said somebody on TikTok sued an ex and got money, so she figured she could do it, too. I told her she'd be better off looking for a job."

"May I ask where you and Leo met?" Bernadine asked.

Alizé hesitated so her aunt replied, "Online. A sugar daddy site."

"Jesus," Lily said softly.

Catherine replied, "Exactly. And she didn't even like Leo. Liked his money, though."

Her niece snarled, "Are you through?"

"Ready when you are. Again, ladies. Sorry for intruding."

Roger and his owner stormed out. The aunt followed.

The stunned Bernadine, Lily, and Sheila sat there in the silence. Lily finally said, "A sugar daddy site."

Sheila said, "A dog named Roger."

"And a woman named after a brand of liquor," Rocky added.

Bernadine said, "I have so many questions."

Sheila replied, "I vote we ignore them and move on."

They all agreed and went back to the wedding planning, but the short visit would be one they'd remember for some time to come.

CHAPTER
13

F riday morning, Reverend Paula was in her office having her coffee and working on the upcoming Sunday's sermon when she heard footsteps on the stairs and a male voice call out, "Hello! Flower delivery."

Confused, she left her chair and stepped out into the hallway. Approaching was a young man carrying a very large something wrapped in lime-green paper. He asked, "Are you Paula Grant?"

"I am," she replied, eyeing the package curiously.

"This is for you. Do you want me to put it somewhere. It's kind of heavy."

"Yes, bring it into my office. There's a table you can set it on."

He followed and set it down. "Let me get you a tip," she said.

"No need. The sender already took care of that. Enjoy your flowers."

"Thank you."

Curiosity rising because she couldn't remember the last

time she'd received flowers, or if she'd ever received any, Paula carefully undid the stapled-together paper. What she unveiled stole her breath. There were red roses, brightly colored lilies, purple stadia, and other beautiful blooms she had no names for. Stunned, she searched for a card. Finding a small white envelope tucked inside she opened it and read. *From a Friend.*

"Aww," she said softly. "You're so sweet, Thornton Webb."

She gave the gorgeous display fresh water and stood before it amazed and impressed. It took up the entire center of her table. She and Thorn had exchanged phone numbers after their lunch earlier in the week, so she sent him a text to thank him.

He texted back. *You're welcome. What time should I pick you up for the movie?*

A part of her didn't want this courting thing to move too quickly. She debated the idea of driving herself and meeting him at the rec, but immediately set it aside. In for a penny, in for a pound. The movie began at 7:30. Doors opened at 6:00.

Six, she texted back.

Your place or the church?

My place.

OK. Earthquake and I will be there at 6. Glad you like the flowers. The friend hoped you would.

She smiled and typed: *See you this evening.*

You got it.

SEATED ON THE sofa in his living room, Thorn set his phone down and smiled. First date. Who would've thought he'd be interested in a woman of the cloth. The few women he'd called himself serious about in his past had all been tall, sleek, high-maintenance types, like his ex-wife, drawn to athletes, entertainers, and men with no-limit black cards. Paula wasn't any of those things and yet here he sat, giddy at the idea of taking her out even if it was only to a showing of *The Mummy* in a small town's recreation center. First though, he had another date. Matriarch Tamar July had invited him over to see some of the town's archival material and since the agreed-upon time for his arrival was less than ten minutes away, he went to get his coat.

Once outside, he decided to walk to Tamar's. She lived only a short distance away. It was cold, but he figured the more he exposed himself to the winter weather, the more acclimated he'd become. On the way, he saw Bobby Douglas putting his twins in their car seats. Bobby waved as Thorn walked by and Thorn waved back. He wondered how long the young family had been in Henry Adams and the circumstances that had drawn them there. Once again, he noted how much he didn't know about his new home and neighbors.

Tamar answered his knock promptly. The day's caftan was royal purple, and she had black fuzzy socks on her feet. Her silver hair was done in a single braid that trailed down her spine, and her face wore a smile. "Come on in." Opening the door, she stepped back so he could enter. "Leave your coat on the chair. How are you?"

"Doing well."

The house was quiet. He noted the fire in the fireplace, and a large flat-screen TV above it. The furniture appeared comfortable, and the walls displayed framed pieces of art, all landscapes that he imagined reflected the local surroundings. Only then did he hear the soft distinctive voice of Sade and it caught him off guard. Tamar a Sade fan? The applause accompanying the singing indicated the performance had been recorded live.

"Sade?"

Tamar nodded. "Yes. Her *Lovers Live*. It's an old CD, but I love her voice. I wish she'd put out something new, but Helen's going to do Helen."

He was confused and Tamar must have seen it. "Her given name is Helen."

"Oh. I didn't know that."

"I'm in the kitchen. Have you had breakfast?"

"I have."

Thorn hadn't expected the kitchen of an older house to be so modern. The stainless appliances looked new, and the large windows looked out over the snowy countryside. The room held the faint succulent scent of bacon. "Nice kitchen."

"Thanks to Bernadine. When she rehabbed this old place, she replaced everything with new, from the cabinets and floors to the appliances. She's been such a blessing." She gestured him to a seat at the table. The tablecloth covering it was blue and accented on the hem by small birds in flight.

In the center was a small vase of fresh flowers and his mind slid back to Paula. There were also what looked to be photo albums.

"Coffee?" she asked from where she stood by a Keurig on the counter.

"Yes. Thanks."

When his mug filled, she set it in front of him. "Sugar? Cream?"

He shook his head. "I take it black."

Tamar sat, added a couple of packets of the sweetener to her own cup of steaming brew, and sipped, her hawklike eyes taking him in. "So how are things going?"

"Going well. Learning my way around, meeting people.

Was invited to a Dads meeting earlier in the week and enjoyed myself."

"Good. I looked through all the archival items I have and didn't find anything that ties your family to Henry Adams."

He was disappointed. "I was hoping there'd be something. It's so weird feeling like this is where I'm supposed to be."

"You may have been led here by the Spirit. Could be there's something here you're supposed to do."

He'd never been very spiritual but understood the concept. "That's possible."

"God, the Ancestors, the Universe, whatever you choose to call the force that sets us on this life journey sometimes moves us around like pieces on a chessboard. And it becomes our job to be open to what shows up wherever we're placed."

He studied her.

"Are you here to give Paula the solace and support she's been needing?"

The hairs on the back of his neck stood straight up and his world seemed to shift. Staring into Tamar's eyes, he sensed a power that made him believe she really could shift into the form of a lammergeier or whatever she chose.

And then as if she hadn't just turned him upside down with the idea of why he was in Henry Adams, she said casually, "Brought you some photo albums and things to look through. If you're going to be a resident, you need to know the historical what's what."

She slid the albums his way. He blinked, gathered himself, and opened the one on the top of the pile. The photos inside were old and yellowed, but the scenes taken when Henry Adams was a much younger community were fascinating. There were men he assumed by their clothing to be farmers driving wagons. Other men were outfitted in suits and hats. The streets were all dirt and the buildings lining them looked like the ones in old-time movies. "How long have you lived in this house?" he asked, leafing through a section of newspaper articles. He paused to view a faded announcement for a concert at the Sutton Hotel by a vocalist named Sissireeta Jones. He made a mental note to google the name when he got home.

"I was born here," she revealed.

He looked up with surprise.

"My father was born here as well. Most Black folks from my era and my parents' era were born at home. Midwives brought us into the world. Hospitals didn't allow us access because of our race."

He sighed and shook his head. The bigotry faced by people of color back in the day, and yes, presently, always resonated with bitter tones.

For the next hour, Thorn looked at photos and asked Tamar questions about people and places that she patiently replied to. He especially liked the ones that showed scenes from what she called the August First parades. She then explained the idea behind the parades that grew during the nation's abolition era.

"Thanks to Bernadine and the kids we've been able to resurrect the parade. We even had the Blue Angels do a flyover."

He was impressed. When he finally closed the last album, he sat back, buoyed by all he'd seen and talked about with her. "Thank you for your time and for answering my bazillion questions."

"You're welcome. Knowing our history is important to us and now you know it, too."

"I do. Not many places have documentation like this."

"A few places probably do. Allensworth in California.

Bayou Mound in Mississippi, the Gullah folks in the low country in South Carolina, and a handful of townships in Texas, too. I'm sure they're as proud of their legacy as we are of ours and have the source material to pass down for the next generation."

"Who do you think you'll pass all this down to?"

"Mayor Sheila is going to try and get Henry Adams placed on the National Registry of Historic Places and build a museum. Some of the more personal family things will be left to my great-grandson Amari. He'll safeguard them for the future."

"Knowing all this makes me proud to be a resident."

"Good. We have a town-welcoming ceremony for new residents, so if you really do decide to stay we'll have one for you in the spring."

"What does it involve?"

"This and that," she said vaguely and gave him a small smile. "You'll have to wait and see."

He chuckled. "I'm not sure whether to be afraid of that or not."

"It'll be fine. Promise."

She studied him silently for a moment and asked, "Are you coming to the movies tonight?"

"I am. Paula's agreed to be my date. I guess it's a date."

"Good to know."

He was glad to have her approval.

Tamar stood then and Thorn took that as his cue that their time together had come to an end. "I'll let you get back to your day. Thanks for coming by," she said.

"Thanks for the coffee, for letting me see the albums, and for your insight."

"You're welcome. I'll see you this evening."

He gave her a nod and, after putting on his coat, left her house and walked home.

Once there Thorn thought back on her words about his purpose in coming to Henry Adams. Had he really been sent to be with Reverend Paula Grant? He had no idea what to make of that idea, but would let things unfold and see where they led.

KATIE SET THE jet down at the small hangar for private planes at the Philly airport bright and early on Friday morning. Preston and his mom deplaned and left the pilot to handle the aircraft's refueling and whatever else needed to be done to prepare for the return flight to Kansas.

They walked inside to an area where a small number of people waited for flights, immediately recognizing Cecily from FaceTime.

Seeing them, his aunt threw open her arms, gave a short happy cry, and rushed to greet him. Preston let himself be embraced and rocked and rocked some more while he held her tight. He didn't know it would feel so good to finally meet his bio dad's family but it did. Cecily drew back and wiped at her happy tears. "Oh, Preston. Look at you looking so much like your dad, my brother." She was shorter than he'd imagined, but her smile was the same as online.

An elderly woman with short gray twists and clear brown skin stood a few feet away. Tears ran unchecked down her cheeks.

Cecily said, "Preston, this is my mother, your grandmother, Grace."

He gave her a smile, closed the distance between them, and she took him in her arms. He felt her shaking as she sobbed. "Finally," Grace whispered. "Finally."

Preston replied emotionally, "I'm so happy to meet you."

"Are you?"

He stepped back. "Yes, ma'am, I really am."

She pulled him back into her arms.

Cecily wiped at her eyes and laughed. "Don't squeeze him to death, Mama. Let him breathe a minute."

Preston then met Cecily's husband, Ed Sr. He was tall and thin. He gave Preston a strong hug and a smile.

"Glad to meet you, young man."

"Same here," Preston replied.

The fourth person was his cousin. Although Cecily said he was fourteen, he was short and looked much younger. He had light brown skin, tiny twists, and a skeptical look on his face. Cecily introduced him, "This is our son, Eddie Jr. We call him JR." He was wearing a nice suit and a pair of Jordans that looked like they'd just come out of the box. Preston wondered if he knew what kind of hit the shoes were going to take in the snow back home.

Preston gave him a nod. "Nice meeting you, man."

"Yeah, me, too," but his voice lacked enthusiasm.

Sensing JR wasn't being real truthful, Preston turned away and said to the adults, "Want you to meet my mom, Mrs. Sheila Payne. My pops had to work. He'll join us this afternoon when we get home."

Sheila was given hugs as well and they seemed to be okay with her.

After all the introductions and hugs were done, Sheila

said, "We have to wait for the jet to be refueled and our pilot to do whatever pilots do before we can take off. She'll text me when she's ready to go."

So they sat and talked, mostly about Preston's life and friends and dreams.

Eddie Sr. said, "MIT is a great school."

Preston nodded. "They have a great physics department and I'll be majoring in that. My girlfriend Leah's going to study physics too, but she'll be at Stanford."

Grace asked, "Does Leah live near you?"

"Yes. We live in the same town. You'll get to meet her too, if you want."

"I do."

Preston was pleased that she wanted to meet Leah. Cecily asked after his bio mom, Margaret, and Preston caught them up on how great she'd been since they'd reconnected. All the while JR had nothing to say. In fact, he was on his phone as if bored.

Sheila got the text from Katie saying she was ready so they walked out of the terminal and over to where the jet was waiting.

Cecily said, "You actually did come on a private plane."

"Yes, ma'am. Ms. Bernadine is a really nice lady. You'll get to meet her."

"Good. I want to thank her for the trip."

Ed Sr. said, "She must have some nice bucks."

Sheila replied, "Nice like you wouldn't believe."

Katie was standing outside in her blue uniform. Sheila introduced her to everyone. The family seemed pleased to meet her but JR said, "A girl is flying us?"

Katie replied in her smooth Jamaican accent. "If you prefer

to not go, have your parents arrange for a taxi or an Uber to take you back home, but make it quick. We'll be departing shortly."

He froze.

His parents shot him a look.

Preston smiled inwardly. He looked over at his mom who sent him a wink.

Grandma Grace asked JR, "Do you want to go home?"

He looked down at his Jordans. "No, ma'am. I'm good."

Moments later, they boarded and strapped themselves into their seats. Preston took in his family's wonderous faces as they stared around at the pristine interior with its white leather seats. He was glad to have Ms. Bernadine in his life.

Across the aisle, Eddie Sr. said, "Preston, I'm impressed."

"On my first flight I was, too. Me and the other kids couldn't believe it. From foster care to this."

Grace asked, "Does she fly you all around often?"

"No, only when there's a need, like bringing you all from Philly."

Katie's voice came over the speakers. "Are we ready back there, Mr. Preston?"

He called back, "Yes, ma'am."

"Alrighty, let's get you and your peeps home."

They taxied out to the runway.

As the plane lifted into the air, the cabin grew quiet. He watched his aunt get comfortable next to her husband and close her eyes. She'd said earlier that she'd worked a double shift yesterday to get the time off to make the visit, so he guessed she was pretty tired. A few minutes later she appeared to be asleep.

His grandmother pulled a skein of yarn and knitting needles from her big tote, then earbuds and her phone. Once the buds were in place, she worked the needles and subtly bopped to whatever music she was listening to. He liked her. His knucklehead cousin, JR, glared his way. Preston ignored him and withdrew a book from his backpack. He got comfortable, put in his own earbuds and began to read to the sound of a TED talk on the new Webb telescope. Everything was fine until JR plopped down into the empty seat beside him.

Preston removed his buds and fought to hide his annoyance. "What's up?"

"Just want you to know I'm the golden child in this family."

"Golden child? Like in the Eddie Murphy movie?"

For a moment, JR stared blankly. Preston guessed he'd never seen the movie.

"No. As in I'm the center of the family's world, so don't think you're going to push me off the throne."

Preston studied him and now understood why he'd been acting the way he'd been. "I don't want your throne. I'm just connecting with my dad's folks. That's it."

"You're all everybody's been talking about."

Preston shrugged. "I can't control that."

"Private jets and MIT. I'm not impressed."

"Okay. Good to know. You can go back to your seat now." Preston had no desire to argue with him over dumb stuff. JR's insecurities were his own to manage.

"Just remember what I said. You don't want to beef with me."

"You don't have to worry. I don't beef with anyone whose mental, verbal, and physical acumen aren't equal to mine."

JR stared blankly again.

Preston shook his head, put his earbuds back in, and returned to his book.

His cousin got up and moved back to his seat. Across the

aisle Preston spotted his mom watching him and he wondered how much of the interaction she'd seen. He'd talk to her when they got home. Grace was watching too, and from the look on her face, she didn't appear pleased. He didn't know if the displeasure was directed at him or JR, and truthfully, he didn't care. His cousin was proving to be a major pain in the butt. They'd be flying back to Philly tomorrow afternoon, but it was going to be a long twenty-four hours.

They landed in Hays a bit after ten, and after saying goodbye to Katie, the group was met by Henry Adams chauffeur TC Barbour, who'd driven the big, gleaming black Suburban.

After the introductions were made and the luggage stowed in the back of the luxury vehicle, they made small talk about the flight, and Grace asked, "How long is the ride to Henry Adams?"

"A little under an hour, ma'am."

She nodded her thanks.

Preston wondered if she was getting tired. Not knowing anything about her health, he hoped she was okay.

TC looked to Preston. "You want shotgun?"

"Yes." He had no desire to be stuck next to his glowering cousin.

Once they were all seated and seat belts secured, TC got them under way.

The snow blanketing the open land lining the highway glistened in the late morning sunshine.

Eddie Sr. said, "Not a lot of houses out this way."

TC replied, "No, there aren't. Most of the state's population is south near Topeka and Kansas City. I'm originally from Oakland and have been in Henry Adams almost two years. All this emptiness took some getting used to, but I enjoy it now."

Cecily asked, "Is Henry Adams this rural, too?"

Sheila replied, "Yes and no. We have our town and a small subdivision where we live, but outside of that it pretty much resembles this."

"The country," JR said disgustedly. "I don't see McDonald's or Popeyes or anything. I'd hate living someplace like this."

TC shot Preston a questioning look. Preston rolled his eyes in response and again wished JR had stayed in Philly.

Sheila came to the defense of her town. "We don't have McDonald's or Popeyes, but we do have the best diner in the county. Food is excellent."

"Yeah, right," JR responded.

"Stop being disrespectful," his dad warned.

"Sorry. I'm sure the food there is very good." The sarcasm wasn't lost on anyone, though. Preston wondered how long it would take Tamar to make JR wish he'd stayed in Philly, too. The kid was way rude.

TC brought up a jazz station on Sirius and JR groused, "Why do old people think everybody wants to listen to jazz?"

TC replied, "Why do you think anyone wants to hear what you have to say?"

Preston directed his smile out the window.

The jazz played and JR kept his mouth shut for the rest of the drive.

When they arrived in Henry Adams an hour later, TC said, "Let me give you folks a quick tour."

Sheila asked, "Afterward, can you swing by the Power Plant so they can meet Bernadine?"

"Sure can."

He drove them past the Dog, and Sheila said, "That's the diner I mentioned."

Cecily said, "Parking lot is full."

"Great food as Ms. Mayor said," TC replied.

"Sheila, you're the mayor here?" the surprised Cecily asked.

"I am."

Preston said, "And she's the best."

As they neared the town's tree, Grace cried, "Oh my. What a beautiful Christmas tree!"

TC stopped the vehicle in front of the rec so they could get a good look at it.

Preston's voice filled with pride. "My mom hooked it up, along with all the other decorations."

"Wow." Ed Sr. sounded impressed.

"Place looks like a Christmas card," Grace said. "Look at all the decorations on the buildings."

Cecily peered out the window. "That is a gorgeous tree."

Sheila explained, "Everyone contributed ornaments. I hope you'll get a chance to see it at night when it's lit up."

As they continued down Main Street, they were shown the church, the school, and the rec center.

Preston played tour guide. "We have two swimming pools, one inside and one outside. We also have an ice-skating rink, and a huge school aquarium that the students maintain."

"That's a big school, Preston. How many students?"

"Not that many; the community college uses it for classes, too." He didn't care if JR thought the place was country. To him, Henry Adams was very special. He'd not be the person he'd become without it.

"Here we are," TC said as he pulled into the parking lot of the Power Plant. "I'll wait out here for you all to get back."

They left the car and went inside. "Bernadine Brown owns the town and the jet we flew on," Sheila said. "My office is in this building, too."

Bernadine's door was open, so Sheila stuck her head in. "We're back."

"Come on in."

Preston and the family followed Sheila inside.

For a moment the family didn't say anything. Bernadine looked to Sheila and then Preston as if seeking an explanation.

Finally, Cecily said, "I'm sorry. With the jet and Sheila saying you own the town, I guess we all assumed you'd be—"

Bernadine said with a straight face, "Taller? Shorter?"

Everyone laughed then.

"I am who you see," she told them, smiling. "Welcome to Henry Adams. I hope you had a good flight."

Now that the ice was broken and introductions were under way, Preston realized they'd thought her white this whole time. It never occurred to him to bring up Ms. Bernadine's race.

Cecily told her how grateful they were for the flight.

"You're welcome. Preston is well loved here. We're so incredibly proud of all he's accomplished and the outstanding young man he's become. I hope you are as well."

JR said importantly, "I'm the president of my debate club back in Philly."

Bernadine paused and studied him for a moment. "I'm sure your parents are very proud."

"I plan to ace my SATs when the time comes."

Preston rarely saw his mother give anyone the side-eye but she did JR, before saying, "We just stopped by for a minute,

Bernadine. I know you're busy. We're going to head to the house, have some lunch brought over, and catch our breath."

"They're welcome to join us at the movies tonight."

Ed Sr. asked, "Movies?"

Sheila explained Movie Night, and when she was done, Cecily asked, "The entire town comes for this?"

Bernadine nodded. "And people from the neighboring communities, too. It's a lot of fun."

Cecily asked, "What's the movie?"

"*The Mummy*," Bernadine replied. "The one with Brendan Fraser."

Grace's eyes brightened. "That's one of my favorites."

Preston smiled. It was one of his favorites, too. He was liking his grandmother Grace more and more.

Bernadine said, "Then I hope we see you this evening. It's been a pleasure meeting you all."

Ed Sr. said, "Same here. Thanks again for the flight. Means a lot."

"You're welcome."

TC drove them home, and once they were inside, they collapsed on the sofa and in the chairs. It had been a long morning. It was now lunchtime, and they were hungry. Preston went to his room for his laptop. When he returned, he brought up the Dog's website and showed everyone the menu so they could select what they wanted.

JR groused, "What kind of place has no chicken nuggets?"

Grace said, "Apparently a place that serves fresh food and not flash-frozen."

JR asked, "Your school lets you bring your laptop home?"

"This one is mine. The one I use for classes is in my desk at school."

"Oh."

Preston saw him eyeing his device with what appeared to be badly masked envy. "Ms. Bernadine provides the ones at school. She makes sure we have everything we need to be successful. I saved up my money from my job and bought this one for myself."

"Good for you," Grace said. "Sheila, so glad you and your husband are raising him right."

"Thank you. Bernadine makes Henry Adams a land of plenty, but none of our kids are just handed things. They earn their way mostly with hard work, or good works."

"What kind of good works?" Cecily asked.

Preston replied, "Basically anything we're asked to do by our matriarch, Tamar July, and her crew. Whether it's a trash detail or helping the seniors with their computers. Leah and I built this website for the diner. We help with the food and the audio equipment at Movie Night sometimes, and with the cleanup after the town meetings. Nobody lets us just sit around. Tamar always finds us something to do. And we whine a lot, but it's really okay because the people here have all been really nice to us from day one, and they didn't have to be. They've taught us a lot about life, too." He saw the pride in his mom's eyes and appreciated it, along with the thumbs-up she shot him in response to his words. He added, "After ten years in foster care, I love it here."

They put in their order. Sheila sent Barrett a text letting him know they were home and asked if he'd pick up the lunches. He sent back a yes.

While they waited, Sheila took them all upstairs to show them where they'd be sleeping. Afterward, the adults went back downstairs, but JR wandered into Preston's room.

"What is that?" he asked checking out the large picture on the wall.

"It's called the Pillars of Creation. It's in the Eagle Nebula in the Serpens constellation."

"Looks like a bunch of weird fingers or elephant trunks."

"Yeah. They're made up of interstellar gas and dust. It's about seven thousand light-years away."

JR came farther into the room and took a slow look around at Preston's work area where he did his homework before moving over to the door that led to Preston's small deck. Beside the door was his telescope beneath its protective tarp. "What's this?" JR asked.

"My telescope." Preston walked over and removed the tarp.

"Ms. Brown give you this, too?"

"No. My bio mom."

"So suppose I accidentally drop it off the deck? Would she get you another one?"

"After I kick your pretentious little Jordan-wearing ass from here to Philly, I'll ask her."

JR startled.

"I don't know who you think I am, but I'm not the one. Better yet, get the hell out of my room. I'm done playing with you."

Eyes wide, JR spun on his Jordans and left.

Wishing Amari was around to help ease his temper, Preston prepared to go back downstairs but paused at the sight of his aunt Cecily standing in his doorway. "I just passed JR in the hall and he looked like he'd just seen a ghost. Did something happen between you two?"

Preston weighed his answer, then decided being true to himself was the only way to go. "He talked about throwing my telescope off the balcony and I told him I'd kick his ass from here to Philly if he did." He waited for her response.

She glanced over at Preston's large state-of-the-art telescope. Her lips thinned and she sighed audibly. "I'm sorry." She then asked, "Do you know what a miscarriage is?"

He nodded.

"I lost three babies before JR was born and I didn't think I'd ever be able to carry a child to term. I was so happy when he was born. Ed and I spoiled him rotten and basically did him a big disservice by not checking his behavior as he grew up. Mama warned us he'd be a handful when he reached his teen years, and she was right. He's disrespectful, rude, mean sometimes. I love my son, but I don't like him. Does that make sense to you?"

"Yes, ma'am."

"His father and I are now trying to undo the little monster we created, but I'm not sure we can."

Preston wasn't sure what he was supposed to say in response, so he chose to remain silent.

"JR's supersmart, but he's smaller than most boys his age so he always feels like he has to compensate by bragging or being confrontational. He's alienated his classmates with his attitude, so he doesn't have many friends."

Preston understood why.

"I'm really hoping he'll mature as he gets older because once he's no longer under our roof, he may have a hard time adjusting to the real world."

Preston agreed. He thought about Reverend Paula and wondered if his aunt could find someone like her in Philly who might help JR get a clue. He'd talk to his parents about it and see if they'd suggest it. His aunt might be more amenable to hearing about family therapy from some adults as opposed to her newly found teenage nephew. "I hope things work out for him."

"Thanks. Me, too. I brought this from home to give to you."

For the first time, he noticed a large manila envelope in her hand. "I have some pictures of Lawrence I thought you might like to see. Do you want to go back downstairs so we can look at them with everyone?"

"I'd like that." Getting to see pictures of his bio dad erased the temper JR left in his wake. Although he now understood why his cousin was the way he was, it didn't make him any more likable or convince Preston to overlook his nasty behavior.

His pops showed up with lunch just as he and Cecily returned downstairs. Preston was glad to see him. He wanted to talk to his parents about JR and what Cecily shared up in his room but not knowing when the time might come, he set it aside for the moment.

They wound up having a great afternoon. Ed Sr. and Barrett bonded right away once Ed revealed that he was a marine, too. They ended up telling boot camp and deployment stories and laughing the entire time. The pictures Cecily showed Preston made him teary. For the very first time, he saw Lawrence Mays. There were pictures of him as a child and as a teen. Some showed him smiling beside Cecily, and others with just him and Grace.

Grace wiped at her own tears and said, "See how much you look like him, Preston?"

And he did.

"You can keep all those," Cecily told him. The idea that he now had images of the man who'd fathered him that were his to keep made Preston even more teary. Through it all the Golden Child didn't say much, which suited Preston just fine. After the pictures and lunch, Grace and the others went upstairs to rest up for Movie Night. Preston took his pictures to his room so he could enjoy them in private and scan them into his laptop.

"Hey, son."

He looked up from the pictures and smiled at his dad. "Hey. Thanks for bringing lunch."

"You're welcome. Are you enjoying the visit?"

"Parts of it. JR's got issues."

He came in and closed the door. "What kind of issues?"

Preston told him everything, including the conversation about the telescope. Barrett wasn't happy. "Does he have any idea how much that telescope cost?"

"I'm sure he doesn't and I'm not apologizing for threatening to kick his butt."

"I won't be asking you to."

Preston then told him about Cecily's miscarriages.

"That certainly explains the behavior."

"I know. I thought maybe she should look for a Reverend Paula where they live and get some help, but I didn't want to suggest it and make her mad or anything. Maybe you or Mom could talk to her about it."

"That's a good idea. If I get the opportunity, I will." His voice softened. "I'm glad she brought you the pictures."

"I am, too. I'm scanning them into my laptop so I'll always have them. This doesn't mean I don't love you or Mom."

"I know. You should have pictures of the man who helped form you. I don't have any pictures of mine."

"Why not?"

"After he had the stroke and before he moved into the convalescent home, my father had everything connected to his life destroyed. Pictures of my mother. Pictures of me. Burned them all."

"That's terrible."

"Yes. The only pictures I have of him are the ones in my memory. I'm glad Cecily gave you those. They're important, and if you ever have children, you'll be able to show them their grandfather."

"Along with the pictures of their other grandfather, you."

"You trying to make an old drill sergeant cry?"

"No, sir."

"Good."

They shared smiles.

"I'm going to go tell your mom what you told me about your cousin and Cecily. You enjoy those pictures."

"I will, and Pops . . ."

"Yes?"

"Thanks for raising me. I wouldn't be who I am without you."

Barrett nodded and said emotionally, "Thanks for raising *me*. Having you in my life has made me a better person." He paused for a moment and the love and pride in his eyes touched Preston's heart with both strength and depth. "Semper fi, son."

"Semper fi."

At five thirty, Paula was dressed and ready for Movie Night. Decked out in her black jeans, white silk blouse, and black velvet blazer she was nervous as all get-out. What in the world was she doing going on a date at her age?

Her phone chimed. It was a FaceTime from Robyn.

"How are you, kiddo?" She was happy to hear from her young cousin.

"Doing good. Are you wearing lipstick?"

Paula chuckled. "Yes."

Robyn appeared surprised. "Is there something special going on there?"

"Just Movie Night. I have a date."

"A date? Like with a guy?"

"Yes."

Robyn's mouth fell open and she laughed. "Who are you, and what have you done with my cousin Paula? Who is he?"

Paula told her.

"OMG! Is he a babe? Look at you. No collar and every-thing. Pull the phone back and show me what you're wear-ing."

The tickled Paula complied.

"Love the outfit."

"Glad you approve."

"How cute is this chef?"

"He's a ten."

"Paula! I gotta come back just to see him. I can't believe you're going on a date."

"Neither can I. Things okay down there?"

"Yeah. I want to buy a car."

Paula paused. "Have you learned to drive?"

"No, not yet but I'm looking at driving schools."

"Well, when you pass the test, I don't see any reason to say no to a car. You need one down there."

"I really do. Hope and I are looking for an apartment."

"Another great idea."

"You think so?"

"Yes. If you're going to be there for a while, you can't keep staying with her family. I know how much they adore you, but getting your own place makes sense."

"Okay. I'll keep you posted on the driving school and the apartment search. One last thing. Do you think I can come visit you for Christmas? Hope and the family are going to Florida to be with her dad's mom and I don't want to impose. I know a ticket to Kansas this late will probably cost a fortune, but I miss you."

Tears stung Paula's eyes. "I miss you, too. A last-minute ticket will cost two arms and a leg but totally worth it to have you here for Christmas. Book your flight, use your credit card, and let me know time and date and all that."

"Will do. Can't wait to see you."

"Same here."

"Hope and I are going to look at an apartment in a few. Her mom's going with us, so I gotta go. I'll talk to you soon. Enjoy your date. I can't believe it."

Paula laughed. "Love you."

"Love you back." And she was gone.

At precisely 6:00 p.m., Paula heard a knock on her door. Swallowing her nervousness, she walked over, opened it, and there he stood—dream date Chef Thornton Webb.

"Hi," he said.

"Hi yourself. Come on in."

He looked around. "Like your place."

"Thanks. Let me get my coat. Are you ready to be the talk of the town?"

"Will it be that serious?"

"That and more, but we won't let it keep us from enjoying ourselves. *The Mummy* is one of my all-time favorite movies."

"Really? You look nice by the way."

"Thanks."

Their gazes met and Paula decided she could stand there and just look at him for the rest of the evening. Instead, she grabbed her coat. Being the gentleman, he helped her into it and waited while she did up the zipper.

"Pretty jazzy boots you're wearing, Rev."

Her black western boots matched her outfit. The small red stars across the toes added a pop of color. "Thanks."

"You ready?"

"I am."

"Then let's ride."

Outside, she reached for the truck's door handle, and he said, "Hold on."

She paused and looked his way.

"The knight opens the door for the lady."

"Thorn—" she protested.

He cut her off before she could say more. "Let me be respectful, please."

He gallantly opened the door and she stepped up and in. Once she was seated, the door closed, and he walked around to the driver's side and got in.

He looked her way. "See. That wasn't so hard, was it?"

"Not used to someone getting my door."

"Keep hanging with me and you will. Practice makes perfect."

She chuckled softly and shook her head.

The rec parking lot was filling up when they arrived. Families, teens, college students, and high schoolers on dates trekked to the doors, followed by a gaggle of little girls wearing their pajamas under their coats, a Boy Scout troop clad in their uniforms, and the Franklin Library Senior Ladies Book Club wearing their blue knitted tams and matching mittens.

Thorn found a spot not too far from the doors and parked. Seeing all the people he asked, "How many people usually show up for these things?"

"By the time the movie starts there won't be an empty seat in the auditorium or an open space in the lot. People come from all over the county. Sheila wants to build a drive-in that we can use in the summer, and that's going to be a big hit."

"Small-town living."

"We're simple folk. Doesn't take much to entertain us."

"Going to take some adjustment for this big-city guy."

"Practice makes perfect."

"Touché."

Her smile met his and she again wondered what in the world she, a girl from Blackbird, was doing with such a splendid guy who was, according to Google, formerly married to one of the most famous supermodels on the planet. But she knew she was worthy and looked forward to a nice time, so not much else mattered.

When Paula and Thorn entered, the auditorium went silent as everyone stopped to check them out. Then someone applauded (Paula would learn later that Genevieve Barbour was the culprit) and the rest of the crowd joined in, accenting the moment with cheers, and calls of yeah! The very embarrassed Paula dropped her head while Thorn laughed.

"I'm doing to excommunicate the lot of them," Paula promised. She turned to him. "I'm so sorry. They mean well, but sometimes they go way left."

He took a few bows, which only encouraged more outrageous applause and laughter. "No need to apologize. I'm having fun."

"Okay, good. Let's find some seats, then get something to eat."

They came under great scrutiny in the food line. Once again, everyone paused to check them out. No one asked questions but Lily, handling the hot dogs, quipped, "Looking good there, Rev. You should bring him around more often."

"Hush!"

Gen, in charge of drinks, asked, "What can we get you?"

Paula chose a hot dog and chips, popcorn, and a chocolate

shake. Thorn took two chili dogs, chips, three brownies, and a soda.

Paula opened her purse only to have Tamar say from behind the tables that served as the counter, "First date's on the house."

"No, they're not," Paula fussed.

Tamar asked, "Have you ever been on a Movie Night date since you moved here?"

That question threw her so she had to admit, "Well, no."

"Then take your food and go to your seats. You're holding up the line, Reverend."

Paula sighed. "Yes, Tamar. Thanks, ladies."

"Enjoy," Gen said, smiling.

On the way back to their seats, Thorn asked, "Do first dates really get free food?"

She shrugged. "Who knows. I'm sure Tamar was pulling our leg, but there's no way for me to prove it because as she pointed out, I've never been on a date here before."

"That's a good thing."

She stopped and looked up at him. "And why is that?"

"Because if you had, you might be sitting with someone else tonight instead of me."

Once again, swoons rose and she admitted it would be very easy to fall for this guy. "That rap of yours is pretty potent, Mr. Chef."

"Trying to make a good impression so this isn't a one-and-done date."

"No missteps so far."

"Good to hear. Keep me posted."

"Will do."

PRESTON AND HIS family entered the auditorium for Movie Night. As his aunt, uncle, and grandmother marveled over the size of the auditorium and all the people, he spotted Amari and the other kids in their usual spot. "Enjoy the movie," he said to them. "I'm going to say hi to my friends."

Sheila said, "Preston, take JR with you, and if you want to sit with them that's okay. Your dad and I will look after Cecily, Ed, and Grace."

Taking JR anywhere was the last thing he wanted to do, and although he was sure his pops had talked to her about JR and his issues, he knew his mom was just trying to be nice. So he sighed and said, "Okay, sure. Come on JR."

Preston took off down the aisle without waiting to see if JR would follow. He did, however, and appeared as put out as Preston felt. Preston had sent Amari a text earlier about what a jerk JR was, and this would be their first face-to-face. Tiff was home with the flu and Leah was backstage working on the audio hookup, but the rest of the kids were there and eyed JR curiously. Preston made the introductions, but JR acted unimpressed and barely said hello. In turn, Zoey's crew chose to ignore him and his bad attitude and went to get popcorn and food, leaving him with Preston and Amari.

Amari eyed JR. "You always this much fun to be around?"

"I don't have to answer to you."

"Preston, you didn't tell me he was so nice."

"Let's go get some food," the disgruntled Preston said.

Loaded down with their popcorn, hot dogs, and sodas, they returned to find Leah waiting for them. Seeing her, JR instantly perked up. After being introduced, he looked her up and down like a snack cake and said, "So how about we sit together, so I can wrap you up like a mummy and keep you close?"

Preston didn't blink. He knew Leah would handle her business, so he waited. Lucas Herman and Zoey, carrying their popcorn and sodas, passed by on their way to their seats. Upon hearing JR's come-on to Leah, Lucas shook his head and declared, "A rap lame as a one-legged camel."

Zoey added, "Game needs work, my man. Lots."

And they kept walking.

Leah, still studying JR as if he were a talking rock, asked Preston, "Is your cousin called JR because he suffers from jargon ridiculisitis?"

Amari screamed, tossed his popcorn in the air, and yelled, "Slap shot to the five hole! Leah Clark scores!"

Gemma Dahl's grandson, Wyatt, stood in the aisle with Devon July and Alfonso Acosta watching this play out. Wyatt turned to Alfonso. "Call your dad. Leah just set this dude on fire."

While they cracked up, Leah eyed what was left of JR, and said, "Do me a favor."

He brightened. "Sure."

"Never speak to me again."

His head dropped.

Preston wondered where teenage girls learned to decapitate dudes so effortlessly.

Tamar walked up and handed Amari a broom and a dustpan before departing without a word. Still chuckling, Amari began sweeping up the mess he'd made with his popcorn.

Devon told JR, "Zoey's dad is a doctor. He can probably give you something for that burn."

JR stalked off to go sit with his parents.

Preston said to Amari, "To quote Zoey: What a dumbass."

"Dumb as they come."

Leah asked, "How can you be related to him?"

"Been asking myself the same thing all day."

With JR out of his hair, Preston sat down and settled in to enjoy the movie.

FROM HER SEAT in Earthquake, Paula took in Thorn's strong profile in the darkness as he drove them home. She'd had a nice time. He hadn't overstepped by attempting to hold her hand or whispering inappropriate sweet nothings in her ear. He'd been respectful and good company. She sensed he might be waiting for her to initiate any physical contact, be it something as innocent as holding hands or a first kiss, and that pleased her because it said a lot about who he was as a person and as a man. "I can't believe that's the first time you've ever seen *The Mummy*."

"Very first and I enjoyed it."

"I watch it every time it's on TV if I can. It's a great story."

"Funny, too. The mummy wasn't playing, though. When he took my man's eyes, I was, like, whoa!"

She smiled.

"Special effects were top of the line for back then, too," he continued. "Loved the face coming out of that sandstorm."

"There's a sequel but it's nowhere near the original. The Rock stars in the third one."

"Does it measure up?"

"Not even close."

"Good to know."

Thorn made the turn off July Road and onto Tamar's property where their trailers were. "Thanks for going with me," he said to Paula.

"Thanks for asking. I had a nice time."

"I had a nice time, too." He stopped the truck in front of her place. Her porch light illuminated the cab's interior just enough to make out his features. "Have dinner with me."

That surprised her, though she supposed it shouldn't have. He'd made it clear from the lunch they'd shared at the church that he was interested in her. "When?"

"Sunday, after you're done with duties at church."

"Where?"

"My place. I want to cook for you, Paula."

Her heart stopped for a moment, and in response to his tone the tendrils of her attraction to him spread and grew stronger, firmer. "You make that sound very . . . sensual."

"Food can be that," he replied quietly. "But I promise to keep my hands on my pots and pans."

She debated silently with herself and decided there really was no reason to turn him down. "Okay. Yes. Dinner Sunday. Your place."

"Good. Now let me get your door, so you can go in."

She opened it. "No need."

"Paula—"

Cold air drifted into the warm cab. "I don't need coddling, Thorn."

"I get that, but there's a big difference between coddling and showing someone you care."

She paused, and admittedly had never thought about the gesture in that way. "If I promise to let you get my door next time, may I go inside now?"

He smiled. "Yes, but remember you said that."

"I will. Thanks again for tonight."

"You're welcome."

Before getting out, she studied him and he did the same to her. She'd wondered how being courted by him, using his words, would play out. Although still unsure, she was enjoying these first opening steps of their journey. "Good night, Thorn."

"Night, Paula."

She noted that he watched and waited for her to unlock her door and step inside before driving away.

FEELING GOOD ABOUT how his evening with Paula had gone, Thorn removed his coat and looked at his phone. He'd missed a call from his sister, Junie. Taking a seat at his kitchen table he called her back. When she picked up, he said, "Hey, Junie."

"Hey you. When you didn't call right back, I was starting to worry if maybe you'd been kidnapped by moose or something out there in Nowhereville. How are you? Where were you?"

"Doing good. Sorry I missed the call. I was at Movie Night."

"Movie Night?"

He explained.

"That sounds like fun. You might be the only person in the world just seeing *The Mummy* for the first time. It's one of the kids' favorites. How are things there?"

"Things are good. So good I went on a date."

She went silent before asking, "With whom?"

"Took one of the ladies here to the movie."

"Okaaay," she replied drawing out the last syllable. "This lady have a name?"

"Paula Grant. Reverend Paula Grant to be exact."

"A reverend? As in a pastor?"

"Yes."

"Okay. Start from the beginning and don't you dare leave anything out."

For the next few minutes, he told her all about Paula, her place in the town's structure, and how well she was loved by the town's citizens.

"You're dating a pastor who's also a shrink?"

He chuckled. Only she would break down the information so succinctly. "Yeah, June."

"Not sure how to process this, little brother."

"I'm equally confused, but getting to know her has been fun. I'm finding myself wanting to know everything there is about her."

"Me, too. And I'm dying to meet her. You go from being married to the witch to being interested in a woman of the Word; that's quite something."

"True. She's originally from Oklahoma and wears cowboy boots." He paused to correct himself. "I suppose I should call them cowgirl boots. She's also a few years older than I am."

"This is getting more and more interesting. Have you told Mama about her?"

"No, but I will when I come for Christmas."

"So you're still coming?"

"Yes."

"Good, because I'm missing you."

"Missing you, too." And he didn't realize how much until talking with her now. "How's the family?"

She caught him up on life with her husband and the kids, and when she finished, he was exhausted after hearing about sports practices, field trips, dance recitals, band concerts, and the two new puppies the oldest set of twins talked their parents into adding to their already chaotic household. She added, "If those two little mongrels eat one more pair of my shoes, I'm selling everybody to the circus."

They laughed. Yes, he was missing Junie a lot.

They talked for a few more minutes until her mom duties called. "Time for me to pick up the kids from swimming. I have to go, but I needed to hear your voice."

"Glad you called. Give everybody my love. The puppies, too. I'll see you in Savannah."

"Will do. See you there. Bye, Chef."

"Bye, big sis."

The call ended and he smiled, grateful for Junie and the love of family.

ON SATURDAY MORNING, the Payne household was up before the sun rose to get Cecily and family to the Hays airport to meet Katie Sky and the jet. Their short visit had come to an end. Even though Preston didn't care a lick about JR, he did wish the others could stay so he could get to know them better, especially his grandmother Grace.

They were enjoying an early breakfast when Ed Sr. said, "Maybe you can come and spend some time with us over the summer before you go off to school."

"I'd like that," Preston said and meant it. "I'll see what my schedule looks like schoolwise and let you know."

JR was being his silent self, which Preston didn't mind at all.

After breakfast, everyone spent the last few minutes sharing hugs and voicing how great the visit had been. Preston shared a particularly strong hug with his aunt Cecily who said, "I'm so glad Margaret passed along your contact information."

"Me, too. Thanks so much for the pictures."

"You're welcome. Keep being great, okay?"

Wiping at the water in his eyes, he replied, "I will."

He also shared a big strong hug with his grandmother Grace, and he told her, "I wish we'd had more time to get to know each other better."

"Me, too," she whispered through her tears. "We'll have more time in the future. Lawrence and your grandfather would be so proud of you. Text me whenever you think about this old lady."

"Will do. Promise."

He and JR shared a nod and left it at that. Preston had been looking forward to having a cousin in his life but the reality of that was not to be, at least until JR grew up and showed some signs of maturity.

Sheila shared hugs as well and Barrett and Ed Sr. vowed to stay in touch.

Moments later, TC arrived with Genevieve. They were on their way to Denver to visit one of Gen's cousins and would be driving there after dropping the family at the Hays airport, which meant the Paynes wouldn't be able to ride along.

TC and Gen loaded the Dardens' and Grandma Grace's luggage, and they all shared a final wave before getting into the Suburban. Dawn was just pinkening the sky when they drove away.

Preston told his parents, "I wish they'd been able to stay longer. Not JR but everybody else."

Sheila gave his shoulders a squeeze. "Maybe next time."

Barrett said, "We talked to Cecily and Eddie about therapy

and they said they'd look into it, but didn't think their health care would pay for it, so . . ." He shrugged. "Hopefully their son will grow up by the next time he visits."

"Let's hope." If not, Preston would be fine never having to be around the Golden Child ever again.

His mom asked, "Are you working today?"

"Yes. Amari and I have a ten-to-two shift."

Barrett said, "I have the day off, but I can drive you two over if you need a ride."

"We do."

"Then let me know when you're ready to go."

"Will do and thanks to both of you for being so nice to my bio family."

Sheila said, "JR notwithstanding, it's easy to be nice to nice people. We both knew how much this visit meant to you."

"We did," Barrett added. "You come from great stock, Preston."

"Great bio stock, great adoptive stock, a kid couldn't ask for more." That said, Preston took to the stairs to go to his room to get ready for his shift at Clark's Grocery.

AFTER WORK, AMARI went to the rec to see if Tamar needed any help with anything before he headed home. He shot his parents a text to let them know his plans. Entering the rec he smiled at the sight of the piñatas hanging up, the tall decorated Christmas tree, and all the other holiday touches filling the gym. The place was empty and quiet but there was a familiar scent in the air that had nothing to do with the celebration. Guided by his nose he followed it to Tamar's office and knocked on the open door. She was seated at her desk. "Hey there. Come on in. How are you?"

Amari didn't think he'd ever love anyone as much as he loved her. "I'm good. Just got off work. Why do I smell pork rinds?"

She froze. "Pork rinds?"

"Yes. Smelled them as soon as I walked in the gym."

She seemed to be avoiding his eyes and he found that odd.

"Your nose must be playing tricks on you."

He shook his head. "I'm from Detroit. I know I haven't lived there in a few years, but pork rinds are one of the basic food groups. Even little Detroit babies know that smell."

Tamar dropped her head and chuckled. "When I finally leave this plane, I'll definitely miss you the most." She reached down and opened a drawer and brought out a plate. On it was a mound of pork rinds. "Close the door."

He complied. Eyeing her bounty, he said, "Those smell fresh. Where'd you get them? I've never seen any like that at Clark's."

"Bing makes them for me."

"Because he has the hogs, right?"

"Yes."

He then asked what he felt to be the most important question. "Are you supposed to be eating those?"

"No, and if you tell your father or Mal, I'll consider you the enemy. Do you want some?"

"Yes!"

She laughed. "Go get a paper plate from the kitchen."

When he returned, she shook a small portion onto his plate.

"Hot sauce?" he asked.

Eyeing him, she smiled and removed a small bottle from the drawer before handing it over. After sprinkling the hot sauce on the rinds, he took a bite and groaned with pleasure. "Oh, Tamar. These are so good."

"Our secret, remember?"

"Forever."

As they munched and enjoyed themselves, they talked in the companionable way they'd built during their time together.

"How'd Preston's visit go with his dad's family?" she asked.

"It went okay. His aunt brought him pictures of his bio dad that he got to keep, but his cousin wasn't real friendly. Called himself the Golden Child."

"Like the Eddie Murphy movie?"

"No, as in spoiled brat. I didn't like him very much. I sorta felt bad for Brain because he was looking forward to having a cousin, you know?"

"I do. You and Preston have become brothers, so it's only natural for you to want the best for him."

"Going to miss him a lot when he leaves for MIT."

"We all will, but your bond with him is true. You'll stay close no matter where life takes you."

"I hope you're right." He thought about his own future. "I'm going to apply to Morehouse."

"Good school. Being around all those Black men will make you stronger."

"And I kind of miss being in a big city."

"That's understandable. In Atlanta you can regrow those parts of yourself you've lost touch with living in small-town Kansas. How are you and Devon doing?"

He sighed. "One minute we're good and the next minute I want to ship him to a gulag off planet somewhere."

"There's a lot going on in him underneath that wig."

"Which should be burned if you ask me."

"Don't be too hard on him. He's got some growing up to do, but I think he'll be okay in the end. I'm taking him on his spirit quest in the spring."

Amari stared. "Really? Maybe a hawk will fly off with his wig."

"Stop being mean," she said smiling.

"I'm sorry, he just makes me lose my mind sometimes." His phone buzzed. Taking it out of the pocket of his hoodie he looked at the screen. It was his mom. "Hey, Mom. Yes. I'm at the rec talking to Tamar."

He listened then said, "Okay. I'll be out front." He ended the call. "I have to go."

"Something wrong?"

"I don't think so but Melody's husband wants to talk to me and my parents. Mom says he said something about her being here for a weekend."

Tamar looked as confused as he felt. "Mom's coming to get me so I can be there when he calls back."

"Let me know what happens."

"Will do." He put on his coat, gave her a kiss on the cheek, and hurried out of the office.

AMARI WAS SEATED at the kitchen table with Lily's laptop open when the link to the congressman came through. His parents were standing beside him.

A few seconds later they were connected. "Good afternoon, Amari. How are you?"

"Hello, Mr. Carlyle. I'm well. How are you?"

Carlyle was wearing a suit and seated in an office. There

were a bunch of bookshelves behind him. "I've been better. I'm divorcing Melody."

"Sorry to hear that, sir, but what does this have to do with me?"

"She said she visited you a few weekends ago? Is that true?"

"No, sir. I haven't seen her since my dad and I visited you in Detroit."

Carlyle sighed and a series of emotions passed over his face that appeared to be disappointment, anger, regret—Amari wasn't sure.

"So she lied to me."

Amari didn't respond.

"I should've known. She was probably with the new boyfriend and tried to use you as her alibi for why she was gone that whole weekend."

Lily said, "She did call wanting to speak with him. I wouldn't allow it."

"She said she flew out, she and Amari settled your differences, and had a good time."

Amari shook his head. "Never happened."

"I'm a pastor; I won't stay married to an adulteress."

Amari was sure he didn't need to know all this but kept his face blank.

"Thank you, Amari, and thank you, Mr. and Ms. July. I won't be bothering you again."

And the connection ended.

Lily said, "He seems like a nice man. I feel sorry for him."

Amari wasn't sure how he was supposed to respond. When he visited Carlyle and Melody, the man gave the impression that he wanted Amari to be his son and no way was that going to happen. He closed the laptop and stood. "You need my help with anything before I head up to do some gaming?"

"No, son," Trent said.

Looking concerned, his mom added, "I'll call you when it's time for dinner."

"Okay." Amari left them and went to his room.

As he sat on his bed fighting aliens on a distant planet, he wondered if Melody had really called to convince him to lie for her. He imagined being the wife of a congressman came with a lot of clout and perks, and that being the ex-wife meant giving up both. He'd never wished ill will on anyone, not even the woman who'd made it known she wanted nothing to do with him, but he hoped the adultery had been worth the life she'd traded it in for.

A soft knock on his door made him look up. "Come in."

It was his dad. "Came up to check on you. You okay?"

"I'm not sure, but I do wish they'd leave me alone."

"He said he'd never contact us again."

"I hope he means it. I don't want their drama splashing on me. I'm just a kid." He looked at the man he considered the best dad in the world and asked, "Do you think I'll ever get over Melody not wanting anything to do with me?"

"Still hurts?" Trent asked.

Amari nodded. "Yeah. Just when I think I'm good with it, they pop back up in my life and it all comes back."

Trent walked over and sat down on the edge of the mattress. "I can't answer that. I wish I could."

"I know. Like I told Mom, I just wanted Melody to like me, that was all."

"I know and I guess all I can tell you is we have no control over how other people feel about us. We only get to control how we feel about ourselves. That's kind of cliché-ish but it's the truth."

Amari thought about that for a long moment. "Maybe once I get older it won't make me so sad."

"Distance can help, but in the meantime, know that there are a ton of people in your life who love you and everything about you."

That brought a small smile to his face. "Thanks for that."

"You're an awesome son."

"Helps to have an awesome dad and a kick-butt Lily Mom."

His dad draped an arm across his shoulder and gave him a strong hug. "I love you, Amari."

"Love you, too. Thanks for checking on me."

"Always. Are you good for now?"

Amari nodded.

His dad stood. "Okay. See you at dinner." He exited.

Feeling much better, Amari returned to his game.

CHAPTER
15

After church on Sunday, Paula made the short walk through the snow to Thorn's place for their dinner. She'd never had a man cook for her before and this was her first visit to his place, so she was experiencing a double set of nerves and butterflies. Upon reaching his trailer she paused for a moment to pull herself together then climbed the short set of stairs. Her knock on the door was answered promptly. "Hi there. Come on in."

The nervousness spiked but she stepped inside then stared around. "Why does it smell like Little Havana in here?" she asked wide-eyed. She took in his grin. "What did you cook?"

Excitement replaced the nervousness. She stripped off her coat, sat to remove her boots, and on sock-encased feet quickly moved into the kitchen. "Is that ropa vieja I smell?" she asked, looking back at him as he watched her with his arms crossed and a grin on his face.

"Maybe."

"Don't tease me, Thorn."

He laughed. "Yes, Reverend. Ropa vieja. Black beans, rice, and fried plantains."

"Oh dear lord! If it tastes even half as good as it smells, I may have to marry you."

"Don't tease me, Paula."

His tone drew her eyes back to his. The intensity she saw there turned her knees to sand. She tried to play it off. "Kidding. Just kidding."

The intensity remained.

Needing to escape the pull flowing between them, she turned her attention to the indigo-colored Dutch ovens on the stove. "May I peek?"

"Go ahead. Everything's done. Grab that pot holder, though. Those knobs on the covers are hot."

Taking his advice, she shielded her hand and carefully lifted the top of the largest one. Inside was the ropa vieja. The flavor-filled aroma of the shredded beef and the liquid it was basking in made her groan with pleasure "Oh, Thorn."

He smiled. "Are you ready to eat?"

She replaced the top, set down the pot holder, walked over to him, and said happily, "I need to give you a kiss. You've so earned one."

He chuckled. "Not going to deny a gift."

He leaned down and the friendly peck she'd planned on bestowing slowly changed into something else once her lips met his. There was warmth, softness, sparks, and so much more she backed away to keep from losing herself. "I'm sorry," Paula said, appalled at herself. "I don't know what came over me."

"You've nothing to apologize for. Natural progression, I'm thinking. Yes? No?"

She supposed he was right. They had been slowly moving

toward this moment, but she didn't know she'd actually be the one to initiate it. She tried to explain. "I pride myself on my self-control."

"Sometimes self-control is overrated."

The echoes of the kiss lingered, leaving her totally untethered, embarrassed, and resonating with a low hum of desire.

"How about we eat?" Thorn asked quietly.

"Please," she replied, needing an out. "Where can I wash my hands?"

He offered directions. When she returned, he gestured her over to the table set up in the living room. Upon her initial arrival, she'd been so carried away by the smells and her curiosity about what he had cooking on the stove, she'd hadn't paid much attention to the beautiful ivory plates, gleaming silverware, and sparkling crystal wineglasses. She'd also missed the vase of beautiful yellow roses in the center.

"This is quite a spread, Chef."

"Wanted our first dinner together to be special."

"It is that," she admitted, looking up into his eyes. It was also quite overwhelming if she were being honest: him, his gallantry, the food, the kiss. Paula Grant had never experienced anything like this before. Ever.

"Let me get you a plate."

"I can get—"

He gave her a quelling look.

Remembering their conversation about the truck's door, she sighed. "Okay. Fix me a plate, but just this once."

"Thank you."

He left and she looked around the room at the tasteful furnishings and art on the wall. She wondered how much he owned personally, and what items belonged to the town.

Thorn came back to the table carrying Paula's plate and set it down on the table. It held the ropa vieja, black beans, rice, and four circles of fried plantains. The scents brought back memories of her life in Miami, and she was in heaven. "Have a seat," he said and helped her with her chair.

Once she was settled, he left for a moment to add the offerings to his own plate, and when he returned he sat.

Paula said, "Give me your hands, please, so we can bless the food." She took his strong hands in hers, did her best to ignore the warmth of the contact, and offered up a short blessing. After they both said a quiet "Amen," they picked up their forks.

Still feeling his hands holding hers, Paula tasted the beef, and again groaned with pleasure. "Lord, this is good." As was everything else she sampled.

"Leave room for dessert," he advised from his seat across the table from her. "There's also enough of the beef, rice, and beans left over for you to take some home with you."

Yes, she was definitely in heaven. "Thank you."

"You're welcome."

"Let me know if this is too personal a question, but did your ex-wife enjoy you cooking for her?"

Thorn took a sip of his wine. "No. She existed on protein shakes and grapes. Can't wear those tiny designer clothes if you eat like a real person. In fact, she didn't like me cooking at all in the house we shared. It was one of the reasons we divorced."

Paula heard the regret in his voice. "Sorry for bringing up bad memories."

"No, you're fine. It was a reasonable question. Have you ever had a guy cook for you before?"

She chuckled. "No. Never."

"Then I'm honored to be the first."

She wondered how many other women he'd graced with his culinary gift but realized it was none of her business, so she didn't ask.

She changed the subject. "Will you be around for Christmas?"

"No. Heading to Savannah to be with my parents and my sister's family. You'll be here to conduct service and Bernadine and Mal's wedding, I heard."

"Yes."

"Family coming?"

"My cousin, Robyn. She'll be flying in from Atlanta. I've been missing her so I'm looking forward to seeing her."

"No other family nearby?"

"No. I have an uncle in Oklahoma, but I'm sure he'll spend the day with his mother." She debated sharing more, then decided to go ahead. "I have an aunt there. She's my late mother's sister and Robyn's grandmother. She's in prison for manslaughter. More than likely she'll die there."

He paused with surprise on his face.

"I shared the story with the congregation so I may as well tell you, too."

When she finished, he said, "That's a sad story. I'm so sorry."

"So am I." The telling put a damper on their mood, so she asked, "Do you mind if we watch the game?"

"Let me grab the remote."

They spent the rest of the meal talking football, the upcoming playoffs, and the Chiefs' chances of returning to the Super Bowl.

"I can probably get us tickets to the big game if you'd like to go. I still have some solid connections to the League office."

Her eyes went wide. "Really?"

"Really."

"I would love to go if you can hook it up. How much more amazing are you? I'm having a hard time keeping up."

He toasted her with his flute. "You ain't seen nothing yet."

At the end of the first game, they cleared the table of their empty plates and switched channels to watch the second game of the day. "How about some dessert?" he asked.

"I don't know if I have room." She was full and happy.

"I can always wrap it up so you can take it home with you."

"What is it?"

"Tres leches."

"You're going to make me move in," she teased.

"I'm okay with that."

She wondered what it might be like to share life with him. "I'll take a small piece and some to go."

"You got it."

Tres leches was a sweet yellow cake topped by meringue and garnished with a single cherry. Tres leches translated to "three milks" to describe the three types of milk used. There'd been a bakery not too far from Paula's church in Miami and every Saturday she stopped in to get a piece to have with her Sunday after-church meal.

At halftime of the second game, she decided to head home. "I'm stuffed," she told him.

"I am, too. I've been looking for a gym. The one in Franklin is pretty poor."

"Maybe you can use the one the colonel has at his place, or Trent's."

"Or I can open my own."

"Are you serious?"

"Pretty sure. I'll talk to Ms. Brown and see if it can be done."

"She and Mayor Sheila have been talking about growing the town. I don't know if a gym fits into their plans, but any new business has to be a plus no matter what it is."

"I agree. Now, come in the kitchen and let me know how much of the food you want to take home with you."

Once that was done, she said to him, "Thanks so much for the great time and the great food, Thorn."

"You're welcome. Hoping this will be the first of many meals we'll have together."

"I'd like that because you're a way better cook than I'll ever be, and I enjoy your company."

For a moment, neither spoke. They stood facing each other while the sounds of the game played behind them.

"May I kiss you goodbye?" he asked quietly.

Shaking, she nodded.

The gentle finger he ran down her cheek was so searing Paula's eyes slid closed. And then Thorn's lips met hers. Small sparks went off in her blood again. He draped an arm low on her back and eased her a bit closer. The kiss deepened. When he finally ended it, her head was spinning.

Still holding her, he looked down and asked, "So where do you want to go first? Rome to see *David*? Or Cambodia to visit Angkor Wat?"

Still reeling from the kiss, she stared up at him in confusion. "What do you mean?"

"Which place first?"

"I can't go to either. One, I can't afford it. Two, I have a church to run. And three, I have kids to counsel."

"Priests and counselors don't get vacation time?"

She studied him. "What are you talking about, Thorn?"

"I'm talking about gifting you with some joy. I'll foot the bill. If you want to go with me, we can book separate rooms so you'll be comfortable. There'll be no hanky-panky, and no expectations other than you enjoy yourself. And if you'd rather go with someone else, I'll still foot the bill. Let me give you some joy to refill your well. From everything I've seen and heard about you here, you deserve that and more. May I do this for you, please?"

She was so outdone she couldn't find the words to respond.

"Will you at least think about it?"

"You want me to go traveling with you?" she asked, finally finding the ability to speak.

"Yes."

Paula backed out of his hold. Her hands covered her mouth, and she stared up at him in quiet awe.

His smile peeked out. "What?"

"You'd take me to Angkor Wat?"

"Yes, I would, or anywhere else you may wish to go between now and the opening of the restaurant."

"Just like that?"

"Just like that."

She was real speechless then, and tears filled her eyes.

Thorn looked stricken. "Why are you crying? Have I offended you? Oh, Paula. I'm so sorry."

She shook her head and waved him off. "No. You haven't offended me. It's just . . ." Her words trailed off as she studied him. Who was this man and why was he in her life? *Ask and ye shall receive* came a voice in her head. "I've never had anyone offer me something like this before. Ever." She whispered, "I . . . need to go home."

"Okay but promise me you'll at least think about it, okay?"

"Okay." Overwhelmed, she got her coat and picked up the brown shopping bag he'd filled with the cartons holding the extra food. He walked with her to the door and she said, voice trembling, "Thank you for a wonderful afternoon."

"You're more than welcome."

Tears rolled down Paula's cheeks as she walked home. Once she entered her own place, she stashed the food in the fridge, removed her coat and boots, and sat down on her couch for over an hour debating how to respond to his offer. She was a priest and a counselor; she had obligations. But something told her if she didn't grab this blessing, she'd regret it for the rest of her life. Decision made, she took out her phone and sent him a one word text. *Yes!* He responded with a smiling emoji. She sent him one in return and stayed there on the couch for a long time.

MONDAY MORNING, BERNADINE met with Sheila to get an update on the proposed warehouse and was disappointed to hear the company had opted to go with a site in Iowa.

The mayor was disappointed as well. "I'm going to have Trent and his crew give me an estimate on the costs of expanding the subdivision to twenty-five homes and the costs of, say, ten condos. We don't want to be overlooked the next time a suitor comes to call."

"How are you going to pay for the build?" Bernadine asked.

Sheila responded, "I'll figure that out once I get the estimates from Trent."

"Give Tina Craig a call. Our group has a real estate arm and we're always looking for sound investments and this could be a project they'd consider."

"Will do."

"Anything else for me?" Bernadine asked.

"Yes. Roni wants to explore adding an outdoor entertainment space to the Three Sisters' plans if it's not too late."

"I'll check with the architect, but I like that idea."

Sheila went on, "Also, Chef Webb called early this morning about the possibility of building and opening a gym in town."

"A gym? That's interesting as well."

"I thought so, too."

Then Bernadine remembered another item. "Jack's canceling the night sky gathering. He said the weather's going to be cloudy for the rest of the week." Bernadine was disappointed. She'd enjoyed the town's previous stargazing events.

"And according to him," she continued, "Nori has agreed to replace Kyrie but only until June."

The mayor said, "That's good news. Maybe by June we'll have found someone to take Kyrie's place. . . . Well, that's all I have to report."

"Thanks, Sheila."

When Sheila left, Bernadine again found herself contemplating her town's future. She agreed with the plan to expand the housing options, and if she had to throw her own money at it, she would. There were probably enough real estate moguls among her Bottom Women sisters who'd also be willing to invest so she hoped Sheila would contact them if their help was needed. "Expansion, here we come!" she said.

OVER THE NEXT few days, the lead into Christmas and Mal and Bernadine's wedding filled Henry Adams with excitement.

Gifts were purchased and wrapped, Preston basked in the renewal of his relationship with Leah, and FaceTiming with his grandmother Grace became a regular part of his routine.

Bernadine and Mal met with Paula about their own housing dilemma and were told to experiment.

"See what works," she told them as they sat in her office. "I recently came across an article about a couple happily married for fourteen years who lived on opposite sides of their hometown. Living apart has worked well for them."

Mal chuckled. "I don't think we want to go to that extreme. Do we?"

"No," Bernadine replied with a smile.

"When you get back from your honeymoon, move in with each other and see how that works," she suggested. "You might be surprised at the outcome. Or make a schedule with designated days together and days apart, and try that. Don't let what is supposed to be the norm keep you from being happy."

When the session ended, they felt better about their situation and vowed to experiment to see what worked when they returned to Henry Adams from their Hawaiian honeymoon.

That evening at the monthly Ladies Auxiliary meeting held in Lily's she cave, President Genevieve went through the designated agenda. When she asked if there was any new business, Paula stood up. "I'm going on vacation the week after Easter."

To her surprise, applause and cheers filled the room.

"About time!" Roni said.

Paula hung her head and smiled.

Lily said, "As the kids say on the internet, go touch some grass. You've earned it. And this vacation better be longer than a weekend."

Gemma added, "And take Mr. Fine Behind with you."

That garnered a round of laughter as well.

Paula said, "Actually."

The room stilled and Marie asked, "Actually what?"

"Actually, this is his idea. We're going to Rome to see Michelangelo's *David*, then fly to Cambodia to visit Angkor Wat."

Genevieve yelled, "What!"

Jaws dropped all over the room, and then all heck broke loose as they shouted questions and clamored for answers.

Laughing Paula responded, "That's all you're getting out of me for now." And she sat.

Lily said, "Bernadine, open another bottle of wine, so we can toast our good reverend."

The wine was opened, the toasts were given, and Paula was content.

The Henry Adams Las Posadas celebration to commemorate Mary and Joseph's quest to find lodging before the birth of the baby Jesus began on the designated night at Bernadine's home. Maria Acosta was this year's Mary, and Lucas Herman had the role of Joseph. Wearing the brown hooded robes Gemma created for the event a few years ago, the two knocked solidly on Bernadine's front door. A small crowd carrying lit candles accompanied them. When she answered the knocking, Lucas, speaking his memorized lines, asked if she had a place they could stay for the night. "I beg you in the name of heaven, may we stay here? My beloved wife is with child and cannot walk any farther."

"Please," Maria said, "I am very weary."

Bernadine looked them up and down critically and replied roughly, "I don't run an inn. You may be thieves. Go away." And she slammed the door.

They left the porch, and surrounded by the softly singing crowd, which now included Bernadine, moved to the next house. For the next little while, Mary and Joseph were turned away again and again, and the residents of each home added themselves to the accompanying assemblage. With no room at the inn, they walked to Main Street under the light of the moon. It was a cold clear night and they were all in need of steaming bowls of Anna Ruiz's flavorful pozole, the celebration's traditional soup.

When Lucas knocked on the door of the rec, it was opened and there stood Anna, Tamar, and Bing leaning on his cane. This time when Lucas and Maria asked for a place to stay, Anna smiled and replied, "Please enter, Holy Pilgrims. Though this dwelling is poor we offer you lodging with all our hearts."

As the festivities began and the rec resonated with laughter and conversations Paula and Thorn warmed themselves with bowls of Anna's pozole. Thorn said, "This is really good."

"Anna's a great cook. This celebration was her idea. She's very proud of her culture and takes great joy in teaching us about it."

"I need the recipe; do you think she'll share it with me?"

"You can ask." Paula glanced around. "She's over there with Luis by the piñatas."

He left and Paula watched him make his way through the crowd and over to where a blindfolded TC was whacking unsuccessfully at the piñata hanging behind him. Thorn and Anna began talking and Paula saw Anna's eyes widen. She then began speaking excitedly. Paula walked to the tables holding the food and got another helping of soup. She was soon joined by Luis who asked, "Did you know that Thorn speaks Spanish?"

Paula was confused. "No."

"Fluent. You'd better lock that man down, Rev, before Anna decides to make him her next husband."

With a laugh, he moved on, and a smiling Paula wondered what other hidden talents Chef Thornton Webb had inside.

CHRISTMAS NIGHT, PEOPLE from all over Graham County piled into the Henry Adams church's beautifully decorated sanctuary for the wedding of Bernadine Brown and Malachi July.

Bernadine was downstairs in one of the basement rooms. She'd arrived three hours earlier, along with Crystal and some of the members of the Ladies Auxiliary who'd come to help her get ready. Kelly Douglas did her hair and makeup and when she finished, she warned Bernadine, "No crying allowed, or you'll ruin your gorgeous face."

Lily scoffed. "She's getting married, Kells. Of course she's going to cry."

"I know but I'm supposed to say that." She hugged Bernadine. "Congratulations and thanks for all you've done for me and mine. Let's hope the twins will actually make it to the altar."

The Douglas's twin toddlers were to be ring bearers. They'd done okay at the rehearsal, so everyone had their fingers crossed that they'd do as well for the real event. "See you all later," Kelly said and departed.

With a choir robe on over her gown and her makeup done, Bernadine was now ready for the ceremony to begin. Her friends departed on words of congrats and hugs that were careful of her makeup and went upstairs to take their seats with the rest of the guests. The only people remaining with her were Matron of Honor Tina Craig and Crystal.

Tina said, "I'm going to check on things in the sanctuary and get in line for the procession. Gen will come down and get you when it's time for you to make your entrance."

"Thanks, Tina."

"You're welcome. Lord, I'm crying already." She grabbed a tissue from the box nearby and, careful of her own makeup, gingerly dabbed her eyes before making her exit.

Bernadine said to Crystal, "Okay, let me get out of this choir robe."

She removed it and set it aside and Crystal gushed, "Oh, Mom. That gown! You look so beautiful."

Bernadine executed a slow full turn so Crys could take in the full effect. "It is gorgeous, isn't it?"

It was fashioned from sapphire-blue silk and flowed snugly from the heart-shaped bodice to midcalf, showing off her voluptuous curves. A matching cape attached at the shoulder and, shot through with threads of silver, trailed behind like a train. Her blue suede Louboutins completed the look along with a diamond-encrusted silver necklace and a matching bracelet and earrings. She was smoking hot and knew it.

"OG's eyes are going to pop off his face and roll around on the floor," Crystal predicted.

"You're looking good yourself, Ms. You." As if channeling Rocky's wedding attire, Crystal was decked out in sapphire-blue leather pants and a fancy short leather jacket. Her silk tank matched the silver threads in Bernadine's cape.

The sound of music wafted down to where they were. "I think they must be almost ready for us."

Before Bernadine could respond, her sister, Diane, came rushing in. "Oh, good. I'm not late. Crystal, I'm going to walk your mom down the aisle." She took off her fur to reveal the fancy white pantsuit she was wearing. "Do me a favor and hang my coat up somewhere, please."

Crystal stood speechless and looked to Bernadine for direction.

Bernadine tamped down her fury. "Diane, we already had this discussion. Crystal is walking me down the aisle."

"I'm your sister. It's my job. What would Mama say?"

"That you're trying to be the center of attention as always. You're even wearing white like maybe you're the bride. You can either sit with the other guests or drive back to Topeka. Those are your choices."

"How can you not want family involved in your wedding? I'm blood. She's just adopted."

"Get out. Now." Bernadine didn't raise her voice but her sinister tone got Diane's attention.

"How can you be so mean to me?"

"Don't make me bum-rush you back to your car."

Looking furious, Diane snatched her coat from Crystal and stormed to the door. "I hope he steals every penny you have."

"God bless you, too!"

In the silence that followed her exit, Crystal stared with wide eyes. "What's wrong with her?"

Bernadine was so mad it took her a moment to speak. "Forget about her. She came to steal my joy and we're not allowing it."

Crystal smiled. "You go, Mom. She can kick rocks."

"Or get her behind kicked. Either way."

Gen poked her head in the doorway. "Time for your debut, ladies. I love that gown! Mal's going to need to be revived after he passes out."

Bernadine laughed.

Standing at the back of the sanctuary, Bernadine's eyes widened at the sight of the musicians music director Roni had brought in. There were strings and horns, flutes and a drummer. Roni hadn't mentioned any of that at the rehearsal. She'd also neglected to tell Bernadine that she'd be walking up the aisle to an instrumental version of L.T.D.'s "Love Ballad." Her hand flew to her mouth at the tune's instantly recognizable opening chords.

The smiling Crystal asked, "Ready, Mom?"

"I am."

"Then let's show these folks what we're working with."

Bernadine chuckled and she and Crystal, stepping slowly and soulfully to the beat, started up the aisle.

"Strut, Ms. B!" someone—maybe Kelly—called out. People stood, clapped, and oohed and ahhed over her gown as she and Crystal swayed their way to the altar where Mal, attired in a fabulous black velvet tux, stood waiting with Reverend Paula, the formally dressed Tina, and Trent, Mal's best man.

Crystal turned her over to Mal who whispered to Bernadine, "You trying to kill me in that dress?"

She laughed.

"You look beautiful, doll."

"You're not looking so bad yourself, sir."

He offered her his arm, she placed her hand on it, and he gave her a wink as he escorted her to their spot before Paula.

When the time came to exchange the rings, he gave Bernadine a necklace featuring a small but perfect sapphire, and she gave him a silver bracelet anchored by its own sapphire. The etching on the bracelet resembled the feathered wings of a bird. His eyes went misty as he looked at it on his wrist.

The vows were next and when Mal got down on one

knee and Kem's perfect voice singing "Share My Life" came through the speakers and filled the church, Bernadine lost it. She had no idea he'd planned to do this. It was a song of devotion and sincerity, and the word *trust* was mentioned time and time again. Her love for him soared, and makeup be damned, she cried like a baby and didn't care.

Kem's song was followed by Roni, Devon, and Zoey singing "If This World Were Mine." Backed by the musicians, their voices blended beautifully and, yes, Devon wore his wig.

At the end of their vows, Reverend Paula pronounced Bernadine and Malachi man and wife and the church erupted with cheers.

Because of the large crowd, the reception was moved to the rec's gym, and like the unconventional wedding rehearsal's waffle dinner, the newlyweds' choice of picnic food was also a hit.

Mal and Bernadine kicked off the first dance to the laid-back sounds of "I'd Rather Be With You" by Bootsy Collins, and once they were done, the party began. After the first hour of Electric Sliding and Wobbling, slow dancing, and whatever dances the young people were doing, the festivities paused for the cake cutting. After the dancing began again, the newlyweds snuck away to begin their honeymoon.

ONCE ON THE plane, Bernadine told Mal, "We're spending the first three days together, then you're going to go play at a bird sanctuary, and I'm going to the spa."

"And if I want to go to the spa?" he asked archly.

"You know good and well being around birds is more your jam than a Brazilian wax."

"Which is?"

She shook her head. "You don't want to know."

Her phone buzzed. She dug it out of her purse and looked at the face. It was a message from Riley Curry of all people: *Cletus and I are in Little Rock and the banks are closed. Can you loan me 200 for gas? Will pay you back tomorrow.* She tossed the phone back into her purse.

"Something important?" Mal asked.

"Spam." Bernadine cuddled close to her husband again and he placed a kiss on her forehead. She was on her honeymoon with the man she loved. Nothing else mattered. Nothing.

Beverly Jenkins is the recipient of the Michigan Author Award from the Michigan Library Association, the Romance Writers of America Lifetime Achievement Award, as well as the Romantic Times Reviewers' Choice Award for historical romance. She has been nominated for the NAACP Image Award in Literature, and she was featured in the documentary *Love Between the Covers* and on CBS *Sunday Morning*. Since the publication of *Night Song* in 1994, she has been leading the charge for inclusive romance and has been a constant darling of reviewers, fans, and her peers alike, garnering accolades for her work from the likes of the *Wall Street Journal*, *People* magazine, and NPR.

ALSO BY
BEVERLY JENKINS

BRING ON THE BLESSINGS
Blessings 1

"[A] heartwarming story of love, community, and family… *Bring on the Blessings* is a tasty reading confection that you'll savor long after the story ends."

—Angela Benson, author of *The Amen Sisters*

A SECOND HELPING
Blessings 2

"A story like none other, and done in a way that only Beverly Jenkins can do. Simply superb!"

—Brenda Jackson, *New York Times* bestselling author

SOMETHING OLD, SOMETHING NEW
Blessings 3

"There is beauty in Jenkins's storytelling that should be the standard by which to judge fiction writing… Brava, Ms. Jenkins, you have done it again and left us wanting more."

—*Romantic Times* (Top Pick)

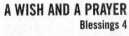

A WISH AND A PRAYER
Blessings 4

"Returning to Henry Adams, Kansas, is akin to attending a family reunion. The characters are rich, and the kids all have a story to be told."

—*Romantic Times*

HEART OF GOLD
Blessings 5

"Her stories are delicious and always leave behind both feelings of satisfaction and want… for her next novel."

—*Fresh Fiction*

FOR YOUR LOVE
Blessings 6

"A wonderful read that combines comedy, drama, historical facts, and where the blessings keep on coming!"

—Romance in Color

STEPPING TO A NEW DAY
Blessings 7

"It's easy to lose hours at a time caught up in this book. An achingly sweet feel-good story of love and redemption of all kinds."

—*Kirkus Reviews*

CHASING DOWN A DREAM
Blessings 8

"Every visit to Henry Adams, Kansas, is like a warm hug... All is not perfect because humans make mistakes, but the knowledge that the people of this town will rise to the challenge, together, is a blessing."

—RT Book Reviews (Top Pick)

SECOND TIME SWEETER
Blessings 9

"If you haven't yet gotten your hands on [this] *USA Today* bestselling author's work, you should do so immediately."

—Shondaland

ON THE CORNER OF HOPE AND MAIN
Blessings 10

"Jenkins's characters come to vivid life, and the town is as well developed as those who live there... Henry Adams remains a place of faith where marriages deepen and relationships are mended. This is the best of the series so far."

—*Publishers Weekly* (starred reviewed)